MAR ZIMMER GETS THE

MARGO ZIMMERMAN GETS THE GIRL

BRIANNA R. SHRUM
SARA WAXELBAUM

inkyard PRESS

ISBN-13: 978-1-335-45365-5

Margo Zimmerman Gets the Girl

For questions and comments about the quality of this book, please contact us at
CustomerService@Harlequin.com.

Inkyard Press
22 Adelaide St. West, 41st Floor
Toronto, Ontario M5H 4E3, Canada
www.InkyardPress.com

Printed in U.S.A.

Recycling programs
for this product may
not exist in your area.

For the ones who never got the rule book—neither did we.

EPIPHANY

(Margo)

I haven't lost a game of dice since I was twelve years old.

If people would pay *attention*, set them with a little science—the perfect grip, the precise moment of release, the meticulously calculated momentum—no one should ever lose.

I've since traded dice games with my parents for rigged games of chance on attic floors, but the principles are the same. So I don't know how the hell, for the first time in five years, I spin this bottle aiming for my boyfriend and it lands on Viv Carter. But it does, and my throat completely knots. Not because she's not, like, pretty. Not because she's not gorgeous, even; I've always kind of wanted to be her. She's my Student Council VP and has the shiniest hair I've ever seen outside a shampoo commercial and this sparkling smile that you can't look away from when she turns it on you. I've also always totally wanted her boobs, let's be real.

But like. What girl hasn't?

It's just that it's awkward. I'll see her on Monday post-tongue down her throat and we'll have to do this *Haha remember what my mouth tastes like? Parties, am I right?* dance and it will be weird for everyone.

Plus, Chad is right here. His knee is touching my thigh, which is fine. He's in the shirt I got him for his birthday, and we made out in the car about a half hour ago. Which was also...fine. Chad is aggressively *fine* at making out, but surprise, surprise, I've never kissed a dude who didn't use *way* too much tongue. Like. Do their tongues actually *expand*? TARDIS style? Do they get bigger on the inside of a girl's mouth? Christ.

Maybe the finesse comes later. And that's when it's all sparks and fireworks and not practically being waterboarded by saliva.

In college, oh, wow, the kissing will be...fine-plus, at the very least.

Anyway. All that is to say, I can't just...make out with a girl in front of my boyfriend. Even if...

"Chad," I say. "I swear to god, are you videoing this?"

His smile is wide and a little dickish, a little eyebrow-waggly. A couple of his freckles disappear into his dimples. "It's the rules, babe. I don't make the rules." He bumps his shoulder into mine and I wiggle away.

"The rules don't say you have to do it on *camera*."

Across the circle, Robbie says, "Wait, who's doing it?"

I roll my eyes and glance at Viv. Her skin is just straight up sparkling. Of course it is. No one can do contours and highlighter like this girl; I've made notes to ask her about it ten thousand times.

And I definitely won't now because Viv is crawling across

the circle, one perfect eyebrow in a perfect arch and I just laugh because suddenly my heart is pounding so hard I think my pulse will tear through my veins like they're tissue paper. I can't... Holy shit, I can't breathe. I try, I make an absolutely valiant effort at an inhale, and what happens is I wind up breathing in *Viv*.

Oh my god, her mouth.

Oh my god, her hair brushing over my neck, tickling my collarbone.

Oh my god, the softness of her arms pressing into mine, her bare knees slipping against the hem of my shorts. I'm going to *die*. Right here at seventeen years old in Robbie Kendrick's basement.

Oh my god, Viv is like, really into this. Is she gay?

Oh my god.

Oh my *god*, I'm gay.

CHAPTER 1

Margo

Three months later

Query: *how to be gay.*

Query: *gay tips.*

Query: *queer culture?*

Did you mean "queen culture"?

I blink at my screen. I slam my face on my keyboard.

At that exact moment, the door to the FROG (the adorable nickname for the Finished Room Over the Garage) opens and closes and my brother, Mendel, and four of his friends descend the stairs. My mistake, thinking 2:00 a.m. meant that the living room would be clear.

I should have known. Mendel spends a third of his time fighting fires, a third hanging out with the family or in his room—a fireman's salary does not pay an apartment's rent—and a third practicing communism in the FROG.

He doesn't even say anything by way of explanation, he

just walks his comrades to the door and whirls back around, slamming a Gatorade. "My goodness, little sister. It's two in the morning."

"Yes," I say.

"What are we googling? School shit?"

I roll my eyes. "Mendel, I'll have you know that I do a lot more with my computer than googling academics."

He arches a dark eyebrow. "At two a.m.?"

I want to protest, but frankly, he's got me there. I just say, "Well. Not tonight."

He waits.

I consider saying nothing, just leaving myself to my own devices and muddling my way through the first four hundred pages of search results like I've been doing for the last two hours. But then I think, *Why?* What's the point of being gay and having an older sibling who's queer in like nineteen different ways if you can't use them as a resource? I blow out a breath and close my laptop. "So, okay. Remember what I... what I told you a little while back?"

He cocks his head.

I lower my voice. "About being gay."

"What?" he fake yells. "You're *gay*?"

"Mendel, god. Yes. That. So I just... Here's the thing. I know I like girls. I know about rainbow flags and stuff and marriage equality and that kissing Viv Carter was a revelation, because—uh. Anyway. I guess I'm just...looking into the rest of it."

"The rest of what?" he says.

I shrug. I don't even know how to explain what I'm looking for. "Just…you know. The whole culture. The lifestyle. How do you like…become a part of that?"

Mendel scratches his head. "Is this one of those autistic things where you're like, *I need to know everything about this before I participate? I'm not going to homo until I can homo right?*"

I roll my eyes. "No." Then, "Yes, probably. Just—I don't know, how do you do this? How do you even signal that you're gay?"

"Ohhhhh," he says. His smile widens until it's bigger than his face. "Like wearing pastel shorts, especially when shorts aren't appropriate. Or asking if anyone in the room knows my good friend Sean Cody."

I blink and make mental notes. "Y-yes."

He thinks for a second. Then he says, "Honestly, Margo, you're fine. You're going to figure this out. It's a lot at first. But the more you, I don't know, live in it? The more you get it."

"Okay," I say. I was afraid that was going to be the answer.

"When I'm not half asleep, I'm down to talk about anything you want, though. You know that, yeah?"

I do. I smile at him and say, "Thanks, big brother."

He tips his chin at me and heads to bed.

I think about what he said, about living it. Letting it sink into my skin. Just allowing myself to become.

I open my laptop again.

On Thursday, I roll up to teen night at the gayest club in Ocala—Willow—wearing the gayest ensemble I could put together. I'm in a white Lacoste tank top and baby pink short shorts and boat shoes, a little leather necklace looped around my throat. I look extremely, perfectly homosexual.

I exit my Lyft and stand outside the club.

All right, Zimmerman, you can do this. You're here to make Human Connections. Shove all that autism behind your Neurotypical Mask. You can look people in the eye and make small talk. Get in there.

I bounce on my toes for a few seconds, trying to get the jitters out.

Let's go.

Willow is a sea of backward ball caps and plaid. There are so many gorgeous girls here—gorgeous girls who actually like girls—that for a second, I have trouble catching my breath.

I mean, okay. No one is signaling that particularly well with their clothing; I'm the only one here dressed like this. But god, whatever. This is Florida. We're like a full generation behind everywhere else. I sigh. This would not be happening in Portland.

I sidle up to the bar and order a Cherry Coke, and a girl with long multicolored hair bumps into me.

"Oh," she says, "hey."

"Hey," I say. She is…beautiful. In this extremely unique way, like her face was put together by a modern artist. She smiles.

"I'm Quinn. I don't think I've seen you around here before?"

"No," I say, "probably not." But I don't want to sound like a complete noob. "The club isn't usually my scene."

"No?" She slides a little closer to me, and I can see the

sweat glistening on her collarbone, lights of the club making it sparkle. "What is your scene?"

Showtime.

"Well," I say, "I just got here from…the gym." I lean against the bar in a way that I know shows off my swimmer's shoulders.

"Oh," she says. "Well. Cool."

"I was there with my workout partner. Sean Cody."

She furrows her brow and glances over her shoulder for a half second.

"Do you know Sean Cody?"

Her face is completely blank. "I, uh…no?"

Crap.

I am going to kill Mendel.

I panic and try to recover. "Anyway, I'm Margo. And I'm a Virgo."

Quinn kind of half laughs and says, "Cool, well, I need to go meet my friends, so…"

Heat springs to my face. "I'm so sorry," I say. "I wasn't trying to push you or something! Are you like…" I take a second to drum up the term. "Masc4masc?"

She blinks.

I hear someone do a spit take behind me, and droplets spray across my shoulders.

I whirl around to find the source and see Abbie Sokoloff, resident Queer Girl™ at S.W. Moody High and fellow swimmer. Add to that: confoundingly hot.

She's raising an eyebrow at me. "I, uh, think you scared her off."

14

I look behind me and see she's right. Quinn is gone. Go figure.

Good lord, this is already a nightmare.

Abbie says, "Do you even know what you just asked her?"

"…yes? Of course."

Her eyebrows climb to her hairline. "Okay, Zimmerman. Let me ask you this: do you know what Willow is?"

I sputter. "Uh. Yes. Obviously. I'm here, aren't I?"

"Margo. Do you know. What WILLOW IS."

I don't know how to answer that, so I go to take a drink from my Cherry Coke, but my mouth misses the straw completely and it stabs into my cheek. I recover, because maybe she didn't notice, and get it right the second time. Except my drink is empty and I sound like a nine-year-old trying to get the last of the chocolate milk from the glass.

"This is a gay club. A *gay club*. For gay girls. Where we can be gay. Gayly."

"Well," I say. "This is just. It is simply." I close my mouth around the straw. Then I remove it from my mouth and slam the cup on the bar. "It's Teen Night and I'm here, and—"

Oh my god, my throat is closing up.

I'm sweating.

Am I dying?

I…

I don't even finish my sentence.

I turn around and leave.

I go the gay hell home.

When I walk through the front door, I am drenched in sweat and covered in glitter for some reason and Mendel is sitting at the kitchen table with a cup of coffee despite the hour, and I just throw my hands in the air.

"Margo," he says. "I—"

That's where he stops.

I don't say shit.

I just stare at him.

"... Why are you covered in glitter?"

"WELL," I say, not able to control my volume, which I absolutely should because my parents are probably asleep. "WHY DON'T YOU TELL ME?"

That doesn't even make any sense, but I'm furious, and I can't call Google and scream at them so I have chosen Mendel instead.

Mendel looks me up and down, from the crown of my head to the tips of my boat shoes. And he says, "Because you're a...gay man?"

I do a double take. "I'm sorry, what?"

He throws his arms up in an exaggerated shrug and says, "You're wearing short pastel shorts and a leather necklace and fucking Sperrys, Margo. You're clearly a youthful male homosexual."

"Ha. Ha ha ha hahahaha, that is hilarious, Mendel. I just went to the lesbian bar and you know what? You know what, Mendel?"

He stares at me and sips his coffee.

"I was the only person dressed like this. And no one knew who Sean Cody was."

He chokes on his drink.

He coughs for a literal 45 seconds.

"Did you... Did you ask the lesbians about Sean Cody?"

"Yes! Like you told me!"

Mendel almost falls out of his chair laughing. "I absolutely did *not*. This—Margo, Sean Cody is… There's a reason girls don't know about that. It's a website that's… Well. It's not for girls, dude. Definitely not gay ones."

I blink. I mumble, my voice small, "But my boat shoes."

He says, "Are great. On a boat."

The kitchen is suddenly very intensely quiet.

He clears his throat. "You can't just learn gay culture off a few websites that, honestly, all cater to cis, gay dudes. That's… I think that's what happened here."

I deflate.

I'm humiliated. This was such a failure.

Mendel sees me crumple and says, "Hey, this isn't a total disaster—"

But I don't stay for anything else. I just go to my room, to be by myself.

I am terrible at this. I'm so fucking embarrassed. I strip out of my shoes and my shorts and my stupid Lacoste and I can't even look at my computer.

I just—I hate this. This is *never* me. I am Margo Zimmerman, the girl who knows what she wants and exactly how to get it. I wanted to get into student government, so I planned a campaign for an entire semester. I ran. I got it. I want to be a large animal vet, so I did everything I could to get accepted into one of the top pre-veterinary programs in the state. I want to have a wife with long flowing hair and a maxi skirt and a golden retriever, hanging up herbs to dry in the kitchen or whatever it is that cottagecore lesbians do, so I researched how to do it.

And I failed.

I failed. So. Hard.

I curl up in my bed, and when I shut my eyes, I see Abbie Sokoloff's face. I hear her saying, *Do you know what Willow is?*

I see her looking perfectly, comfortably, gorgeously gay, like she belongs. Like she's gay and it's real, and no one would question her presence at a lesbian bar.

Not like me. I need help.

And...

And I have an idea.

CHAPTER 2

Abbie

She's waiting for me when I climb the aluminum ladder out of the pool. Margo Zimmerman, student body president, best butterfly and backstroke *and* freestyle on the team, Chad Wilson the quarterback's girlfriend, and archetypal Hot Girl is waiting for me when I get out of the water.

I'm immediately suspicious. We might swim together, but I can count on one hand the number of interactions we've had—including last Thursday at Willow. If I were into girls like her, I'd say she was way out of my league. And that's exactly what she'd say, too. We're not friends, but not just because I'm not cool or pretty or popular enough. We're not friends because we have nothing in common.

She's standing there, clearly waiting for *me*, hands on her hips (like I need anything to direct my attention to her hips, Jesus), her auburn hair pulled back into a tight French braid, her tiny olive green bikini damp but not dripping. Her time out in the sun has made the spray of freckles across her nose stand out even more.

She is just absolutely beautiful.

She says, "Hey. You're gay."

I choke.

She waits. She's not wrong.

I say, "You're Margo."

"I need a favor," she says. "Can we talk?"

"Uh. Sure. Let me get my towel." I wind my hair into a rope over my shoulder and wring it out. Her eyes flicker, and I swear she looked at my chest, or my hands. Or my hair.

Or she was distracted by the movement. That seems most likely.

She follows me to the chair where I've left my bag of stuff and looks anywhere else while I shake my towel out and squeeze the worst of the water from my swimsuit top. And who can blame her? If I were straight, I wouldn't want to watch a girl squeeze her own boobs.

I wrap the towel around me and say, "So what's up? You got a friend who needs a date to Homecoming or something?"

She finally looks back at me, her brown eyes serious. "No." She closes her eyes, and takes a deep yoga breath, hands and all. Then clears her throat. Jesus, a speech is coming. I know the *I've been practicing this* look. "I'm gay."

Everything I saw at Willow that night, that weird night Margo showed up there, finally sort of clicks into place. But not like, easily. It doesn't make sense. This has to be some kind of elaborate prank. I look around for one of her douche-nozzle friends holding up a phone and snickering. I don't see anyone, but that doesn't mean there isn't anyone.

So I just say, "Oh, come on."

She blinks. "Excuse me?"

"This is a joke, right? You're Margo. Margo's—you're *gay*?"

"I am Margo and I am gay."

"Boy." I'm looking at her face, and it's reading as. Well. Completely sincere. Does Margo Zimmerman even know how to lie? "Boy," I say again, because, *boy*. And then it clicks. "Oh, so that's why you and Chad broke up."

She huffs, her brows drawing together. Oh, dammit. That clearly struck a nerve. I clear my throat and pretend that didn't just happen. "So, uh. What's the favor?"

"Well," Margo says, crossing her arms over her chest, "not that it's any of your business. But yes. That is why we broke up. Put it in the school newspaper or whatever."

There is a beat of silence.

Then, "Oh my god, don't. I was joking."

"Okay, but if you don't want people to know, why did you just come out to me?"

"Because. I want you to teach me."

"Teach you? What, exactly?"

She wrinkles her pretty ski-slope nose and rolls her eyes. Like it should be obvious. "To be *gay*, Abbie."

I blink. "You just—I don't know. You're just gay. You said you're gay, so you're gay. I don't know what you're asking for. If you're gay, you're gay. Congratulations, you gay."

"Right. Right, yeah, and that's why you're here doing laps at the community pool. Because you swim. You're a swimmer. No one ever told you how to do a backstroke. Congratulations. You swimmer."

"It's not the same thing at all. You're comparing a skill with…" I don't even know what, but it hits me and I smirk. "A talent."

She's been cool and collected this whole time, confident. But at that, her eyelashes flutter and she looks at the wet ground. Her professionally polished *too long to be gay* nails tap at her thigh, then her thumbnail goes to her teeth. "I don't… It's not a talent for me. I don't—I don't know what I'm doing. It's like you guys have this whole lingo, this whole world, and—I know how to get a guy to like me, okay? But I don't know how…" She swallows. And stops short. "You know what? Never mind. This was a bad idea. I'm just… I'm just going to go. So. Thanks. Or whatever."

She doesn't give me a chance to respond before she turns and walks away. And, yeah, I watch. I consider going after her and telling her she's not as clueless as she thinks she is, tapping her bare thigh, touching her mouth. But I don't. Because she'll figure it out. Or—considering how hard she fumbled at Willow—she won't. Either way, it's not my problem.

The house is quiet when I get home. That doesn't necessarily mean no one's here—it could be that my parents just aren't speaking to each other. Which, to be honest, is usually better than the alternative.

I don't bother to find out and head upstairs to shower. I'm exhausted; I busted my ass out there in the pool, working on my front crawl, which is definitely my weakest stroke. And then Margo Zimmerman asked me how to be gay? Like, I don't know, dude, buy some high-top sneakers and tell everyone you think Kristen Stewart is hot. Congrats, you've nailed being gay.

When I get out of the shower, it's no longer silent. Kitchen cabinets and pots and dishes are being slammed around, punctuated by Mom's Angry Voice, where she overemphasizes every third or fourth word. Then a lull, in which I assume Dad has said something—something *very* inadvisable, if Mom's *OH MY GOD, BRIAN* means anything.

Like, my car is here. They had to have heard the shower. They *know* I'm here. They know I can hear them. They just don't care.

And then the front door slams. Mom, probably, because no more dishes are being crashed around. Ten bucks says Dad will just leave the carnage as is and retreat to their bedroom to put on his favorite crypto vlogger.

I throw on an old T-shirt and pajama shorts and venture into the kitchen to scavenge for food.

I was, of course, right: the dishwasher is still sitting open, half-emptied, and I can hear Jimothy the Crypto Bro shouting from behind my parents' bedroom door.

Honestly, it's better this way. I have no interest in either of them asking me if I'm all right, because if they gave a shit about me being all right, they wouldn't do this. I'm their *kid*, and like, I don't care if they fight, everybody fights, but god. Close a door for fuck's sake.

A stack of mail sits on the island, a letter addressed to me from Florida International University on the top. I pour a glass of water before I open it, and I guess it's a good thing I don't take a drink first, because when I read what it says, I completely choke.

Dear Ms. Sokoloff,
It has come to our attention that you have not maintained the grade point average you had upon admission to our university. Our standards are high, and slots are in demand, so we cannot afford to admit a student who

cannot keep up with the academic demands placed on them. Therefore, if the semester's final grades do not reflect a renewed dedication to your studies, we will revoke our offer of admission.

Sincerely,

I don't care, dean of whatever, I hate my life.

I'm so glad my parents are too pissed at each other to worry about me because I suddenly don't have the spoons to interact with any human in the world. I need to figure out what the hell is going on with my grades and how to fix them because I can't not go to college next year. I can't not get out of this house and away from my parents.

We're coming up on midterms, but I can check my grades through the student portal in the meantime. I pull my laptop out of my bag and don't even sit to open it.

My grades load, and I stop breathing. C's across the board, except my AP US History class.

I have an F. And not like, a *two points from a D* F. A solid, glaring, undeniable F.

Shit.

Okay, Abbie. Okay. How did we get here? I knew I'd been struggling. I have been for a while, and not just because I've been sleeping like shit. Mr. Cameron's AP US History class is the only one I can't bullshit my way through, and well. It sure shows.

An F.

Why did I even think I could swing an AP class? Maybe I could talk to Mr. Cameron, see what we can figure out, see if—

I can't think about this right now. I need to get out of here, blow off some steam. Get my skateboard and go, go see if Oscar's out there, see if his parents are home, maybe we can go back to his place and—

Hold on. Hold. On.

Margo Zimmerman.

Margo Zimmerman is in my AP US History class, and she's probably killing it in there. No way she's not.

She wants to learn how to pick up girls? Cool. I need to pass this class.

CHAPTER 3

Margo

You're gay.

I rehash it in my head approximately ninety-seven times.

Abbie Sokoloff popping up out of the pool in a two-piece that kept dragging my gaze down toward the softness at her hips and then right back up to the pretty cut of her collarbone. Frowning at me.

And my brilliant decision to declare, *You're gay.*

Not, *Hey, Abbie, it's Margo. We have class together?*

Or even, *Oh my godddd, Abbie! What are you doing here?*

Just, *HEY YOU UTTER LESBIAN.*

YOU'RE GAY is absolutely Rickrolling me while I wait for AP US History to start, my forehead becoming intimately acquainted with the fake wood of my right-handed desk. Less risk of having to make eye contact with Abbie, Who Is Gay.

I pointedly do not notice when she walks in.

I am paying more attention in this class than I ever have; I am absolutely fascinated by the Constitutional Convention and all the intricacies that didn't manage to make it into *Hamilton*. Mr. Cameron actually furrows his brow at me once or twice, and that's only because I'm probably giving him *serial killer* eyes, which, as it turns out, have a lot of overlap with *tell me more about the Constitutional Convention* eyes, and even more overlap with *fuck oh fuck let me not look at Abbie Sokoloff, three seats to my right,* eyes.

I don't know if the clock ticking down is merciful or not.

Every minute that goes by means one more minute I don't have to deal with the consequences of my extremely recent past, but it also means one minute closer to the bell and therefore the hallway anarchy that occurs before the next class. Those three minutes are high-risk. It is no man's land. It is making me sweat. It's making me stim so hard I think the teacher is going to tease me for missing my calling as a percussionist. My fingers are going wild on my desk.

Thankfully, I did this week's reading two weeks ago so this is all review. It doesn't matter that by the end of the class I couldn't tell you more about Thomas Jefferson than I could when it started, because I already could have told you everything before the starting bell rang.

I am not concerned.

Well, not about that.

My *murder you* eyes drift over to the clock.

Three minutes left.

Two minutes.

Mr. Cameron announces, "Eh, I'll let you go early."

Of course he will, that son of a bitch.

I jump up out of my chair and bite down on my tongue

when I catch my thigh on the edge of the metal. And I power walk out of the class as fast as humanly possible.

And then, of course, of course, I hear Abbie say, "Hey, Margo," like everything is normal and I didn't proclaim her gayness at the edge of the swimming pool yesterday.

I say: nothing.

"Margo?"

N-o-t-h-i-n-g.

Then her hand is on my arm, in the crook of my elbow, and I can feel all her fingers against my skin, and she's pulling me and I'm ignoring her because if I keep ignoring her, this will all stop happening.

But it doesn't. Her grip tightens and I have to stop.

She says, "Hey. *Margo*."

"Oh!" I say, like a total dickhead. "Abbie! Yeah, hey!" *Why! Am I saying everything! With an exclamation point!*

"Hey," she says again, her brow furrowed because of course it is; everything I've done in the last fourteen seconds has been absolutely Martian. "You remember what you asked me yesterday?"

I swallow. I choke. I don't know if it's on the question or my own spit.

I wait, because it's obviously rhetorical.

She blinks at me.

Which I know, because for once, I am not staring deeply into her eyebrow. I'm looking right at her eyeballs. Very intentionally. Left—right—left. The eye contact is so…purposeful that for a second I forget why I'm doing it and what we were talking about in the first place.

She blinks again.

Oh. Right. I say, "… N-noooo?"

She narrows her eyes. She doesn't believe me. Why would she? Everything is bad.

She says, "Okay? Well. I think you do. Anyway. The answer's yes, but I need something from you."

I purse my lips. And I glance down at where her fingers are still pressing into the crook of my elbow. Not just pressing. Squeezing.

Abbie drops her hand from my arm and it's not quite a relief. It's—it settles somewhere between a relief and a loss.

I mentally add that to the list of things to pointedly ignore (which also includes the aggressive buzzing of the fluorescents and the cloying scent of the Harvest Apple school bathroom soap clinging to my hands).

I blow out a breath, and I say, "What. What do you want?"

"Help," she says. "You need my help, and I need yours."

And now I'm feeling, well, just a total crap ton of things and it's too many things, which means that I'm feeling catty. So I say, all prim and bitchy, "I thought you said I didn't need your help. That I'm just—well." This hall is too crowded to be flinging around sentences like *I'm gay* before I'm sufficiently adequate at it. I finish, "That I'm."

"Okay," Abbie says, saving me. "Listen, let's not do this here." She pulls her phone out of her back pocket and adds, "Give me your number and we'll figure something out. Meet up after school or something. Just to talk. Okay?"

I take her phone and enter my info. It's ridiculous that giving this particular girl my number feels like *any* kind of achievement, different from giving any other girl my number pre-queervelation. Because this is a purely professional exchange.

And well, let's be honest. Abbie has probably gotten a *number* of girls' numbers in her life. Maybe even this exact way. If I know anything about her, it's that I should like…put my last name in the address book to make sure she doesn't mix me up with three other Margos.

I give her my number (under Margo *Zimmerman*, thank you very much) and I try not to be weird about it and I just say, "Okay."

Her fingers brush mine when I hand her phone back and her lips kind of curl up on one side and she says, "Cool," and I wonder how many times that line has worked. How many girls she's *met up after school or something. Just. To talk.*

I know, because everyone knows, that it is, at minimum, a lot.

I mean, who could blame them? Abbie Sokoloff is *hot*. Her dark hair is always in this kind of devil-may-care cluster of waves to her shoulders and her eyes—just a tad too big for her face—are always…up to something. And she's too small to take up as much space as she does. It's overwhelming.

It's… Yeah, well. *Overwhelming* is the word.

My hands betray me and give her *finger guns* for fuck's sake, when I say, "Well. See you." She smirks. And turns to walk away.

What I do is watch her.

Totally freaking weird about it.

CHAPTER 4

Abbie

I don't text her immediately. I don't even do it right after the final bell rings and the school vomits students out into the sweltering afternoon. I wait until I'm at home, in cooler clothes, my feet on the coffee table, the TV looping whatever show Netflix is trying to push on us today—that's when I pull out my phone and find Margo's number.

I type, Hey. You're gay. And hit send.

I can't control the shit-eating grin on my face, and frankly, I don't want to. When I don't get an immediate answer, I drop the phone on the couch next to me and pull my US History book out of my bag.

The chapter is supposed to be pretty straightforward, but I can't focus. All I can hear is Lin-Manuel Miranda's giddy, *I was chosen for the Constitutional Convention!* on repeat in my head. Instead of the Virginia Plan. I've read "the rights of suffrage in the National Legislature ought to be proportioned to quotas of contribution, or to the number of free inhabitants" like fourteen times when my phone buzzes next to me.

Well with your help I will be.

And immediately on top of that: I mean I am.

Three more buzzes, right in a row: Gay. Not that I need your help.

Well, I do.
But I'm gay. Anyway.

Finally, a full ninety seconds later: lol.

This is certainly not the Margo Zimmerman I'm used to. I don't think I've ever seen her off-balance. About anything. Ever. My gut tells me to give her shit, but I can only kind of commit to it.

I reply: You're doing great, killer.

Then: Make sure you're free Wednesday afternoon.

She writes: What's Wednesday?

I reply: The day after tomorrow.

Then I decide to keep going, because it's so much fun to mess with her, to flap the unflappable Margo Zimmerman.

Hump Day. The day of the week between Tuesday and Thursday. Derived from Wodinsday, referring to Wodin, or Ødin, the Norse All-Father, portrayed best and most recently by Anthony Hopkins. https://en.wikipedia.org/wiki/Wednesday.

Three dots.
Nothing.
Three dots.
Nothing.

Finally: SIR Anthony Hopkins.

Followed by: You've come to me for history tutoring and assume *I* don't know my Norse mythology PLS.

Then: Why am I canceling my pedicure on All-Father's Day?

It's easy to think Margo Zimmerman is humorless. That she's rigid, uptight, hyperfocused. That she's less than the sum of her parts.

Apparently not.

Because you can reschedule a pedicure, but you can't reschedule the Westford field hockey match.

Almost immediately, I receive, Oh. Right. Okay.

Then: Gay Lesson Number 1: Field Hockey.

If she were here, in front of me, where she could see my face, I would scoff and be absolutely offended that she would assume such a thing about field hockey. But she's not here, and I'm not offended, so I do the next best thing: I dissemble.

Um, my best friend is on the team and I just want to support her okay.

The actual *second* I hit send: Yes.

Of course.

Totally.

I just meant because we're like doing the lessons.

There at the field.

You know.

If my phone had been next to me on the couch, it would have buzzed right off the side. Calm down, Zimmerman, both my best friend and field hockey are pretty fucking gay, so yes, that is where Queer 101 starts.

Oh.

Three dots. For…a while.
Then: ha ha.
I put my phone facedown and go back to my textbook, but I don't have any more luck than before. It's been, I don't know, twenty minutes, and then my mom bursts through the front door, laughing, plastic bags rustling. I don't have to look to know that it's not groceries in those bags. I don't have to ask to know it's not my dad on the receiving end of that laugh. I don't have to look up to see her not notice me as she breezes through the living room, chattering about yoga positions or something.
The bedroom door closes.
I turn off the TV.
I still have no idea what the Virginia Plan is.

Wednesday afternoon, and I'm sitting on a towel on the hot metal bleachers, watching the teams warm up. My best friend, Charlie, really does play field hockey, and I really do try to make it to as many matches as I can. Her girlfriend, Adriana, who is also my ex-girlfriend, is here, too, down by the field. She's pretty invested in Charlie, which I appreciate, and I'm not mad about how our relationship ended. Just because you're friends with a hot girl, doesn't mean you should date her.

34

The match doesn't start until six, but I told Margo to meet me here at five. If she wants to observe some gays in their natural habitat, this is a pretty low-stakes place to start.

It's the fall semester, and softball's a spring sport, after all.

I see her as she spots me, and I watch her climb the bleachers to where I'm sitting. Even from here, her legs look ten miles long in her denim shorts, the edges of the pockets hanging out. That's not usually a look I go for, but listen: swimming does a body good. She comes closer, and I can make out the embroidery on her tank top, and I can hear her flip-flops before I can see what color they are.

Oh, look. They're the same yellow as her tank top.

She sits down next to me, not too close. Her hair's up in a ponytail.

"Did you flat-iron your hair?" I ask, because I can't not say anything. "And then? Put it in a ponytail?"

She turns to me and furrows her brow. "I'm sorry, do you *not* live in Florida? And therefore not experience humidity?"

"Look at my hair. You don't need words to answer that question."

"I... I need *something* to answer that question. Your hair always looks extremely good."

"Thank you," I say. "But yes, I experience humidity, and no, I don't flat-iron my hair, because who has time for that? Do you know how long it would take to straighten my hair?"

"No—"

"Me, either," I interrupt her, "because I've never done it."

She shrugs and looks down the field stubbornly. Almost defiant. "Well. Some of us like looking smooth and shiny. Even in our ponytails."

"It looks good," I say, and I'm surprised at how sincerely I mean it. "I'm not saying it doesn't. And I'm not saying you can't—okay. Look. I'm not saying you can't do this whole like…high femme thing. I'm just saying you might be in the minority in a lot of circles. Queer circles. You know?"

She pauses a beat. Then reaches into her bag and pulls out an honest-to-god notebook. "No," she says. "I don't know." She turns to the first page and poises her pen over the paper.

Like she's going to take notes.

I blink at her. She's just. Staring at me. Waiting.

"Well," I say. "Okay. I assume you've seen me. And how I dress?"

She's still staring, like she thinks it's a rhetorical question. It's not.

"I assume?" I say again. "You've seen me and how I dress? You see me, now, and how I am dressed?"

She very visibly looks me over. I feel like I should be self-conscious, or flattered, or something, but it's for science, so I force myself to hold still and be observed in my *I woke up this gay* muscle tank and Owl House snapback. "Oh," she says. "Yes. I can see you right now. You're in jeans. In this humidity that we've established does not affect you." I open my mouth to protest and she holds up her hand. "No. We've established it."

"Okay." I point down the bleachers at Adriana. "You see her? Tell me what she's wearing."

"Not jeans." She smiles a little, like she's pleased with herself. Then says, "Shorts. A men's button-down. High-tops. Damn, that's a good look."

"That's my ex-girlfriend."

She raises her eyebrows. "Oh. Well, shit, should we like, go?"

I call her name and she looks up in our direction, and I wave, and she waves back, and starts up the bleachers toward us.

I think Margo's going into full panic mode. The muscles of her legs tense, and the idea of her getting an adrenaline dump over this is so absurd I almost laugh out loud.

But Adriana reaches us and says to me, "Hey, I was wondering when you were going to get here." She looks at Margo and says, "I've seen you before. Aren't you on the swim team with Abs?"

"Yup," says Margo. "Yes. We're not dating."

I choke.

Adriana's eyes narrow slowly. Not mad; confused. She says, "Okay. I mean, obviously. Aren't you dating Chad?"

I say, "They broke up like three months ago."

Adriana puts her hands up. "Okayyy."

Ugh, now Adriana is going to think I have a thing for Margo. Which I don't, because she's totally not my type. And she should know better, because she knows how I am around girls I'm into. "I'm just saying, everybody knows that."

Adriana's eyebrows go up, but she doesn't ask any more questions. She's cool like that; she'll keep secrets to the grave and doesn't give a shit about gossip. Clearly. "I think they're starting Charlie today," she tells me. "I'm pretty excited."

"Yeah," I say. "She's gonna do great."

Adriana glances over her shoulder to the field, sees something I don't, and is already going back down again when she calls back to us, "Nice to meet you, Margo. Abs, I'll see you later?"

"Yeah, man."

I turn to Margo and spread my hands. "Behold. Tell me what you've learned."

Margo glances down, then forces her eyes back to my face. "Well. That was...shockingly civil."

"Shockingly civil," I repeat. "Well, you'll be delighted to know that Charlie is the one who's my best friend. She's why I'm here."

"I'm sorry. Your best friend is dating your girlfriend? Ex-girlfriend."

"Very ex-girlfriend. Adriana and I are better as friends, and we both know it. And I've known Charlie since I moved here. And yes, she observed Girl Code and asked before she started going out with Adriana."

Sure, she *asked*, but like, what was I going to tell her? No? It doesn't matter that Adriana and I are better as friends; it was kind of shitty of Charlie to do that, considering she was the one who introduced us.

"Oh." Margo starts scribbling something; who even knows what. "That's...okay then."

"And while you're taking notes, inexplicably, write this down—if you don't want people to think about your sexuality, maybe don't awkwardly announce how you're not dating the queer girl you're talking to, without any prompting whatsoever. Do you need me to repeat any of that?"

She starts a new line, then stops halfway through and stares at it. "Jesus Christ," she says, and she drops her head into her hands. "Listen, I'm not being weird, okay?"

"Are you not?"

"I WASN'T BEING WEIRD." Her voice is so loud Adriana and Charlie both look up to where we're sitting. I wave

38

back at them. Margo looks like she wants to crawl under the bleachers and never come out. She grunts in frustration and when she speaks again, it's much quieter. "Not like I didn't want her to think that... It's not because *you*... I mean. Well. It's because I'm sitting here with her ex-girlfriend and I just didn't..." She shifts, and her knee bumps mine for the briefest second before she pulls it away. "I didn't want to start anything. It's not because I couldn't stand the thought of someone thinking we were together or something. Obviously. So, you know like—"

As entertaining as this has been, it's clear Margo is in like *full panic, can't shut up* mode, so I put my hands on either side of her face. Her mouth closes, so sharply I can hear her teeth click together. I say, as gently as I can, "Stop. Talking."

She follows directions.

"Do you trust me?"

She opens her mouth to answer, and I say, "No. No words. Do you trust me?"

She nods.

"Do you think I would have called over my ex-girlfriend-who-is-dating-my-best-friend if I thought it was going to start drama?"

She pauses. Shakes her head.

"Good." I drop my hands. "You can talk again."

Margo purses her lips and stares down at her pencil, her half page of notes. She breathes out through her nose and says to me, "Well. Are we just going to sit here talking about my flat-ironed hair and your ex-girlfriend or are you going to start today's lesson?"

I blink. "Today's lesson?"

"…yes?"

"There's no lesson," I say, and when she opens her mouth to respond, I don't let her. "Listen, I know what I said the other day sounded like I was being an asshole, but I don't know, man. I don't know how to teach anyone to be gay. Shit, sometimes I don't know if *I'm* being gay correctly. I figured we could come out here, hang out, absorb some gay via osmosis or whatever. It's a field hockey game. It doesn't get a whole lot gayer than this."

She cocks her head, and her expression wipes into total neutrality.

She shifts her body so she's facing the field. Like she's really going to absorb it. Crosses one long sculpted leg over the other and says, brightly, "Okay."

"Okay?"

The corner of her mouth turns up. "Okay. Give me just one sec." She pulls out her phone and scrolls for a minute, then types something out very decisively, and my phone buzzes in my pocket.

"I just thought," she says, suddenly standing and swinging her bag over her shoulder, "that you could use those."

She sent me four links.

The first one is literally just to the Wikipedia page on The United States Government.

"To absorb some United States History? By osmosis."

She wrinkles her nose, sweet as fuck.

And just.

Leaves.

CHAPTER 5

Margo

If I didn't leave, I was going to cry, and I was absolutely *not* going to cry.

Not in front of her—a girl who knows everything, who knows who she is, who's gotten a million girlfriends with her absolutely Giant Dick Energy and won't stop swinging it around for everyone to trip over. Not in front of a girl who looked at me like... I don't know.

Like I was straight.

Because I flat-iron my hair.

I am in Old Navy with three of my best friends because standing in rows of clothing makes me feel good. It makes me feel comfortable, like I can pick who I show the world with $12.99 and a discount code and some floral. Usually, this calms me down: retail therapy.

But right now, it doesn't.

Even the familiar murmurs of my favorite people in the background (*You've already got the best ass in this entire store; you can't buy THOSE and totally wreck our self-esteems forever.*

Oh my god, you're right. I'm getting them.

Do you guys think this shirt would push me closer to Euphoria Zendaya or Spider-Man Zendaya? I'm not sure about it—) doesn't comfort me like it usually does.

I keep seeing Abbie, flicking her eyes from the top of my high ponytail to the big cushy soles of my flip-flops, and I can hear her thinking: *this girl likes girls? Please. Even her hair is straight.*

Maybe the problem isn't that she can't teach someone how to be gay; it's that she can't teach *me*.

So now, here I am in the Old Navy, staring at rows of plaid. At boyfriend cut button-downs. And I keep being pulled to the white eyelet sundresses in the front row. I keep leaning toward this pretty, short shift that would fall right at mid-thigh, in this deep yellow with flowers that would make my skin absolutely sing with life. It's on clearance because these aren't fall colors, but I don't care. There's a whole display of jewelry that's funky and girly and calms my fluttering pulse and that is what I want.

I keep my eyes on it when I hear Aaliyah asking me to chime in on the Zendaya debate, coming *this* close to replying, to reaching for the familiar.

But I stop myself.

It's not what I came here for.

I came here for this freaking plaid.

I yank one down off the rack, stealing a last glance at those sundresses, and run my fingers over the fabric. It's soft, nice even. I think, holding it up against my chest and looking in the mirror, *I'd fuck me.*

But then I hear Abbie's voice in my head again: *I'm not saying you can't do this whole high femme thing. I'm just saying you might be in the minority in queer circles.* But all I can focus on are the words *you can't do this whole high femme thing*, and that's great because I don't even know what "high femme" means.

I can figure it out from context, I guess.

It means me.

And the shittier thing is that I don't even know if I'm reading it right or if I'm being completely judgy and projecting *all* of this.

Because I do feel like the minority in queer circles.

I don't even have a queer circle.

I go on the internet and it's like everyone is speaking a completely different language and using phrases like "high femme" and I've never even kissed a girl outside of a game of spin the bottle. And maybe I'm wrong.

Maybe I'm not even queer at all, because it sure as hell just feels like...like I bought a rainbow hair band and when I wear it, I'm lying.

I don't... I don't know.

Aaliyah starts to get understandably annoyed at my lack of *any* kind of participation in this girls' shopping trip and says, "Margo!"

I spit out, "It's giving *Euphoria*" without looking.

I clench my nails around this stupid *I'd fuck me* plaid shirt and they dig into my palms. It hurts a little bit, and so does my jaw.

A voice from six inches behind me says, "Are you...going to buy that?"

It's Julia, who would never be caught dead in plaid. She's actually holding the yellow sundress I was lusting after earlier, and she should be. Her legs go on for ages, and it would be perfect for her skin tone. For her everything. She's very...

swan. Basically, Jameela Jamil if Jameela Jamil were seventeen and Black. She deserves the beautiful heterosexual dress.

I say, "Well!" as though I've got anything saved up to come after that.

Chloe, who can pull off a pixie cut better than Tinkerbell, tiny pale elf that she is, says, "No judgment or anything, it's just like…different, isn't it?"

Aaliyah calls from the shoes, "Wait, have we considered doing like a Seattle hipster ensemble for Halloween? 'Cause I could be into that."

Chloe and Julia have now launched into the hipster stereotypes they would choose to signify, and while Julia considers aloud how she might best personify the abstract concept of "The Linux Operating System," I wring the shirt in my hands. I could tell them the truth.

I could! I will. They'd probably be more confused that I'm looking at *plaid* than that I want to bang girls. And they'd be right. These girls know me better than anyone outside of my family, and they get to enjoy my Full Authentic Autistic Self™, which I can't say about a lot of people.

There's already Student Council Margo (very smiles and type A), Swim Team Margo (competitive, yet encouraging), Party Margo (playing make-out games knowing full well everyone in the room has a tiny video camera in their back pocket)—why can't there be Gay Margo?

But I look back at them, and I just—can't.

I don't know why.

It feels bad that I can't say it, that something in my stomach is telling me it isn't the right time.

But it's not the right time.

And so I don't.

G-d, this whole thing was such a wash. How do I feel worse now than I did before?

Aaliyah says, "Margo? Margo Zimmerman? Can you come out and play—okay, there you are. We're going to the Orange Julius, babe. Are you gonna buy that?"

Julia says, "Oh, no, if you actually are, it's okay!"

I shake my head.

I hang the shirt back up.

I go to the Orange Julius.

And then, I just…go home.

On Sunday, I go to Jamal's; it's kind of a tradition. Neither of us goes to church on the Lord's Day (I'm Jewish; my Lord's Day is Saturday, and Jamal is agnostic; he says his Lord's Days are Tuesdays, Thursdays, and every other Wednesday if it's raining) so we switch off hanging at each other's places instead.

Jamal's older brother, Nadir, broke his PlayStation last week in some kind of unfortunate parkour accident—their mom is *still* muttering angrily about the indignity of parkour! In the living room!—which means the traditional gaming Sunday is not exactly an option.

I'm okay with that, because if gaming, which I'm medium about, is not an option, that means Jamal's horses are.

"All right, horse girl," he says, and cocks his head toward the back door.

"Are you using that as an insult?"

He shrugs, ropes of muscle in his shoulders pushing their way through his short sleeves. "I'm just calling it like I see it. Some girls are horse girls, and some—"

"Please," I say. "All girls are horse girls."

He quirks his eyebrow and says, "Sounds like something a horse girl would say."

I groan and shove him out the back door.

The Tahans own a considerable amount of land (surprise, they have horses), and they use it for their Arabians. I've loved paints the most since I was a little girl, (also known as "pintos," which is Spanish for "painted, dappled, or spotted") because something about paints makes them seem...wild. (Probably the aforementioned chaotic and multicolored dapples and spots.) But Arabians are *majestic*.

Spirited and powerful and lean.

My pulse races just getting close to the stables, which Jamal thinks is absolutely hilarious. Sure, he hangs around these living unicorns every day.

But to the rest of us mere mortals, or to me at least, they're magical.

My hair is back in a ponytail and I'm in some pretty unflattering torn-up jeans and boots, the kind of thing you can wear in a stable without being too concerned about a paycheck going down the drain.

No one gets to see me like this.

No one but Jamal and the family I muck stalls for in the summer.

I practically skip into the stables, and the horses are snorting and stomping at our arrival.

"Hi, pretty girl," I say to Rascal, the truly unfairly named. Rascal is a tall (for an Arabian) chestnut mare who would be more likely to pet you than throw you, if her hooves allowed. It's Whiskey you've got to watch out for.

Whiskey is a less exciting tan, and is, of course, Jamal's favorite because Jamal is a freak who loves anything you have to watch out for.

I pet Rascal's velvety nose and I swear she smiles.

I address the older gelding behind me, saying loudly for Jamal's benefit, "Best Friend Black Horse."

I can never say it without smirking.

"Ugh," says Jamal from Whiskey's stall. "I was four, man, what do you want from me?"

"I think it's a regal name," I say.

Jamal's mouth curves into a smile and he leads Whiskey out. "Come on," he says. "Take Rascal."

My heart freezes, and that's so embarrassing. He does this every time because how on earth can you be a *horse girl* without wanting to ride a horse?

I do want to.

I will; I totally will.

Just.

Not today.

"I want to watch today."

"Kinky," he says.

I growl in the back of my throat and he laughs. "Come on," he says. "Rascal is practically an old woman. My baby sister could ride her."

I play with my nails. "Not—not today."

Jamal eyes me and just kind of purses his lips in acceptance, nods, and leads his horse off.

I follow him, horseless, to the outdoor pen and lean against the split-rail fence while he saddles Whiskey. He then slides a helmet down over his shiny black curls—that's what happens when you never use a flat iron: Jamal's perfect hair.

He mounts Whiskey, and I just...watch.

Jamal works the massive horse into a trot, and I can name every muscle moving to make it happen. My mind races through them on its own accord: the extensor muscles, the flexor muscles, the cranial pectoral. I can feel them under my hands.

But I can't feel them shifting against my legs—not that my legs would hang that far front, anyway, but... I don't know why I freeze like this every time. Why every time I watch Jamal crouch into Whiskey the untamable colt's back, I feel this nearly unbearable spike of jealousy.

I could ride.

I could do it right now.

I haven't been on a horse since I rode a Shetland pony around a pole at a carnival when I was four and I knew I wanted to be a large animal vet. Horses are huge and powerful and remarkable, and I want to understand them.

Before...before I get on one's back again.

Jamal has a jumping track set up and Whiskey gears up for one. Jamal's got two scars on his face from that damn horse—one across his lip and one on his eyebrow—and several more up his legs. But they're a unit now. He slides down so he's practically about to breathe Whiskey's mane into his mouth and they jump, and *god*, the longing is palpable.

Jamal lands. "Chickenshit!" he calls.

"I'll ride one day! I'm on my period. I'm cramping today."

"No, you're not. You're a chickenshit." They gear up for another jump, this one higher, requiring that they move together even more fluidly, more intentionally, than they already have been.

They soar.

The landing sounds in my ears and reverberates in my chest, and goddammit.

I *am* a chickenshit.

"I'll ride when I know how to ride."

Jamal narrows his eyes and guides Whiskey into a trot, right up beside me so I can feel how connected they are, how horribly jealous I am, how badly I want it, how afraid I am. Even with a tame horse, there's a risk, there's a wildness, there's... there's no way to prepare.

"You know how to ride. You've studied horses for ages, Miss Future Veterinarian. You know more about these things than I do."

"Not yet," I say.

He mouths "C-h-i-c-k-e-n-s-h-i-t," and kicks Whiskey back into a gallop.

Is it so completely absurd, so totally cowardly, to want to know how to do something before you take a dive into it? So you don't just...fall on your face? In front of G-d and everyone?

Whiskey and Jamal jump one rail, then two, then three.

And I watch.

CHAPTER 6

Abbie

The other three links Margo sent me are:

https://en.wikipedia.org/wiki/History_of_the_United_States_(1776-1789)

https://www.preceden.com/timelines/74647-american-history-from-1492-1877

https://apcentral.collegeboard.org/courses/ap-united-states-history/exam.

I have literally never been spoken to like this in my entire life.

The thing is, if I weren't desperate for help, this would definitely be our last interaction. If my entire college admission wasn't dependent on me getting that AP US History grade up, I would never *ever* speak to Margo Zimmerman again.

Is this how straight girls talk to each other? Because *yikes*. I'm so glad I figured out I'm bisexual before I got accidentally wrapped up in that melodramatic shit.

Maybe her first lesson should be How To Be Civil To Other Girls.

By the end of the field hockey match, my bleary rage has coalesced into something crystal clear and sharp.

The thing about Margo Zimmerman is that she's used to winning. And if her winning eases my path to passing history, then I'll let her win.

But she'll hate it.

It takes me four days to set up, but the following Monday, I send Margo two texts. The first just says, You win. The second says, Room A24, today at 4 p.m.

I don't get a response, but that's okay. I don't need one.

Margo will, of course, be early, so I run from my last class to my locker (and take twenty full seconds staring blankly into its depths before I remember why I'm even here: *oh, right,* my change of clothes) to the bathroom and get to A24 at 3:40 p.m. She's not here yet, but I don't know how much time I have before she arrives, so I rush through my preparations.

And I'm ready. I'm in position—sitting at the front of the classroom, my feet on the teacher's desk, a biography of Sappho open on my lap—when Margo pushes the door open.

I look up, like I'm surprised. The bright clear green of her Henley makes her auburn hair even more vibrant than usual, makes her brown eyes almost gold. "Hey," I say, taking my feet off the desk. "Come in. Sit down."

Margo hesitates. "I…" She peers around the classroom, as though she's looking for an empty seat. There are like, twenty. Literally, every seat is empty. "Where?"

"How about up near the front?" I say. "That way I'll know you're paying attention."

She narrows her eyes. "Abbie. Are you joking?" She

clutches her book bag to her chest and examines the front row, because she knows I am not joking.

But what I say is: "Of course I'm joking. You can sit anywhere you like." I glance at the clock at the back of the classroom. "But go ahead and pick one. We start at four o'clock sharp." I put my feet back on the desk and pick up my book again.

I wasn't reading when she walked in, and I'm sure as hell not reading now. I see her turn her head to look at the clock, which I know says 3:51 p.m. She's got nine minutes to pick a seat. She spends two of them waffling, when she and I both know she's going to land right in the front row. It would be way too weird to sit anywhere else.

I'm trying not to watch her worry about it, but it's so delightful. It's 3:53 p.m. and I can barely contain my smile. I turn a page I haven't read, and she sighs kind of passive-aggressively, like she wants me to hear it and feel guilty about this situation I've concocted, but she doesn't want to, you know, *confront* me about it.

One of the desks scrapes against the floor, and she mutters, "Jesus Christ," and I let my eyes flick up long enough to confirm what I knew would happen: front and center.

I don't respond, because why should I? It's nice to see her sweat after that shit she pulled with me last week. She can wait.

(She can wait, but can I? I'm pretty much vibrating in my seat, absorbing absolutely nothing on the page I'm staring at. On the best of days, it can be a struggle, but right now, I'm too many *things* to pay attention to the words on the page.

Too nervous, too delighted, too drunk with power, too…
whatever the adjective for Schadenfreude is.)

Margo's definitely nervous, too. She's sitting at that desk,
three feet away from where my feet are propped up, straightening her notebook and pencils, crossing and uncrossing
her legs. And she's doing it in a denim skirt that would be
fingertip-length if she had her hands on her hips.

I run my knuckle between my throat and collar.

The clock hits four o'clock, so I close my book and stand.
Margo glances up from pointlessly rearranging the four pencils on her desk, and the look on her face is eloquent. Her eyes
skip from how harshly my hair is pulled back to how the bold
lines of my suspenders curve over my chest to how sharply
my button-down nips in at my waist. Rarely have I been so
clearly, so unsubtly, so thoroughly eye-fucked by anyone like
I am being right now by Margo Zimmerman.

But it doesn't have to mean anything.

I turn to the blackboard and write *Ms. Sokoloff* in letters
large enough that she could have read them if she'd chosen to
sit in the back. Under that, I write *Queer 101.* I put the chalk
down, dust my hands off, and face Margo again, resting the
heels of my hands on the ledge under the board.

Margo's face is still absolutely out of control, but she manages to scoff. "I am *not* calling you Ms. Sokoloff."

"I don't know how other teachers do it, but in my classroom, you need to raise your hand before speaking."

Her face goes pink and she clenches her jaw. I can see her
wrestling with a decision and *god* is it a struggle not to grin.

Extremely, painfully slowly, she raises her hand.

I lift my chin. "Yes? In the green."

"I am not. Calling you. Ms. Sokoloff."

It's too much. I can't help the laugh that escapes me. "Good. Look. You wanted lessons, so you're getting lessons." I walk back to the desk and grab one of the two sheets of paper I brought with me, delivering it to her.

Margo says, "A syllabus?" But not with heat. With total unmitigated glee. Like her voice literally cracks with joy.

The syllabus is set up for nine weeks, with readings and papers and the whole thing. And she's *excited*. I was only half married to the idea, but she's so into it that now I feel like I have to follow through.

She's reading it already, so I don't say anything else. It occurs to me that I'm concerned about how she receives it, like it matters. Like it matters how Margo Zimmerman feels about my fake syllabus for this fake class that only exists because I couldn't let her win. But she's so delighted by it, leaning over her desk as she reads, her flat-ironed hair escaping from behind her ear to hang in her face. She doesn't move it.

Is it warm in here? It's warm in here. The air's too thick, or something. I have to loosen the knot in my tie to be able to breathe.

It's not better when she looks up, her eyes bright. She really is objectively pretty. Gorgeous, even. Just not my type.

I clear my throat. "Are you ready to get started?"

Margo tucks that hair behind her ear again, picks up the pencil closest to her—the one farthest to the left in the little picket fence she's constructed on the right side of her desk—and smooths the top page of her open notebook. The perfect picture of the perfect student.

She says, "Yes."

"We're going to start today by defining some terms." I turn back to the board, pick up a piece of chalk, and write, even larger than I wrote my name, *HOMOSEXUALITY*.

CHAPTER 7

Margo

HOMOSEXUALITY.

Homo. Sexuality.

Honestly, screw you, Abbie Sokoloff, I know what *homosexuality* means and I know what lesbians are and I DEFINITELY know what French kissing is, *Jesus*.

Homosexuality.

I have spent the last hour being talked down to and expected to take notes on it, and I absolutely hate that I have. My notebook has two pages' worth of stuff I already know because I didn't want to miss anything.

And because I love this syllabus.

I found myself staring at every line that Abbie planned out, getting excited. Excited to write literal essays. Excited to learn about queer history and sexuality and dress code and Sitting Like A Gay, whatever that means. And secret gay slang. And *Thor: Ragnarok*—a scientific study in Tessa Thompson and Thor, Lesbian Ally.

I want to learn all of this. And my heart flutters in my chest at the idea that Abbie, for vengeance or otherwise, worked on this for... I don't know. Hours.

At least.

It's unsettling. That she did it, and that I'm reacting to it.

Not as unsettling as the feeling in the pit of my stomach watching her in those suspenders. The lines of her chest and her waist and... *god.*

I don't know if she could tell.

Shit, I HOPE she couldn't tell.

She can't know that the last hour left me absolutely dying, crossing and uncrossing my legs and forcing myself not to look at her so I didn't actually choke.

Like I said, it's unsettling.

I didn't come to Abbie Sokoloff because I like her; I came because she knows things—specifically, things I want to learn. At the conclusion of this arrangement, she can go back to her world and I can go back to mine, but maybe with a girlfriend.

I am not thinking about the curve of her thighs in those jeggings.

I am thinking about...about.

Literally anything else.

I have swim practice today after school, but there's time to kill before I need to get there, so I head to the library. Now that a couple days have passed since my first lesson with Abbie (it's "ØDINSDAY", after all) and dulled a little of the total fury of the event, I am left to focus on the goal at hand.

Our school library doesn't have a queer section at all. This is the Bible belt. There's no way our governor—who doesn't even want us to say the word *gay*—would let any public school library have a whole labeled section of books for people like me, so I'm pretty surprised that I find any of the books on Abbie's reading list.

Then I get curious: I google "under the radar queer YA" and spend some time poking through the shelves, finding a surprising number of titles that haven't been banned by PTA Pam and the Campus Crusade.

I check them out. All of them.

I don't know what they're about, I don't know what I'm about to learn, or even who the authors are.

What I do know is that Abbie put some real thought into the syllabus. She seems to play pretty fast and loose, but she clearly wants to help me, however she can.

And...that just. Really matters.

After last week, and the total disaster that was the field hockey game, and the BULLSHIT that was the classroom learning experience, it matters.

Not...not in any way beyond academic. Professional.

It matters medium.

I check out my books, halfway between proud and embarrassed to hand them to the librarian, and run off toward swim practice. The locker room is close to empty when I get there because I'm almost late, which never happens.

It's only *close* to empty, so I duck into a stall and change comfortably alone behind a locked door like I always do. I come out of it in my swimsuit, clothes wadded under my arm.

And I stop short, because Abbie is directly in my line of sight, just a few paces away. My mouth actually falls open— the way a straight girl would when presented with her very attractive, regular, platonic friend. She's pulling the royal blue swimsuit up over her shoulders, and I've always considered these swimsuits kind of ugly. I was just...*extremely* wrong.

Well. Maybe not about the swimsuits.

I've never put much thought into the muscles of Abbie's shoulders, or the little lines at the small of her back, or the way that swimsuit traces over her shoulder blades.

But my *gosh*. Am I sweating? I don't know; it's the pool locker room. It's humid in here.

Wow, it's humid in here.

I am staring.

I'm still staring like a lesbian deer in the headlights when she turns around, swimsuit mercifully pulled completely up over her chest.

I don't know what I expect her to say, but it isn't, "Zimmerman, did you change in the bathroom stall?"

"Yes."

Her eyebrows go up. "Huh," is all she says.

I narrow my eyes, because I'm already tired of her. "What?" I don't know if I intend it to come out as a semi-growl. Well. Maybe I do.

"I just thought you weren't going to come out for a while."

I roll my eyes. "Har har. That's a bathroom stall, not a closet."

"Oh, I know," she says, that infuriating smirk on her face, "it's just that only gay girls use the bathroom stalls to change."

"You didn't," I say, as if that will score me any points.

"Were you watching me change, Zimmerman?"

"Shut up." My face is probably bright red, and would be even if I hadn't watched her slide those straps up over her shoulders, even if the memory of it didn't make my throat close up. "I wasn't watching you change. But I could have, because you didn't change in a stall, and if you didn't change in a stall, then changing in a stall can't be—" and I do like, jazz hands, I guess "—*queer culture* or whatever."

"I said gay girls were the only ones that did it, not that gay girls were incapable of doing anything else."

I roll my eyes, because. Well. G-d. All I want is to get out of here and into the pool because if I was running late before, I'm definitely actually late now but for some reason I can't make myself just. Walk away.

"Hey, you came to me," she says.

"Yes, you are the expert," I say, deadpan. "Let me grovel before your superior knowledge and wisdom. I know nothing. Please diagram the clitoris for me again."

She puts her hands on her hips and sort of tips her head toward me in a way that I'm pretty sure is supposed to be funny, but here I am, following the lines of her fingers. Just, gay as hell, looking at where her fingers are pointing. Her smirk has taken on a life of its own, like she *knows*, and I can actually hear it in her voice when she says, "Are you flirting with me, Zimmerman?"

A tic of anxiety pulls at the back of my brain, but she thinks she's winning. And the only thing stronger than my anxiety is my desire to win. Specifically, to beat her. So I swallow it and summon the boldness that ran through my veins when I thought I liked boys. I take a step toward her, narrow my eyes just a little, and say, "If I was flirting with you, you'd know it."

Abbie laughs a little, and I kind of hate her for it, and she just says, "Would I?"

I clench my teeth and I'm probably blushing. Because I'm mad, not because I'm... Anyway. Whatever. I'm mad. I say, "Listen. When are we doing the history tutoring?"

Abbie bites her lip, but it's clear she's not fake-flirting with me anymore. Her eyes go somewhere else, and she says, "Well, I mean. The sooner the better, right? What about after practice?"

I shrug. "Yeah, I'm free tonight. Why don't you give me time to take a shower and come over to my house?"

Her face brightens again, and vulnerable Abbie is gone in a flash. She gives me finger guns (I'll never live that down, oh my god). "Hey!" She nods, a wild grin as bright as the high beams on Chad's dumbass truck spreading across her face. "You're right, I *could* tell when you were flirting."

I let my expression relax back into Resting Bitch Face and just spin, mumbling, "Good lord," under my breath.

I stretch my arm behind me and flip her off, and her laugh follows me to the pool.

CHAPTER 8

Abbie

Margo lives in a neighborhood not far from mine: solidly middle class, if that even exists anymore, filled with teachers and not quite C-level businesspeople. The Zimmerman front yard is nicer than most on their street, no weeds in the garden beds and mulch that is definitely not what the builders threw in there.

They've left their front porch light on, and there are little solar-powered lights on either side of the walkway from the driveway to the porch. I ring the doorbell, and the dog that starts barking sounds like it's the size of my car. The door opens, and an older, taller, musclier version of Margo is standing there in front of me.

"Hey," he says. "You must be Abbie?"

All I can do is nod, because *damn*, good job, Mr. and Mrs. Zimmerman. A+ genetics.

He opens the door wider and it's pretty hard not to watch

the lines of his arm when he does. Especially in that sleeveless undershirt. "Come on in," he says. "Margo's in the kitchen."

"Thanks," I manage. I touch the glass mezuzah as I walk through the doorway, and then I'm just standing there, in the windowless vestibule, with Zimmerman the Elder, and I don't know where the kitchen is and man, if that's what Margo's eyes look like in the dark...

"I'm Mendel," he says as he leads me through the house. "The older brother. Margo said y'all are in AP US History together?"

"Yup," I say, which is all I can say, because his nightmare medium-slung sweatpants are ruining my bisexual life.

And then we're in the kitchen and Margo is sitting at the kitchen table, bent over her notebook and an open textbook. All I can see is her hair draped over the fist her head is propped up on and then she looks up and I've forgotten all about Mendel's sweatpants. Because I've never seen Margo like this. Casual and air-dried and relaxed. She's wearing leggings and a deliberately oversized crop top and her feet and face are bare, a handful of freckles scattered over her nose and cheekbones, and I guess I can't breathe.

"Abbie? Abbie."

Oh no, Mendel's talking to me. I turn to him and why is everyone in this room so attractive? The eternal bisexual struggle. "Yeah? Sorry. What's up?"

"Are you a dog person?"

Margo meets my eyes and her body language shifts, her shoulders bunching up, and she touches her hair, her face. Like something needs fixing.

Nothing needs fixing.

"Dame Julie Andrews is totally cool," she says, fingers worrying at her earlobe. "She's absolutely massive but she swears she's a lap dog."

Dame. Julie Andrews. The dog. Sure. Why not.

"That's fine," I say. "Whatever is fine. I mean it's your house."

Mendel nods. "Cool. I'll let her out, then. Plus, you won't have to listen to her whine the whole time you're here."

"You know Julie Andrews," comes a female voice from another room. "She hates to not be the center of attention."

As if on cue, a long baying howl echoes through the kitchen.

Mendel and Margo say in stereo, "SHUT UP, JULIE ANDREWS," and Margo collapses into laughter.

I...don't know what to do. We were never a dog family, and I don't know—it shouldn't make me think less of us, but here, in the Zimmerman house, with this lovingly delivered, comfortably exasperated chastisement. It feels like we never got a dog because there wasn't enough love for one.

Mendel doesn't say anything else, just walks out of the kitchen, shaking his head and laughing.

"I'm sorry," says Margo, and then she literally snorts. She covers her mouth and her eyes widen just a little but she manages to catch her breath and says, "Sit down. We're very regular around here. Sit at the regular kitchen table."

"Yes, all the most regular people I know name their dogs after celebrities who have achieved damehood." I drop into the chair across from hers and shrug, like this is all somehow not the exact opposite of my house. I'm overwhelmed and I don't know what to say so I just say the first thing that comes to mind, and it's somehow, "You should see my neighbor's dog, Judi Dench. She's constantly getting out of their house and shitting in everyone's yards."

Margo laughs again, bright and unbridled, and says, "You haven't even met my sugar glider, Sir Michael Caine."

Holy shit, my joke landed. "I can't wait to see him with the Muppets."

Margo laughs so hard she pulls a Chris Evans, falling back against her chair and grabbing her own boob about it. It takes her a second to pull herself together, but she finally catches her breath and kind of karate chops the textbook in front of her. "Focus!"

But how am I supposed to focus when this whole brand new human is sitting in front of me? I can't meet her eyes as I pull my notebook from my bag. I'm *nervous*, of all things, as if I don't want her to know how badly I'm tanking this class. It's literally why I'm here. If anyone's going to know my level of fail, it's going to be Margo.

"So," I say. "Where do we start?"

She pulls this meticulously laid-out timeline out of her bag and says, "Here," pointing to the beginning. Like. The *beginning*. "In the beginning, there were no white people here. And then came Leif Erikson. And then came Christopher Columbus. And syphilis. But that means we have to go to Spain, which is not where he was from. He was licensed for exploration by the same monarchs that kicked the Jews out of Spain. Did you know that? And they couldn't go to the new colonies, so they went to England, which is why there are so many old Sephardic—"

"Oh," I say, somehow simultaneously caring and not caring that I interrupted her. "No. I don't—Margo. Wait. So many Sephardic what?"

"What?"

"You said there are a lot of old Sephardic something, and then I cut you off, which, sorry."

Her eyes narrow, but not like she's mad, like she's thinking, like she's rewinding through the conversation. Then they relax, and she goes, "Oh! Families. Old Sephardic families. They came from England with the early waves of settlers."

"That's really interesting, and I am glad you told me, but like—listen. I'm not—" I scratch the back of my neck, because I need something to do with my hands, because I hate admitting to this kind of stuff. My face feels like it's on literal fire. "I'm failing, and that's unacceptable. So I just. You know. Need help with the next test. Or paper. Or whatever he assigns."

"Oh," she says. "Okay. Sure, let me just…" She examines that timeline and shuffles some papers around and doesn't give me a single bit of shit for any of this. "You want to nail the test next week. Sorry, I should have probably, like, asked before I went Extreme History Nerd on you and wrote a tome on the history of the continent."

This is not the same Margo Zimmerman that sat next to me on the bleachers before the field hockey match. Or the one who was waiting for me to come out of the pool and shouted *you're gay* at me. Or the one in Room A24. Or the one in the locker room. Or any Margo I've ever seen.

Lucky for me, she's not my type.

"Yeah. I guess it's going to be on the Constitutional Convention? I've been trying to do the reading, and I just can't get anything to like, stick in my brain. Like, I just can't focus for shit."

She nods. "Textbooks suck. You don't need ninety percent of it, anyway. If you just want to pass, what you need is the really boring stuff. So let's start with definitions." Her mouth twitches up and I half expect her to write in loopy cursive over the full page: AMERICA.

But she doesn't. She writes out *Declaration of Independence* on one side of a T chart, and *Constitution* on the other.

She slides it to me and says, "Okay. Fill in what you know. Not complete sentences or anything, just—"

And that is when Dame Julie Andrews comes galloping down the hall. She's all ears and jowls and legs, everything flopping and drooping like a half-melted dog candle. She careens up to the table, her big nose snuffling and snorting and rooting against my legs. Margo's laughing but also trying to get her hundred-pound dog to calm down and not push me out of my chair. Julie Andrews finally takes the hint, but turns her excitement on Margo, her giant paws up on Margo's thighs, waterboarding her with kisses. Margo leans back from the onslaught and Julie Andrews notices her book bag and buries her nose in it like she's rooting for truffles. A type A collector's set comes sliding out: three-ring binders, a pencil pouch, a *pen* pouch, two textbooks in book covers for god's sake.

And the olive green of Audre Lorde's *Sister Outsider* peeking out from under a thick black hardcover of James Baldwin's early novels and stories, both of them wrapped in shiny library plastic.

She...checked out the books I assigned her? I don't know

if I'm going to laugh or... I don't know. Cry? I've only read a few of the books I put on there; most of them came from some "40 Queer Books To Read Before You Die" list Google showed me. I want to read them. I want to read widely and deeply, and I've tried. I have. But a lot of nonfiction is like wading through half-dried concrete, even when I'm interested in the subject matter.

Margo's laughing, sputtering, and finally says, "My gosh, Julie Andrews, get your life together!"

I'm laughing, too, because I can't help it. This big dopey-ass bloodhound is named Dame Julie Andrews, and Margo hasn't given me crap for failing this class that she's doing so well in, and she actually, like, seems to care? About so many things.

It's like...maybe Queer 101 isn't just about getting laid for her. She wants the *community*, and she wants me to show it to her.

Mendel comes back into the kitchen and whistles sharply and Julie Andrews vacates Margo's lap and galumphs over to him. He rubs her head and ears and jowls, and I've never heard a dry dog sound so wet.

Mendel says something about treats and Julie Andrews loses her mind a little, and they disappear from the kitchen.

In the Julie Andrews–less quiet, I glance back at Margo's book bag, and her eyes follow mine to the books she checked out.

"Oh," she says, suddenly going a little pink. She tucks a strand of hair behind her ear. "I'm going to get the rest. That's just all they had in the school library."

I can't figure out why she's self-conscious about that, and I can't figure out why I'm so distracted by how her blush makes her freckles stand out. "No," I say, "I—I'm surprised they had any in there."

"Nineteen copies of *Lord of the Flies* but nary a rainbow spine in the library." She shrugs. "Anyway, I just didn't want you to think I was like...slacking. I'm going to the real library tomorrow. So."

I blink. "Slacking? Dude, listen, the fact that you looked for the actual book instead of the SparkNotes is impressive. You don't slack. Nothing about you is slack. Why do you think I asked you to help me pass this class?"

She swallows hard. "Oh." Her face goes redder somehow and she just looks at me for a half second too long. Then she clears her throat and says, "Okay. Right. Yeah, this—this class. The Constitution."

She blinks down at the sheet she gave me and slides it across the table. "Show me what you got."

CHAPTER 9

Margo

After Abbie leaves, I slip up the stairs and into bed, and I crack open *Sister Outsider*. The introduction is about identity, in a hundred different ways. Ways that don't apply to me at all and ways that do. Then she goes into this trip in Russia, and I'm not sure what I'm supposed to learn about queerness from it. Not at first.

It's good.

Then it becomes about identity again, and people, and her experience as a Black woman. It's a story that I can get swept away in, and Audre Lorde, it turns out, is a lesbian. Like… like me, I guess. Though that still feels nerve-wrackingly false, like I don't have enough experience to call myself that.

Either way, just reading something that someone *like me* wrote makes it suddenly feel Big and Important. Even though I don't get it right away. Even though the correlation to my own life doesn't come particularly easily tonight.

What comes easily, what keeps punching through the text, is Abbie.

She wasn't Jerk Professor Abbie in my kitchen.

Wasn't *Are You Gonna Keep Doing This Femme Thing* Abbie when she leaned over that piece of notebook paper and started scribbling what she knew about US history in stop and start fragments of thoughts. She was vulnerable, and she was listening, and she was… god, I don't know.

A lot.

What's also *a lot* is how much I'm thinking about the interaction. And I can't focus.

That's not good; how am I supposed to figure out any of my shit if I can't stop thinking about Abbie long enough to get through two chapters of a book that's supposed to explain said shit?

I stare back at the page, and I cannot get the personal application through my thick skull, and now I feel like I'm going to fail.

As though this is a real class!

As though I'm going to come home and go, "Sorry, Mom and Dad, I really screwed up Bein' A Gay 101. I'll never get a scholarship to college now."

But that's what it feels like, and anxiety curls in my muscles, thrums through my veins with every word I read.

I blow out a breath, and I close the book.

This is just… It's fine. It's not what I need tonight. A couple chapters is enough; it's satisfactory.

I lean over the side of my bed, halfway to falling off, and pull Abbie's syllabus out of my bag.

She's assigned several essays for me—of course she has—and the first one hits me like a baseball bat: How I Knew I Was Gay.

It's patronizing on purpose. In the same vein as "HO-

MOSEXUALITY," and defining the acronyms LGBTQ-IAP (which I actually thought was more patronizing than it was; that's kind of a long acronym, and the primer was helpful. Lesbian-Gay-Bisexual-Transgender-Queer/Questioning-Intersex-Asexual/Aromantic/Agender/Definitely Not Ally-Pansexual) and the perhaps more inclusive and less of a mouthful GSRM (Gender-Sexual-Romantic-Minorities).

But it doesn't feel basic to me.

My pencil hovers over my paper, and I realize that I have no idea how to start it. I know I kissed a girl in a game of spin the bottle.

But before that, what was normal and what was a crush?

What was wanting to be a pretty girl and wanting to be *with* one?

What was...when? When was I just Gay?

I don't know. I don't know how to figure it out and I don't know how the hell to put it on paper.

So, cool.

I crumple that, too.

And I go to sleep, and by "go to sleep" I mean lie awake until 4:00 a.m. doing nothing but finding faces in the speckles on my ceiling.

And thinking about how on earth to write this essay.

And why. It is so impossible.

It's Sunday again, and this week Jamal and I hang at my house. He sits beside me in a white tank top and basketball shorts, gaming on my PlayStation that *my* brother did *not* parkour into. He's blasting his way through *Mass Effect* for the thousandth time, making the same exact decisions he's made the last 999.

"Oh, romancing Liara," I say. "We're really branching out."

His mouth curls up and he keeps his eyes on the screen when he flips his middle finger at me. He says, "Khara alaik," one of the only phrases in Arabic I know (it technically translates to "shit on you") because if your best friend is Palestinian and bilingual, you learn the swears real fast.

I grin and lean back against the couch cushion, toes pressed up against Jamal's leg. This is how we've always sat. And maybe that's normal, or maybe it should have clued me in—being able to sit next to a dude who looks like *Jamal*, toes on his outer thigh, without feeling a thing that wasn't, "Keep shooting like that and you're gonna die—get better at this."

Not like if I were into guys, I would be required to be into every single pretty one, but Jamal is…ridiculous. He's lithe and tall and has a baseball player's ass and shoulders. And his smile is the distillation of mischief. Golden brown skin and eyes that match. Jamal looks at a girl and she melts.

But… I never did.

The signs are everywhere now that I *know*.

I've been able to avoid this before, but now Abbie and her lessons and that pointless essay are in my head and they're all I can think about.

Jamal yells at the screen after getting blasted by a Geth (which I could have told him was coming with *that* weapon) and I shift.

I wonder if he can hear me thinking this. Thinking: I'm gay, I'm gay, I'm gay, and you don't know and hardly anyone knows and all of this feels HUGE. It feels like a sign on my head. It feels like it's fake, like I don't know anything about myself and like I'd be making too big a deal out of what I'm feeling if I said it out loud. It's all wrong and right and chaotic, and it's a conversation I kind of want to happen with him. But on the one hand, it's like a betrayal that I haven't told him already. On the other, this is my own and no one is entitled to it, and I'm so freaking *insecure* after the classes and the field hockey and the Old Navy disasters, respectively, that I don't even know HOW to approach it. Or what will happen if I do.

It is Pandora's gay, gay box.

I roll my shoulders and take a deep breath, and my toes curl with tension.

"Jesus Christ, Margo," says Jamal. "Are you trying to pull my leg hairs out?"

"Sorry," I say.

He turns back to the screen.

It's not like there's a guide to coming out. There should be maybe; maybe I should have asked Abbie about *that* to begin with. Or Mendel. I'm so nervous. Coming out to Mendel was nothing because, I don't know. He's queer, too. And he's my brother. Abbie was easy because it didn't count. It was a professional necessity. Jamal has been my best friend since the seventh grade.

This? This counts.

I don't know why I can't breathe getting ready to say it.

Like somehow this is going to change anything.

I stare at the side of his face, and what I intend to say is, *Hey, can we talk? I just need to tell you something.* And work my way up to the queerfession after a lot of background and waffling and preparation.

He side-eyes me, like he can feel the stare lasering out from my eye holes. "Can I—can I help you?"

What comes out of my mouth is, "I'm gay."

He's so unresponsive for a second that I think maybe he didn't hear me and I'll have to work up the nerve to say it all again, and I don't even know if I can.

Then he says, "Whhhhaaaaattttt?" in the same way that you'd *whhhhaaaaatttt* a professional football player telling you he liked sports. He glances at me one more time and half rolls his eyes, then gets back to playing.

"I… Excuse me?"

Jamal kills a Geth.

He blows out a breath through his nose.

He presses Pause and sets the controller down, then shifts so he's facing me, knee bumping over my bare foot.

"Of course you're gay," he says.

"What?"

"What do you mean, *what*?"

"I just don't think you could have known. I didn't know until a few months ago."

Jamal raises an eyebrow at me and says, "Dude, I've known you since middle school. You've been gay forever."

"How?" I'm almost offended. Almost violated, like how dare he know this private information before I did? How dare my best friend's own brain out me to him?

He shrugs. "Well, I mean. For starters, you could resist all this." He waggles his eyebrows and gestures down his torso. I groan. "Seriously, have you seen the way you look at girls?

75

And you just… I don't know. It's a vibe. You're gay. Of course you're gay, M."

I chew on my lower lip and look over his shoulder at the blank living room wall. "What about Chad? And all my other boyfriends?"

He goes super deadpan. "Please, dude. Chad was always a fuckin' beard and you know it."

I snort. "Or whatever that term is for girls."

Jamal laughs and bumps my shoulder. "Your face is red." He glances down at my wrist and slips his thumb over it. "And your pulse is going about a million miles an hour. Were you seriously that nervous to tell me?"

Suddenly, I feel bad about that. Like I didn't trust him or something. "I don't know."

He furrows his brow, just for a second. "You think I'd give a shit?"

I consider it. No. No I didn't.

I wasn't afraid he'd disown me or something.

I was afraid it would be fake. I was afraid I would tell him, and he'd be completely shocked, or worse, not believe me at all. And if my best friend, who knows me better than anyone, who knows me sometimes better than I do, didn't believe it, it would all feel impossible.

My chest loosens. I actually tear up, which is kind of embarrassing.

"Hey," says Jamal. He curls his hand around the back of my neck and says, "Good for you, okay? I love you, man." And he kisses my forehead.

I lean my head on his shoulder and whisper, "Okay."

And suddenly it is.

Okay, I mean.

Suddenly, no matter what anyone else says or implies, it's real.

I am real.

I am going to DO THIS. I am gay, and Jamal knew, which makes it valid, somehow, and I am going to get myself some gay as hell gear and Gay with the best of them.

Because I am Margo Zimmerman and I. Like. Girls.

There's a few seconds of silence, just the quiet sounds of the washer and dryer in the background and the tick of the giant clock we never look at because it's ugly but also because cell phones exist, which Mendel and I told our dad a thousand times, but he still insisted on putting one up in the living room, anyway.

Mass Effect comes back on.

Jamal mutters under his breath, *"I'm gay,"* in this mocking tone of voice that's like it was the most obvious thing in the world.

I flick his ear. I say, "Khara alaik."

CHAPTER 10

Abbie

We're sitting at the dinner table, all three of us. We almost never do this. Usually somebody is pissed off or eating with friends or whatever. The last time we were all together at a table was probably Passover, which was six months ago.

I guess this sounds like a good thing, us all sharing a meal together. It's not. It's me at one end, two boxes of pizza in the middle, and my mom and dad very obviously halfway to second base at the other end. This is how it is: they're either yelling, not speaking at all, or fucking. They never just…talk. Sometimes it seems like they barely know each other.

And that's fine, I guess. I'm not trying to tell anyone how to live their life, but like, when you've got a kid, maybe you should at least *try* to act like you like each other.

Once, my dad got up in the middle of dinner and walked out of the house. They'd been fighting about something all day; I don't remember what it was, or if I ever knew. What I do remember is my mom bursting into tears and somehow suggesting her nine-year-old daughter should go after him, bring him back, she loved him so much, why would he do this, she knew he didn't mean it, she loved him, she loved him, she loved him.

I didn't go after him. How could I? I was *nine.*

He spent the night at a hotel and came back while I was at school. I don't know who apologized to whom, or if anyone ever did, but when I got home, I was on my own for the rest of the day. They were too busy making up to say hello, or help me with my homework, or fix me dinner.

Maybe it's selfish to want your parents to pay attention to you. A lot of classmates over the years have told me how lucky I am to not have a curfew, to not have any rules. And that's nice, I guess, but I would like to know what it feels like for someone other than Charlie to look at me and see a whole sentient human.

They finish eating before I do, or get tired of eating, I guess, because when they get up, we all know what's about to happen. My dad chases my mom, laughing from the dining room down the hall, goosing her to make her squeal. The bedroom door slams shut.

I'm staring at the pizza. No one asked me what kind I wanted. They just ordered it. It's ham and pineapple, and I've been picking all the ham out of it because I don't like the way it tastes and, well, we're not supposed to have it. It's not kosher. And my parents don't care and so I didn't care and I don't know, maybe I still don't, or maybe I do.

G-d. I need to get out of the house. What I want is to go to the skate park and blow off some steam, just skate until my legs feel like jelly. Maybe find somebody to blow off some steam with in another way.

But I can't, because it's raining, so I text Charlie.

Help, my parents are getting along

I can hear way too many sounds coming from my parents' room, so I put on some music, loud, while I wait for Charlie's response.

She replies: Gross come over.

I want to ask if Adriana is there, but I know it'd be rude. I like Adriana, but I don't want to have to share Charlie right now. I don't want to have to share anyone. I just want—it sounds naive, but I just want someone to *see* me.

I'm in pajama shorts and a tank top but I don't care, and neither will she. And neither will Adriana, if she's there, because why would she?

I stuff a change of clothes and my toothbrush into my backpack, just in case. My parents won't care one way or the other, and we've had enough spontaneous sleepovers that Charlie's folks won't think it's out of the ordinary, even on a Sunday night. I text my mom, knowing I won't get a response, to tell her where I'm going, and then I text Charlie to tell her I'm on my way, and then I am.

Charlie lives with her mom and grandmother and three sisters in a duplex about fifteen minutes from my house. Her grandfather died before she was born, and her father's done so many tours in Afghanistan I've lost count.

Their house is small but well lit and meticulously organized. Charlie shares a room with two of her sisters—the youngest one, Emma, still sleeps in her toddler bed in their mom's room—and it's so optimally arranged it looks like an IKEA catalog. Or the inside of Margo's backpack.

Adriana isn't there, and I feel bad for how grateful I am. Charlie seems to instinctively know I need some one-on-one time, so she sends her sisters into the living room and gives them permission to play whatever game they want on the Xbox. She closes and locks the door and flops onto the queen-size bed she shares with Morgan. I lie down next to her, my fingers laced behind my head, and we're just...silent. I can hear her sisters playing *Super Smash Bros.* in the next room, but that's okay.

I already feel better.

I say, to the ceiling, "I can't wait to get out of here."

"You just got here."

I grin and kick her foot. "You know what I mean, you jerk."

"Sorry about your parents," she says. "You staying tonight?"

"I don't know." It's the truth. I don't want to sleep on the foldout couch. I want my own bed. I want my parents to be normal.

"You know you're welcome to."

"I know. Thanks, man."

We're both silent for a few minutes. Emma shrieks with delight, probably, and I can hear Charlie smile. "You need to talk about it?"

"What do you think of Margo Zimmerman?" The question's out of my mouth before I can stop it. Before I even knew that's what I was thinking about.

There's a moment before Charlie responds. "I don't know,

dude. I haven't really interacted much with her. She's pretty hot, but like. I don't know. Not my type." She turns her head to me, hair whispering across the pillow. "Not yours, either, I didn't think?"

"No," I say quickly. I'm not lying. Margo's not a ponytail basketball girl, and she's not Ferris Bueller, and she's not a devil-may-care skater, so.

"Hmm." She faces the ceiling again. "Besides, she's straight. Hasn't she been dating Chad the Impaler since last year?"

I roll my eyes because, honestly, I can't help it. "Not that that means anything, but—"

"*Yes*, Abbie, I know, you're bisexual, bisexuals exist, I get it."

"Charlie, come on—"

She cuts me off, and I'm not even sure if I can be mad because I'm muttering. I hate that I'm muttering. She just says, "But like, *Chad*?"

"I don't think they're together anymore." She always does this, because she's a gold star lesbian, and somehow that always makes me feel like the asshole, like I'm trying to convince her to be bisexual or something. As if that's how it works. "I mean, I know they're not. Together. Everyone knows that."

"Well, Chad's a douche."

I don't say anything because at this point, what can I say? She turns her head toward me, her cheek resting on the pillow. "Abs, I mean this in the nicest way possible, but why do you give a shit about Margo Zimmerman?"

I press my lips together. I really want to tell her what I'm doing. That I'm giving gay lessons to last year's Homecoming Queen. But I can't, because you don't out other people. I should include that in the lesson plan: Keeping Queer Secrets.

But I can't say anything, and I can't say nothing, so I go with, "She's helping me out in AP US."

Charlie turns all the way over on her side, her head propped up on her hand, and looks at me. "Is that it?"

"No, Charles, I'm totally banging it out with Margo Zimmerman." I roll my eyes and hope it's convincing enough that she won't press, even though just saying the words has conjured...unexpected imagery. Unexpectedly good imagery. So I do the healthy thing and ignore it and just barrel through. "Yes, of course that's it. Cameron's class is a lot harder than I thought it would be and Margo's the most overachieving human I know."

"Hmm."

If I protest, it'll make her more suspicious. Knowing Margo is gay is the biggest secret I've ever kept from Charlie. Maybe the only one of any consequence. And I feel all this pressure to Be Good At Being Gay so I can mentor this Baby Gay correctly. But half the time I feel like I'm not that good at being gay—because I'm not *gay*. I'm bisexual, and the amount of baggage that exists in the queer community about bisexuals is exhausting. We're crazy, we're greedy, we're slutty, we're actually lesbians, we're actually straight, we're just doing it for male attention. (I swear to god Charlie once told me I was *appropriating lesbian culture*.) Everyone at school knows I'm bi, but the last thing I want is for Margo Zimmerman, the lesbian, to look at me the way Charlie does. To feel like my attraction to people who aren't girls is some kind of covert straight girl op to infiltrate the gay community, and… What? Tell them to dress in florals—

OH MY GOD.

I have been a huge dick to Margo Zimmerman.

Charlie says…something, but I don't know what it was because I was too busy thinking about the checklist of things I gave Margo to change about herself in order to be *a proper gay.*

"Sorry, what?"

"I said," she says, "you don't need an A. Spaghetti brain."

I snort. "I know I don't need an A. But I do need to pass. And I'm not right now." She doesn't respond, and I take a deep breath, because I'm about to tell her the thing I've been trying not to think about since I saw my midterm grades. "Like, I don't give a shit about the AP exam. If I don't pass this class…my acceptance to Florida International is conditional on me maintaining a reasonable GPA. And what I've got in there right now? I did the math. I need at least an eighty. I've got a fifty-six."

Charlie blows out a breath. "Shit, dude."

"Yeah," I say. "That's pretty much where I'm at."

She reaches over and squeezes my forearm. "You got this, man."

I don't know what to say. It's such a medium, vanilla reassurance, but also somehow exactly what I needed to hear from her. I just want to know someone takes my success seriously. As a given. I just want to know someone believes in me.

My phone dings. I want to ignore it, but it might be Margo. Or my mom. So I roll off the bed and dig my phone out of the side pocket of my backpack.

"Everything all right?" Charlie asks.

Come home rigth now

"No," I say. "It's my mom. She wants me home." I'm just staring at the phone, because I know what's going to happen when I go home. She'll tell me she and Dad had another fight, and she needs me there with her, and she'll cry, and I'll have to play the role of the adult, and I just—I don't want to do that. I'm tired.

"Are you going to go?"

The screen darkens. "I don't know. I don't want to."

"So don't."

Abigail Rebecca, come home this instant

"She's pretty adamant."

"Abs."

I look over at Charlie. She's sitting up cross-legged on the bed. She says, "If you don't want to go home, don't go home. Tell her we were watching a movie and your phone was on silent and you passed out and didn't wake up until the morning."

I want to. Desperately. But she's my mom, and, well. That's it. She's my mom.

And she needs me.

I reply: Leaving Charlie's now.

I say, "Sorry, Charlie."

She grins despite herself, but I can tell she thinks I'm making a mistake. To be fair, I definitely am. She stands up and comes over to me and hugs me, tight. "You know I love you, right? You've got this. All of it. You're only here for another

85

eight months. You're gonna kill this AP class, and you're going to get into college and get the hell out of here. Okay?"

My eyes are burning and I hate it. "Thank you," I whisper, because that's all I can manage without totally losing my shit. We stay like that, arms around each other, until I can pull myself together and I back away from her. "I'll see you tomorrow."

She smiles, but I can see right through it. Just like she can see right through mine.

After all, what are best friends for?

CHAPTER 11

Margo

Student Council has been underway for a half hour and I'm trying, I am *truly* trying to give a shit about the Homecoming theme and the budget and ticket sales and all the things I am usually extremely skilled at giving a shit about, thank you very much. But I have a lesson with Abbie after school and I'm so… I'm so distracted by all of it.

I'm sitting here in my normal, apparently heterosexual clothes with a change in my bag, waiting to spring some real homosexuality on her, and I can't stop thinking about it. About…all of it.

Viv Carter snaps in front of my face and says, "Earth to Margo?"

I blink. "Right. Yes. Yes, I agree."

She quirks a perfectly shaped eyebrow and says, "You agree?"

I purse my lips and glance furtively around the room. Aaliyah's and Julia's are the only specifically friendly and encouraging set of eyes here. "Y-yes?"

"Okayyyy," she says. "So one vote for the decor budget to be set at *I agree*. Anyone else?"

Blood rushes to my face, because 1) embarrassing, and 2) I'm so focused on being a freaking lesbian that even after being totally called out in front of everyone, I can't stop looking at Viv's legs. Her shorts. Are so short.

And thick thighs, my *god*, they save lives.

I can't stop looking at her mouth. Even twisted in disapproval, I can't stop thinking about how my tongue was in it, and it was *good*.

Sydney kicks me under the desk and whispers, "You okay?"

And *great*; I am literally too gay to function because now I'm thinking about how hot Sydney Arollo is, too. She's tall and slender and has this glowing brown skin and jet-black hair cut in this beautiful, smooth A-line that sharpens her jaw and softens her cheekbones, and she's leaning over my desk, tapping her slightly long fingernails on it, on *my* desk, like that's totally okay, like it's acceptable and normal.

IT IS. Get it TOGETHER, Zimmerman!

"Yeah," I say. "Yeah, I'm fine. Just got some stuff on my mind."

Like your ridiculous perfect face and Viv's ridiculous perfect legs and a thousand strategies to cope with this lesbian nightmare of a Student Council meeting.

"Okay, well," she says, and she kind of shrugs and her mouth curls up in this way that I now recognize as flirting.

Sydney has always been astoundingly hot, is the thing.

In the ninth grade, I remember looking at her thinking, *Now* there *is someone I'm legitimately into. There's someone I want to* touch.

Then she came back in the tenth with a new wardrobe and a new haircut and new pronouns and a new name, and I thought, *Well, I'm not into girls, so I must have been misinterpreting my own hormones.*

No, Margo. Nothing had changed. You wanted to touch her because she was always a *girl*, whether or not you knew it.

And you were always gay.

And now she's in my space, smirking at me in a way that makes me wonder if she knows, and between her and Viv and my upcoming lesson with Abbie, I'm about to burst out of this chair in a Sapphic cyclone of "Sweet mother I cannot weave; sweet Aphrodite has overcome me with longing for girls."

I stare down at the desk and then shut my eyes so tight my *eyelids* hurt. I can do this. I am not literally too gay to function. I can fake it like I'm doing 70 percent of the time, anyway.

I stand and brush my skirt off, and say, "Apologies, guys. I think I'm running low on sleep. I'd like to hear from the treasurer about budgetary concerns, then we ought to have time to go over the caf reforms that were proposed last month."

Aaliyah smiles at me from down the table.

I am smooth Student Council Margo; my mask is firmly in place, and all is well.

But behind my rib cage, I am utterly wigging the hell out.

The second the bell rings, I leave.

I just get the absolute fuck out of there.

I try to avoid noticing every attractive girl in a two-hallway radius, which is challenging, given that two of those girls are Chloe and Julia, and the only reason Aaliyah isn't on that list is because she's still gathering her stuff from the

Student Council room. Thankfully, even though my friends
are all beautiful, I've never been into any of them. So I can
at least begin to snap out of my homosexual panic around
them. I pull myself together, or try, while Aaliyah catches up
and says, "You okay?"

"Yeah!" I say. I feel like my tone is too bright, like I over-
compensated just a little, but no one says anything about it.
So we walk along, and I try to come up with a good reason to eventually deviate from the group and duck into the
bathroom.

"Well," says Chloe, "how's student-counciling? Dance
budgets approved and like healthy school lunches adequately
campaigned for?"

Julia laughs, "Chloe, is that all you think we do?"

Aaliyah says, "In fairness, it kind of is."

I spit out a laugh and screw my face into what I hope comes
out as mock offense, and it is at that moment that Jamal comes
down the hall.

He's usually this cool devil-may-care guy around campus.
He wouldn't have to put a single bit of effort in to start a cult,
and a popular one at that. Scientology wishes it could. But
the second he lays eyes on Julia, in any context, he turns into
a complete buffoon.

That himbo face replaces the one I'm familiar with as he
walks past us, and he chin tips us, saying, "Ladiesssss," then
proceeds to walk headfirst into our absolutely jacked PE
teacher.

Or he would have, if Mr. Fletcher hadn't performed an epic
last-second dodge that sent Jamal flying as he tripped over
the guy's foot. We all watch it happen in slow motion—the

shocked changes on Jamal's face, every piece of paper he's stuffed into his books exploding into the air, his crash flat on his face. I swear, he slides so far, it's like a *Family Guy* bit. I didn't know friction even worked that way in nature.

The hallway is in chaos.

Jamal is apologizing right and left and desperately trying to gather the shreds of his dignity along with his stuff. The girls are cackling, and I'm trying so hard not to laugh that I can feel my face going red with the effort.

"He's a beautiful disaster," says Chloe through gasps for air.

Julia giggles, too, but she shrugs, eyes on him as he walks away. "I don't know," she says. "I think he's kind of cute."

I file this information away for Jamal, and we all part ways at the school entrance. Then, when I'm out of their eyelines, I double back to the bathroom to change before my lesson.

I walk into Room A24 a Full-On Authentic Gay.

Cutoff shorts, high-tops (both of which I did already own, thank you very much), a purple and gray plaid button-down, (which I did not, in fact, own until yesterday), and a backward Captain Planet snapback I stole from Jamal.

I try to run my fingers through my hair but my nails bump up against the closure and duh, I'm wearing a hat.

How do the Gays get volume, dammit?

I sit front and center, like I did last time, organize my pencils in perfectly symmetrical order, and open my notebook. I also crack open a giant Gatorade because I'm still recovering not only from the Student Council disaster but from fasting all day Tuesday for Yom Kippur.

I take a long, *long* drink, and look up when I hear some-one enter the room.

Abbie's in a too-big vintage adidas T-shirt and black skin-nies and high-top black Vans, which is at the very least medium-key gay. It's high-key *I-Can't-Stop-Looking-At-Her* even though it's not like anything she's wearing is designed to draw attention to any particular part of her.

It doesn't matter. My attention is maddeningly, unsettlingly drawn.

Of course, it is. That's the day I'm having, I guess.

Here's the thing about Abbie and her medium-gay outfit: it looks like she just yanked some stuff out of her closet to put on her body. She's relaxed and normal, leaning against the chalkboard. This is just *what she wears.*

What I have on, well. It doesn't feel like *what I wear.* It's like…what I have put on in order to dress queer.

It's different.

But this is what I'm supposed to do, and I'm doing it. It's not like masking is a new experience. Watch me make eye contact, gayly.

It takes me a minute to realize that Abbie's staring at me. Like, not in the same way I'm staring at her, I don't think. More like…confused.

She says, "Hey. What…are you wearing?"

"Clothes from my closet. What are you wearing?" Which I mean to come out like a real attitude-filled retort, but it comes out kind of hoarse and defensive like, "Clothes from my CLOSETWHATAREYOUWEARING."

"Clothes. From my closet." She gives me kind of a brow-furrowed once-over, but has to tilt her head to take in my

shorts and shoes and legs. Legs? Maybe. I mean, she's probably not looking at my legs, and if she is, I don't want her to
be *confused* about them.

Not that she's looking at them.

Or that I want her to be.

Do I want her to be?

Jesus Christ, ANYWAY, she's craning her head to look at
my SHOES.

"Uh, Margo?"

"Yes?"

"You do realize there's not like...a *literal* uniform, right?
Like, you can dress however you want and still like girls."

I twist my face into the closest facial approximation of
DUH, OF COURSE I can manage. "Ha. Yeah. Yes, *obviously* I know that, Abbie."

(Of course there's a uniform, which evidently does not
include Lacoste and boat shoes. There are rules here. There
are always rules.)

"O...kay."

"It's 4:01," I say into the inexplicably awkward pause that
springs up between us.

"You're right," she says, and pushes off the chalkboard
ledge. "You know, I wasn't planning on covering gay fashion,
but it seems like..." Her eyes sort of narrow, like she's thinking, and says, "Okay, so there's a few different like, vibes."

I open my notebook to a blank page and write *VIBES*.

"High femme, which is...well. You. Makeup and heels
and dresses. Lipstick lesbians. There's tomboys, which is more
me. It's more of a gender-neutral thing. You might hear the
phrase *chapstick lesbian*."

"Chapstick lesbian. Got it."

"And butch. Think Kasie Callihan."

Ah yes, Kasie of the shaved head and men's band T-shirts, who wears a tie for every yearbook picture. Butch.

"But it's up to you because it *is* you. Any questions?"

I stare at my notebook, and open my mouth to ask. But honestly, this is kind of my area of expertise. "I think Google and I can take it from here, thanks."

"Great. Let's move on and talk about how to move like a gay."

"I'm sorry—how to *move* like a gay?"

"How was I standing at the start of our lesson?"

"Leaning, one foot on the wall." Once the words are out, I realize that maybe this is too detailed. Maybe this makes it seem like I was paying too close of attention to her. But it's too late now. And…well. I like…want to get an A. "You had your hands on the ledge of that chalkboard."

"Have you ever seen a straight girl stand like that?"

"I don't know. I don't usually walk up to girls and ask their sexual orientations."

"No, I know. You just walk up to girls and declare them instead."

If I were drinking anything, I would have spit it out. As it stands, I didn't have time to run by Starbucks so I'm just laughing. Abbie's smirk widens into something a little more genuine.

"Look, even if I didn't have a reputation, I doubt very much you would assume I was heterosexual, right? So, no, you've never seen a straight girl stand like that. Straight girls don't have Big Dick Energy."

I write down the phrase, "Straight girls don't have Big Dick Energy," and grin into my notebook. "Is it Big Dick Energy if you claim it out loud?" I ask, arching an eyebrow.

"Yes," she says emphatically. "Why do you think the word is *cocky*?"

My left eyebrow jumps up to match my right and I just say, "Noted."

"Get up."

I narrow my eyes. I would like to respond with, *You get up.* But she's already up.

So I just get the frick up, but I don't conceal my annoyance.

"Relax, Zimmerman. Just stand like you would normally. Not like you're auditioning for the lead in *Mary Poppins.*"

"This is how I stand! Normally!" My spine is straight because good posture is important, dammit. My shoulders are square. My neck is freaking regal.

Abbie bites her bottom lip, and then bursts out laughing. What the hell is it now? I'm trying. I'm GAY-ING.

"Fine," I say, and I march across the room, just about taking one of the desks with me.

There is no hope that Abbie missed that near-collision, but I don't care; I'm on a mission.

I examine the wall and lean against it, then fold my arms. I prop my heel up, slipping like an inch and then recovering. And stand there. Like a kid in a leather jacket who smokes behind the school or whatever.

Abbie's eyes sweep over me again and I'm blushing so hard I think I could give her a tan. But she doesn't seem to notice; she just walks over to me, almost lazily, and leans against the wall next to me. Her foot propped up next to her knee. Her shoulder just a couple inches from mine.

She turns her face to me, and she's so *close* and there's no way she can ignore the thirty-seven shades of red I am right now. There's no way *I* can ignore the little bump on the bridge of her nose, the way it's just slightly too large for her face. Just too interesting to be perfectly symmetrical.

I am holding my breath.

I…well. I stop doing that.

"What?" I say. I don't know if it comes out defensive or aggressive or breathless but I am certain it doesn't come out *regular*.

"You look uncomfortable, Zimmerman," she says, and her eyes drop to my mouth, then back up again, and I don't know what I'm doing with my face. "Am I making you nervous?"

Yes. "No." I shift against the wall, trying desperately to look relaxed, to look like I belong in this stance. To capture the vibe that Abbie projects so freaking effortlessly—the kind that makes her seem three inches taller than me when she's actually a good six inches shorter. To show her that I can. My foot just manages to slip lower, so the toe of my left shoe is now resting on the heel of my right.

A+ 11/10 Gay.

"Look," she says, and pushes off the wall to stand in front of me. "Relax. Relax your body."

I breathe out, like I do in yoga. Like that will work.

Like literally anything could counteract the immediate tension in every muscle I possess hearing Abbie Sokoloff say the words *your body*.

She puts her hands on my shoulders and I guess I could get

more tense. But she just sort of shakes them, trying to loosen them up for me. "R*elax*."

She's so close to me, her face just right there, and I can't look past her like I do most people, because it's too obvious, so I stare at her hairline instead. It's not even like, a sexy place? It's just that she's SO CLOSE TO ME and looking at her face/eyes/nose/mouth would be completely overwhelming and I wouldn't be able to focus on the words coming out of her face/eyes/nose/mouth.

I guess we'll find out if she's offended. But right now, I don't care, because I physically cannot.

So I focus on her hairline, and I breathe.

I let my shoulders drop. "Okay," I say, and my voice comes out way too quiet.

"Almost there," she says and lets go of my shoulders.

And puts her hands on my *hips*. And pushes them back against the wall. And lets go.

My breath actually *hitches*; Jesus Christ.

She crouches next to me and I'm so glad I shaved my legs this morning and also I've forgotten how to breathe? She wraps her hand around my back ankle and pulls it away from the wall.

I lose my balance completely and my right hand slaps the wall—echoingly loud in this quiet room. My left finds purchase in Abbie's hair.

In Abbie's goddamn *hair*.

I jerk my hand back like she bit me and say, "Sorry. Sorry."

"You got it?" She's still holding on to my ankle.

I swallow past a truly untenable knot in my throat. "Yeah. I got it."

She puts my foot on top of the other, so they're crossed at the ankles. And she finally, finally lets go of me. She stands up and examines her handiwork. "How's that? Tell me how it feels."

I wriggle my shoulders against the wall and test the balance. Forcing myself to think about how the posture feels and not how my throat or my stomach or anything south of my stomach or you know what? Anything *north* of it. Feels.

The posture.

Feels fine.

I say, "Good. I don't feel like I'm about to fall over." I glance up at the ceiling and give myself a few seconds to settle into this. "Behold," I say, one side of my mouth ticking up. "My Big Dick Energy."

"Very impressive," she says, and I actually kind of believe her. "Walking is easy—just walk fast. But you do that anyway, so good job, you gay."

I say, "Thank you. I've often been told I walk homosexually fast."

"I would be surprised if that were the case," she says, but keeps talking so I don't have a chance to retort. "Go sit back down. Next lesson is sitting wrong."

I furrow my brow and peel myself off the wall. My brow is still furrowed as I walk to my chair, and my confused face, I actually *have* been told, looks more like a pout than anything, so I probably look downright chaotically dramatic.

But, in my chaotically dramatic defense: how to *sit wrong?*

I stand beside my desk, considering for a moment if there's a way to nail this before she introduces the topic.

But nothing comes to me.

I just sit.

...correctly.

Abbie pulls the cushioned chair out from the teacher's desk and stands in front of it, arms extended. Then she folds one leg up under her as she sits down in one smooth motion. "Behold. Sitting wrong."

I manage to cross one leg over the other under this tiny desk, and say, "All right. Yes, you are sitting wrong. I'm not sure what this has to do with being gay?"

"We're all incapable of sitting correctly in a chair," she says. "Don't ask me why. But I've caught myself so many times in so many uncomfortable positions because like hell will I put my damn feet on the floor like a heterosexual."

I snort and find myself instinctively trying to remove my feet from the ground in response, like when you're a kid and the floor is lava.

My feet hover and my calves start burning quickly but here we are: grown up, gay, and the floor is Heterosexuality.

"Okay, you have to at least be able to tell yourself halfway convincingly that what you're doing is more comfortable than sitting regularly, and that. That is not it."

I twist to peer below the desk, like I need visual evidence of my on-fire muscles. Then I shift, pull my calf up and my knee knocks against the desk—hard.

It hurts.

I decide not to start with my right leg (because this is a right-handed desk; that was not my best idea). I go with my left. I half stand and pull my left foot so it rests under where my butt is supposed to go, and, one foot on the ground, maneuver so I'm kind of sort of sitting—perching, really—in this desk, and somehow now my right thigh is higher than it was so it's just slowly *bruising* under this desk, but whatever. I'M SITTING.

It's DEFINITELY wrong.

I glance down at my desk and decide to rest on an elbow. Then I look up at Abbie.

The look on her face is…infuriating. Like she knows this big secret about Gay Life™ that I don't and she's just so fricking delighted by that. And, of course, she does. She knows all the secrets. That's why I went to her. But she doesn't have to look so damn *smug* about it.

"Is this—is this wrong enough? Or?"

"Oh," she says, in that particular tone of voice that only people who are desperately holding in a laugh have, "it's pretty wrong. Sure. Yeah. But, uh, listen. You look pretty uncomfortable. And you look like you're *trying*."

"Of course I'm trying!"

"Of course you are," she says. "You just can't look like you are. The wrongness of your sitting has to look natural, like, of course this is how you sit because, of course it's the most comfortable way of sitting."

I clench my teeth together to hold in an actual groan. This should not be so complicated. Being a lesbian should not be rocket science. And yet, here I am.

I pull my leg out from under me and the legs of the desk clatter on the ground, and I know the floor is Straight Lava, but my right foot plants itself there.

I situate my left so that it's on top of the desk and kind of try to lean back, arms behind my head. Like, Cool.

I think I'm going to fall.

Oh, fuck.

Oh, shit, I'm going to fall.

FUC—

I yank my left leg off the desk in a total panic and scrape it on the way to the floor, but luckily my absolutely *profane* combination of shouted words is drowned out by the thump and crash of the desk as it settles back from the precipice of disaster under my even posture.

Now I'm just pissed.

I grab the desk with both hands and flip the thing around backward, then plant my gay ass in the chair so I'm straddling the seat back. There is a tiny sliver of writing surface left from the L-shape of the desktop and I gather up my entire notebook and set of pencils and slam them onto the two square inches of space, line each pencil up in the notebook crease, and crouch over it.

I force my face into a solemn, defiant line and look up at Abbie.

"Next."

She bursts out laughing.

I can't keep that straight line on my face no matter how hard I will it. The thing is, she's not laughing *at* me. She's laughing because this is ridiculous and because I'm funny. She's laughing and I am just a little stunned at how viscerally I feel it.

My smile cracks and then I'm laughing, too.

"Well," she says after she's caught her breath, "there's good news and there's bad news. The good news is that there is a correct answer for wrong sitting in that particular desk. The bad news is that you haven't gotten it." She doesn't wait for a response, just comes over to sit in the desk on my right. She holds up one finger and says, "Watch," and props her heel on the outside edge of the wire basket under the chair.

And…that's it.

I can feel The Pout coming on.

I stand, just to get a good look, and to be really, deeply, satisfyingly furious. I put my hands on my hips and circle the desk, to be sure I haven't missed anything—a subtly placed elbow or foot. But no. It is a heel. A knee, as a result of said heel, peeking just above the desktop.

That's it.

That's visual homosexuality.

I want to protest.

But I just find myself sighing. "Well, what do you know," I say. "You really do look like a freaking Gay."

CHAPTER 12

Abbie

We don't go to Willow every Thursday for Teen Night, but we do go to most of them. Charlie and Adriana and me and half the field hockey team and half the softball team and a handful from the marching band. It's a big crowd, and they know us. The cover is five dollars, which is shitty, but it's the only place in town where girls who like girls congregate in any kind of comfort.

We usually lose track of each other within a few minutes of arriving, but Charlie, Adriana, and I stay close.

Charlie says (shouts), "You should dance with someone tonight."

Adriana is sipping a Sprite, looking around. I can't help but think Charlie's only suggesting this because she doesn't want to babysit me. It's uncharitable, I guess. I shouldn't begrudge her for wanting to dance with her girlfriend.

"You look good," Charlie says. And she's right: I'm wearing a pinstripe button-down open over this distressed *Teen-*

age Mutant Ninja Turtle tank top, and these black skinnies I live in. But I live in them for a reason, and that reason is my thighs. "You should find somebody to dance with."

"Maybe," I reply. The thing is, she's right. I keep coming to Willow because it lets me blow off steam and when you have parents like mine, you end up with a *lot* of steam to blow off. Maybe I'm giving a bad rap to bisexuals everywhere, but sometimes you just have to close your eyes and let someone else's hands and mouth be the only thing you think about for a while.

But tonight? I don't know; I don't really feel like dancing. I don't feel like having a stranger press their hip bones into mine, even if there's not an unwelcome boner. I don't feel like having to fend off someone's mouth, and I don't feel like being disappointed at the end of the night that I didn't have to. It's bad. All the options are bad.

I don't even know why I came tonight.

I mean, I do, and it's because my parents suck.

"Well, if you don't want to dance with anyone, dance alone," Charlie says. "You might change your mind. Besides, it's been a while since you've gotten any, hasn't it?"

It hasn't, actually, and Charlie knows that, but because the person I hooked up with two weeks ago wasn't a girl, Charlie doesn't count it.

And I just hate that *you might change your mind* shit. Yeah, I *might* change my mind, *Charles*. But that's not the point. The point is my mind is set right now, during this actual conversation.

I've made a choice. Respect that choice.

I just shrug.

Charlie leans closer. "Are you okay?"

I shrug again. I mean, I guess I'm okay. I'm okay as long as I'm not at home. "I'm fine," is the best I can do.

That's when she knows that I'm not, and I guess that's when I know, too. "Come on, Abs." She nods toward the bathroom.

I start to protest, but she won't hear it. This is a more familiar level of bossiness, one I'm more comfortable with. We skirt the dance floor, and a girl bumps into my shoulder, moves over to get a good look at me, then tries to tug me in to dance with her.

I shake my head and shrug and kind of show her my hands like "I can't; it's not my fault," and she pouts playfully before turning away again, dancing with a girl with blond curls piled on her head.

It's early, so there's no line for the bathroom yet. Charlie pulls me into the wheelchair-accessible stall and locks the door behind us.

She folds her arms; she means business. "Talk to me."

"I don't know, I'm—" I don't know what I am. I'm upset, I guess. About a lot of things, I guess. About my history grade and my parents' fucked up relationship and I don't know. Margo, maybe. I don't know. When I was showing her how to lean against that wall, she seemed so affected by—I don't know. *Me.* And she's not my type or anything, but she's hot, and I'm human, and being that close to her, our shoulders an inch apart, our faces turned toward each other's, just so… *close.* And I put my hands on her hips…

Well. This is a business transaction but—

"You're what?"

But I'm not *dead.*

"I don't know, dude." I start to say more, but I don't. I don't know why I don't.

"Do you want to go home?"

"Jesus, no." I shake my head. "I don't want to be anywhere near that dumpster fire."

Charlie spreads her hands like, *Well, then what?*

"Dude, my options aren't just *go home* or *make out with a stranger.*"

"Are they not? Listen, I'm not trying to be an asshole here, but making out with a stranger is kind of your stress relief MO."

That's not 100 percent untrue, but she'd never say a half-pipe is kind of my stress relief MO. Charlie's like, *obsessed* with what I do with my mouth and feels pressed to remind me of it, but starting a fight in a bathroom stall isn't going to make anything any better. It's not going to make her less biphobic.

"Dude, I'm not trying to tell you what to do. I'm telling you that the reason we're all here is for escapist purposes. So escape. Dance, or don't. Check out girls, or don't. I don't give a shit. But moping isn't going to do you any favors."

"I'm—"

"Not. Yes you are." She grabs my shoulders and says, "Do yourself a favor and go out there and just close your eyes and think about anything besides your parents or whatever's fucking you up so much."

She has a point, I guess. I have to live with my parents, and I'm not there with them now. I shouldn't give them this time that's *mine.*

"Okay," I say. "Fine."

Charlie smiles her *I've won* smile and I groan in disgust

106

as she opens the stall door and pulls me out behind her. We come onto the dance floor and the pounding bass we'd felt in the bathroom resolves itself into a Hayley Kiyoko remix. Charlie's already making her way back to her girlfriend and I watch them put their arms around each other and kiss briefly, their hips swaying in unison while they dance. I don't know if I'm jealous. Not of either of them specifically, but of the thing they have. The thing I've never quite been able to grab hold of.

The girl who found me on the way to the bathroom finds me again. She's in a black collared shirt buttoned all the way up, sleeves rolled back to her elbows. Her hair's straight, but it's hard to tell what color it is, the dance floor lights painting it red and blue and green.

She leans in far enough that I know she's for sure hitting on me and says, "Who's your favorite?"

"What?"

She looks pointedly at my chest, then meets my eyes again. "Who's your favorite?"

Ah. "Donatello," I tell her. "That big stick energy."

She laughs. "Mine's Michelangelo." She sticks out her thumb and pinkie like *hang ten, dude.* "Tell me your name."

"Abbie," I say.

"I'm Erin. You want to dance?"

I hate that Charlie was right. I hate that after standing here long enough with the lights tattooing my eyelids and the music sinking into my bones that now suddenly I don't *not* want to dance. I hate that I'm saying, "Sure," and that I'm letting her take my hand and pull me into the crowd.

What I don't hate is how freaking pretty she is. I don't hate that she's six inches taller than me, lean and muscular, like she definitely plays a sport. Maybe basketball. I don't hate how her hands feel on my hips, waist, shoulders, thighs, throat, how her breath heats my skin but cools the sweat.

I don't hate it, but I don't love it. It's taken me two songs to realize I'm somewhere in that nebulous gray area of medium. Dancing with Erin is a solid five. Six, I guess, when she turns her head and that tendon in her neck stands out.

"Hey," I say, right in her ear, "I have to go to the bathroom?" I don't know why it comes out as a question.

She says, "Cool," and lets me go and the bathroom feels like sanctuary. The music is muted, just the thump of the bass and the occasional three-second shout of treble when the door opens.

I lock myself in a stall—I don't actually have to pee, I just, I don't know. I need to be alone. My phone buzzes and I pull it out and it's an email I immediately delete. But there's a couple texts I haven't seen since we've been here: from my mom, and a girl in my pre-calc class, and Margo.

I open hers first. It could be about studying. We're supposed to meet up tomorrow at her house, and I need to know if that's off.

But it's not about that. It's…no text at all.

It's a picture. Of Margo. Sitting in her desk chair.

Wrongly.

It's so cute and ridiculous and so freaking *Margo Zimmerman* I burst out laughing. It's set up like a candid, but there's no way it actually is. This must be her room—she's pretzeled up in a desk chair, elbow on the desk in front of her. The desk is a minimalist's wet dream. Her hair is up in a haphazard, unstraightened knot at the crown of her head and she's in an olive green racerback tank top and black shorts and her shoulders are. Wow. Maybe it's the lighting or I don't know. Maybe it's her *shoulders*.

I swallow and even though it's almost midnight and probably past her bedtime, I reply:

Good job, homo

Almost immediately: Does that officially count as an A
And then: Because I'm marking it down in my gradebook.
I can't tell if she's joking. She's probably not. I reply: I thought I was the one who was supposed to have the gradebook.

Well. Is there an A in it under sitting or?

As if sitting gay is a thing. As if how you dress or how you move or how you talk means anything about who you love, who you want. This whole thing is snowballing into absurdity, and I almost feel bad because I'm obviously the only one who's benefiting. But if I say, *I can't teach you to be gay, no one can teach anyone to be gay*, would she still be willing to help me with history?

Now that we've started this...whatever it is, transactional friendship, I guess, I can't imagine not doing this. Not mean-flirting with her or saying stuff just to get a rise from her, just to see the blush bloom high on her cheeks. If she weren't getting something out of this, something from me, would she still want to see me at all? Or would we go back to barely even realizing we're in the same class?

Wow, I hate that idea.

There's a line in this bathroom. I don't care. I said "supposed to" have a gradebook, not that I DO have one.

I wasn't sure after that four-page syllabus

Somebody bangs on my stall door. I yell, "I'm taking a shit!" There's a muffled "Jesus," but they don't knock again.

Margo's texted me, I'll have to take you school supply shopping.

I assume she'll be able to see my smirk through the phone when I type, Is that what you do for fun, Zimmerman? Go shopping for school supplies?

Well, how do YOU spend your wild Thursday nights if not in the stationery aisle at the Office Depot?

I decide to tell her (mostly) the truth: Trolling for bitches.

Then I pocket my phone and unlock the stall door and come out. There's a girl waiting with long acrylic nails, giving me a nasty look; I assume she's the one who learned about my fake bowel movement, but I don't care. At least I keep my nails appropriately trimmed for this crowd.

Social contract says I should go find Erin, but I kind of don't want to. I don't feel like dancing anymore, and I don't want to deal with her trying to get my number or something. The thought makes me feel conceited, but the way she was dancing was not an *I don't care about this person's number* kind of dancing. I'm standing in the shadow of the speakers and I text Charlie.

I'm getting a Lyft and going home, I'm exhausted

Margo has replied: Same obviously. In the stationery aisle at the Office Depot.

I won't get a response from Charlie until she and Adriana are ready to leave, so I go ahead and order a ride. I text Margo: Leave it to you to find the one late-night office depot in Ocala.

Desperate times, desperate measures. Where else is one going to *troll for bitches* around here in the middle of the week?

I can't stop the chuckle that bubbles up as I reply. You remember Willow, don't you, Zimmerman?

Then I think, maybe that was *too* mean. So I soften it with, Don't worry, I'll bring you sometime.

Margo takes longer to reply than she has been, which just means: longer than fifteen seconds.

Oh. You're actually out. Don't let me interrupt your trolling
Hope you're having a good time
!!!
Sorry, I hit send too soon.

My ride has arrived and I take a screenshot of his details and send it to Charlie and Adriana both. I climb in and text Margo: I'm actually headed home now, so, you know. Bitches got trolled?

LOL well congrats

This, after her last spurt of texts—I don't know how to read them. Tonally, I mean. They're all over the map. Or maybe they're not. She sounds a little put out, but contrary to what Charlie thinks, I'm not trying to bang every queer girl in central Florida. Besides, if Margo wanted me, she'd say something. She's always *saying things*. She sure wouldn't have picked me to teach her how to pick up *other* girls. She's using me for my Big Gay Energy and that's it.

My head hurts. It's the music and the sweating and.

And that's it.

My head hurts, and I can't sleep. The house was silent and dark when I walked in three hours ago. It still is, and I don't know what that means. I don't even know if my parents are here, together or separate, but it's not like it matters.

I wish... I don't know. I kind of wish they'd just get divorced. Everyone would be happier.

I mean. Probably.

It's four o'clock in the morning and I'm staring at the ceiling. What I want to do is get in my car and drive to the skate park and just...skate until my legs give out. I can't, because it's four o'clock in the fucking morning, and I need to go to sleep. I've tried every trick I know of—audio books and mid '90s British murder mysteries and masturbation and I'm just. Staring at the ceiling.

I'm thinking about Margo and her perfect family, and it's not helping. It's probably making it worse. I'm thinking about the picture Margo sent me tonight, about how much effort she must have put into it, the framing and the pose and everything. How she clearly didn't take it herself, so she had to have someone take it for her, someone she wasn't embarrassed to ask. I'm thinking about Erin, the girl I danced with, and how it might be to dance with Margo. If she'd be handsy or not.

I blink, and the dark blue light has shifted to gray. It's got to be close to six o'clock now, and honestly, I might as well just get up. I'm so tired and desperate for sleep I could cry.

I can hear my parents now, moving around, snapping and sniping.

"What's the matter?"

"I asked you to clean out the coffeepot last night."

"I'm sorry. I forgot."

"Seems right."

"I'll clean it out now, if you want."

"No, it's fine. I'll do it."

"Barbara—"

"It's fine! It's not like it's a complicated task!"

"Jesus."

"There are just more direct ways of saying fuck you, is all."

"Barbara, that's not—I literally forgot! Sometimes I forget things!"

"Sometimes!"

"I'm sorry I can't have a perfect memory, okay? I'm just grateful you never forget anything ever, including mailing my mother's birthday card on time."

"That was four years ago, Brian! You remember that, but not the very simple task of cleaning out the coffeepot?"

I can't—Christ. I can't listen to this anymore. I roll out of bed and take a shower, and when I come downstairs, they're still arguing, or arguing again, or who gives a shit. I'm leaving the house like an hour earlier than I need to, but I *have* to get out of here.

I park in the school lot, the only other cars here this early belonging to the football players and JROTC kids. I blink, and the lot is full of cars and empty of people and *fuck*, it's almost eleven o'clock and I have definitely slept through my AP US class.

As if it matters.

My phone buzzes, and it's Margo. Too hungover for history? ☺

That cheesy winky face makes me smile.

Please, what kind of girl do you think I am?

The kind who spends her Thursdays *trolling for bitches* and getting too hungover for history?

Texts suck, because you can't read tone at all. If we were face-to-face, I would know what was happening. How she meant every word. I almost want to believe she's flirting with me, but it's pointless.

All I can do is assume she's joking.

I see my reputation precedes me.

Why do you think I came to you in the first place? ☺

Fuck. It's probably because I've gotten like twenty minutes of sleep, but I'm suddenly on the verge of tears. It's stupid, and I hate it, and I hate this conversation, and why did I agree to teach the hottest girl in school how to be gay. What was I thinking?

Obviously I wasn't.

She says: Seriously, though, are you feeling okay?

Cool, now I am actually crying. Cool. Good. Great.

I manage to only make seventeen typos while replying, Yeah, I'm fine. Just didn't get a whole lot of sleep.

Margo doesn't respond. The bell's probably rung for the next class.

So I crank up the car and drive away, and I do what I've wanted to do for the last twelve hours: I skate.

CHAPTER 13

Margo

"Did you know," I say, scooting just a little closer to Abbie, "that Aaron Burr has this reputation for being an asshole because of well, the murder, but actually he was kind of amazing?"

We're sitting on the carpet in the bonus room (even though the floor is lava), academic detritus all around us while night darkens outside the window.

Abbie's eyebrows go up. I don't know if it's *ooh, tell me more,* or *oh Christ here we go again.*

I choose to believe it's the former because my mouth and brain are already going, and there's no stopping either of them when somebody starts me in on:

1) The American Revolutionary War (you're welcome, Abbie),

2) Fashion theory (obviously),

3) Horses (shut up).

I hear the excitement in my voice. I can't tone it down.

I used to find it embarrassing. Now, like, I don't know. I mean, I'm not going to open conversations with facts about horse gestation, but we'll probably get there eventually. Cope, or leave.

"Like, once, some friends of his couldn't take care of their grandkids, so Aaron Burr, who was SUPER broke, by the way, took the watch out of his pocket, pawned it, and gave all the money to them that night. And that was like, a regular thing for him—being broke because he wouldn't stop giving his money away. He was also a total abolitionist, and— anyway. Anyway, that's...important. For your tutoring. For... essay questions."

Abbie's sitting cross-legged next to me, elbow on her knee, chin on her fist, and just... I don't know. Listening? Watching? Whatever she's doing, she's not bored. She's not exasperated, I don't think. Amused, maybe. Because the ever-present smirk is almost there, but not in a shitty way.

She waits a few seconds after I finish blathering before she says anything. And what she says is, "Essay questions? Is *name five reasons Aaron Burr isn't America's biggest asshole* a common test question?"

I look primly at my nails. "It's never appeared on any published exam, but you know. Best to be prepared."

It's ten after nine, but I can't stop talking, and I don't think Abbie's noticed. I mean, she's definitely noticed that I can't stop talking, but I don't think she's noticed it's ten minutes past when we were supposed to be done. Our books and notebooks are still on the floor in front of us. Not so much between us. They maybe started out that way but somehow that's not where they are now and I don't know how that happened.

I notice the not-space between our knees and glance back at the clock and cough. "Well," I say, "now that I've kept you ten minutes late with my riveting speeches about the Found-ing Fathers…"

"Oh," Abbie says. She sounds genuinely surprised. Or dis-appointed? Or I don't know, I must be losing it. "Sure. Of course." She starts shutting books and notebooks and putting them back in her bag, and I can't help it.

I have one more thing.

"Okay, Aaron Burr."

Abbie's almost-there smirk is now 100 percent definitely there. But still not in a shitty way. She stops packing her bag and gives me her full attention and says, "Oh, sure. For the essay. Please, go on."

"He was a *total* feminist. Like, he and his wife, Theodosia, were super into Mary Wollstonecraft, who by the way, was Mary Shelley's mom. The woman who wrote *Frankenstein*? Which, did you know that Mary Goth-Ass Shelley lost her VIRGINITY on her mom's GRAVE? Anyway. Crap. What was I… Mary Wollstonecraft. She wrote this whole book of really radical feminist essays and Aaron Burr was basically an evangelist for it. Anyway. I just thought you should know." I stop and take a breath. "You know. That Aaron Burr gets a bad rap and that Mary Shelley fucked on her mother's grave."

"These are some intense essay questions you're imagining, Zimmerman."

"It's important to be thorough, Sokoloff."

"Well, I guess I can't argue with that." She finishes pack-ing her bag.

I have moved on in my head from *I'm just such a history nerd!* To *Stay, though*, and I know it. That awareness is why I literally bite my tongue to keep from telling her, like a super regular person, that Mary Shelley was so metal that she kept her dead husband's heart wrapped in one of his poems until the day she died.

Why would I instinctively reach for, "Hey, do you want some ice cream?" when I COULD reach for, "Calcified heart!"

Jesus Calcified Christ.

I choose, instead, to say nothing.

I just keep my mouth shut and walk her down the stairs over the garage to the main floor, and then to the door. When she leaves I say, "Bye," like a normal person, instead of "Did you know that Herman Melville and Nathaniel Hawthorne were banging it out? All authors throughout forever are apparently queer and banging and Nathaniel Hawthorne was an absolute thirst trap; did you know that weird thing about history, Abbie?" like a batshit person.

She leaves and I just stand at the door for a minute, wishing that she hadn't.

I am certain it's because she's a ridiculously attractive girl, and she's paying attention to me, and she knows I'm gay.

It's not because of the shape of her nose, or the way she kind of pushes me around when she talks to me (or literally arranges me against the wall), and it's not because she sounds like she's keeping a thousand little secrets every time she laughs. It's not because she's Abbie Sokoloff that I'm standing here wishing she'd stayed longer.

It's because I'm gay.

And like I said. She's a pretty girl.

That's it.

And that's something I guess I need to get the hell under control.

I rake my hand through my hair and head through the living room to wind around to the back of the house.

I clunk my head against my brother's door. "Mendelllllll," I say.

He mumbles something back.

"You're not asleep. It's 9:15."

"I'm playing with Angela Lansbury."

My mouth quirks up. "Well, I hope you have a safe word."

He opens the door and I almost fall on him but I catch myself on his doorframe. It would have been unfortunate for both of us, but none more so than Dame Angela Lansbury, who's five pounds and sixteen inches long and is currently clinging to Mendel's shoulder, long green tail curling down his chest.

"Dame," I say to the iguana.

Dame Angela Lansbury stares me down in the way that only a reptile can. Mendel gives me this look, fake evaluating me, then finally says, "Enter. This time."

I roll my eyes and he laughs when I push past him into his room and plop onto his spinny chair. He sits on his bed and says, "Margo, you look half dead."

"Jesus, is this what happens when I don't straighten my hair?"

"Nah, it's the pallor."

"Ugh."

He lies back and says, "Dude. What's up?"

I spin slowly, eyes on the ceiling. It's better than looking at the firemen calendar on my brother's wall. "Have you ever been a lesbian, Mendel?"

"I cannot say that I have."

"It's complicated."

"It's Abbie."

"What?" I stop spinning and sit straight up. "No, I don't know what you're—what do you mean?"

Mendel raises himself onto his elbows to look at me and his eyebrow creeps up. "What do you think I mean?"

"I don't know." I say it too fast. I can hear myself. "I'm not in your head."

"Please," he says, "you're in my head like seventy-five percent of the time."

"You think I like her or something?"

Mendel says, "See?" and smirks.

I groan. "I don't."

"Why the hell not?"

"Mendel. G-d—"

"Godddddddduuuhhhh," he mocks me, and I resolutely ignore it.

"What kind of question—"

"You guys are tight, right? She's hot. You made me take a solid seventy-five shots of you at your desk the other night so you could send her a selfie, and I'm sorry but it doesn't count as a selfie if—"

"It wasn't seventy-five."

He gets this challenging look on his face and goes for my phone and I snatch it back and slice my hand through the air because I'm getting nervous. For some stupid reason. "No. Seriously, I'm not into her. She's not into me. That's not... That's not how it is."

Mendel leans back onto his bed, looking straight up at the architectural drawings he has taped up there. The Rage Against The Machine shirt he's wearing is about a size too small for him, but that's what happens when you suddenly get into lifting over the summer, I guess. "Maybe I'll ask her out then."

My throat closes up. "No. Do not." It comes out a little strangled, which, great. What does that mean? Why does that thought make me want to die just a little? It shouldn't; she's gay.

Right, *that's* the reason it shouldn't make me want to die.

"I'm messing with you," he says, and his laugh rumbles in his chest. "But please, go on about how you definitely don't like her. Angela and I have the evening and you have the floor."

I roll my eyes and say, "It's not about Abbie. It's about..." I feel naive. I feel young, and I feel inexperienced, and I don't know that I have ever felt so deeply, plainly like the Little Sister. "It's about just not knowing what I'm freaking doing. Or like, who I am."

"Come on," he says. "You know who you are." He sits all the way up and scoots to the edge of his bed. Angela Lansbury shoots her murder eyes at me. "I mean, as much as anyone does when they're eighteen."

"Almost eighteen."

He waves his hand at me dismissively.

"It's hard," I say. "Being one person forever and then just figuring out you're something else altogether."

He leans forward, and Angela Lansbury has to crawl back on his shoulder to balance. "You're the same as you ever were, Margo."

He was the first person I told.

The night I broke up with Chad, Mendel came outside to the front porch and found me on the swing crying, and

I said, "I broke up with Chad," and he said, "Thank G-d," and I said, "I'm gay," and he said, "Welp."

And we just sat out there on this swing where Mendel once told me it was him who'd lost Grandma's *wedding ring* (which had been passed down to Mom) and I couldn't tell a soul, and I'd suggested that maybe faking a robbery was the right call. And we'd decided it was not, because who wants cops around the house, but I still hadn't told anyone; I would take it to the grave. The same porch swing where I'd snuck an iguana home because my best friend in middle school had gotten it but her mom had said no because she had a reptile allergy (which I'm pretty sure is not real). Mendel fell in love and declared her Dame Angela Lansbury right then and there.

On that swing.

Where he'd once chipped my tooth pulling the swing so far back that it had bounced while I was on it and I clacked my teeth together, and a couple years later sat up with me 'til 4:00 a.m. yelling about which zodiac signs the entire cast of Star Wars were—and I mean the *entire* cast of Star Wars.

("Obviously, Han Solo is a Sagittarius," he said.

"And Obi-Wan is a Taurus. Darth Maul, clearly a Leo."

"What?"

"Someone is forgetting The Clone Wars. You're telling me Frat Boy Spider-Maul is like, a Libra? Please.")

I sat in that porch swing and I cried and I told my big brother I was gay, and he said, "G-d, Margo, I love you. Okay? You're my favorite person. My favorite gay, gay, lesbian person."

And I spit out my iced coffee all over his shirt.

"If it wasn't June, I'd kick your ass," he'd said, staring down at his soaked shirt.

And I'd just laughed harder.

Mendel *would* say something like *you're the same as you ever were.* To him, I am.

To me, I feel…a little lost. A little…panicked.

I say, in his room, "I know. But I just don't know what I'm doing. I don't even know how to speak the language. I don't even know how to tell people I'm gay because I feel like I should have to take a test. Like there should be some kind of official assessment or like, a brain scan."

"A brain scan?"

"Yes. Like I could make an appointment, go in, and the person in charge would say, *Oh, wow. Wow, yeah, there's no questioning these results. You're DEFINITELY gay. Congratulations.*"

He scoots a little closer to me and reaches out with his long, jacked arms and spins the chair. I pull my feet up closer so they fit inside the big seat. (Like a gay!) "Don't chip my tooth," I say.

He says, "Go fuck yourself."

I laugh.

"You'll figure it out. You know yourself. You're gay and you don't need a test. You don't need someone else to tell you who you are. You just need to trust yourself. I trust you."

I'm glad this room is big and clean enough to spin in.

He shoves the chair one more time.

I sigh.

The room spins.

"You haven't freaked out like this in months. Not about like, being gay," he says.

"I know," I say. "I don't know what my deal is tonight."
Why am I so…so freaking insecure?

He stops the chair when it slows down. Makes me look at him. "Abbie?" he asks. Slowly. Like it's the most obvious thing in the world.

I bite my lip.

"You sure she's not in your head?" he says. "A *little*?"

It's not her.

It's not about her.

Even if it was, it wouldn't matter, because she is Abbie Sokoloff and I am Margo Zimmerman, preppy baby gay, who she can laugh at because I can't lean against a wall. I am not someone she would be interested in any way other than academically.

Abbie very obviously wants me for my brain.

And please. I know *exactly* why she didn't get much sleep the other night. She made it…super clear.

It's not Abbie Sokoloff.

It's just *A Girl*.

And I am the one in my head.

"No," I say, and Mendel doesn't say anything.

I get up eventually and make for my room and Mendel says, dramatically, "Angela. I thought she'd never leave."

I groan and shut the door behind me, Mendel's belly laugh following me through the hall.

Margo Zimmerman
Queer 101
For: Abbie Sokoloff

How I Knew I Was Gay

~~Webster's Dictionary defines "gay" as~~
~~A wise person once said.~~
How do you even know... How do you know something so big?

I could tell you that it was when I wound up with my tongue down Viv Carter's throat during a game of spin the bottle over the summer and for the first time maybe EVER, I actually felt something below the waist when I kissed someone.

I could tell you that it was before that. That I really *knew* when I couldn't stop watching *Keeping Up with the Kardashians*, over and over and over, and spent three hours online looking desperately for those thigh-high boots. So I could, you know. Look like her. The most beautiful woman in the world.

I could tell you that it was the first time my first boyfriend knocked braces with mine and I thought, *This is like doing algebra. Logical and sequential, no fire, no nothing. It's tongues and teeth and math.*

The thing is, Abbie, that I don't know when I *knew*.

I know when I acknowledged it.

I think I know when I should have known—and that is *always*.

But how should I have known when the entire world has been coupling me up with boys since I was in diapers? How should I have known when everyone kept asking me what age I wanted to get married to a boy and how many babies I wanted to have with him and everyone kept telling me how exactly to walk and talk and think and put on lipstick for *boys*.

How was I supposed to know? When everything, everything is for boys?

I don't know when I knew I was gay.

Do you? Do you know? Was it forever? Did you just come out of the womb knowing exactly who you were and exactly who you wanted to kiss and exactly who you didn't?

I don't know how I knew I was gay, Abbie.

Maybe one day I'll be able to look back and figure out that exact moment my gut was whispering something my brain refused to catch.

The thing is I know now.

The thing is that I can't go back.

The thing is: I never ever want to.

CHAPTER 14

Abbie

I guess I never noticed how frequently Margo and I crossed paths before she verbally assaulted me at the pool. I had plenty of time to notice, every year since seventh grade when my parents moved us here, but she never felt...consequential like she does now. She never felt like she mattered. Like she does now.

Sometimes a floor tile is laid sideways or a picture is hanging crooked or a church sign letter is out of place and it draws the eye—the thing about Margo Zimmerman is that she's never out of place. Margo, Teenage Social Chameleon. She doesn't acknowledge cliques, but flits from social circle to social circle without so much as batting an anxious eyelash. She was Homecoming Queen. She's on Student Council, she's setting records on the swim team, she's bouncing back and forth between valedictorian and salutatorian. She has friends everywhere, whether or not *they* know it.

That's why she had the confidence to stand in front of me

at a public pool and say, *You're gay.* What was I going to do? Get mad at her? At Margo Zimmerman?

No one gets mad at Margo Zimmerman.

She has always been everywhere, but now I *notice* her everywhere: in the hallways between classes, casually flirting with other girls, outside before the first bell and after the last one, in the cafeteria with her Too Cool friends, at Dive Team Alyssa's Halloween party.

Alyssa always has a Halloween party, every year since the fourth grade. The necklines get lower and the skirts get shorter, but everything else stays the same. Her parents still put out bowls of candy and punch even though Jeeps and Focuses and F-150s line the street outside their house, and they still insist on playing *Ernest Scared Stupid* and *The Nightmare Before Christmas* in the background.

I couldn't have told you last year what Margo Zimmerman's costume was. But this year, she and her innermost circle of friends—who are now, and will forever be, forward and backward in time, *far* too cool for the likes of Abbie Sokoloff—are all dressed in sexily disheveled school uniforms. And holy Jesus, Margo's pleated plaid skirt is a little too short, and her shirt is unbuttoned just a little too far, and her tie is just a little too rakish, and when she walks in, it's just a little too hard to breathe.

It doesn't matter if she's my type or not. Anybody who looks like that, dressed like *that*, is 100 percent everybody's type. I'm only human.

I'm standing with Charlie and Adriana (dressed as Yara Greyjoy and Danaerys from *Game of Thrones*) and I'm trying hard not to feel like the world's least sexy third wheel in my Members Only jacket and nail-studded baseball bat, and boy, Margo sauntering over here sure as hell doesn't help that.

"Expecting a Demogorgon?" she says, tipping her chin at my bat.

My brain short-circuits because. I mean. Look at her.

My mouth, independent of my mind, says, "A what?"

She blinks, and I realize what's happened.

"No," I say. "I mean, yes. I mean, I've seen the show. I'm not just—I wouldn't wear a costume of a character in a show I hadn't seen."

Charlie kicks my foot, and my mouth snaps shut.

Margo says, "It wasn't a quiz," half laughing.

I say, "Well. Obviously." Charlie kicks my foot again, and I think Margo notices, and I clear my throat. "And you're gender-swapped Prince Harry."

"One—he abdicated, Abbie. And two…" She laughs again and messes with the knot in her tie. "You know what, he's the hot brother, so I'm just going to take that as a compliment? I'm—we're *Gossip Girl*. Well. The cast of *Gossip Girl*. The original one. I'm Serena but you can't tell Chloe because she's convinced she is."

I force a laugh, like I get the joke or like, have any idea what she's talking about. "Would that we all could be Serena."

Adriana chokes behind me, and it's not fair, because if anyone should get to die in this moment, it should be me.

It's just that Margo Zimmerman's legs make me…head empty, only vibes.

"Well," she says, stepping just a little closer to me. Close enough that she can lower her voice in this crowd. Close enough that I can smell her coconut shampoo. "I was going to be Mary Shelley but I couldn't find a calcified heart on short notice."

I burst out laughing, because I frankly have no idea what she's talking about. I can *feel* Charlie's gaze on me but I don't care because all I can think about is how absurd and hot Margo would look dressed as the Original Goth. But like, accessibly hot, which is way different from how she's dressed now. Except *I couldn't find a calcified heart on short notice* somehow snapped me out of whatever weird schoolgirl uniform trance I'd been in, and she's suddenly just Margo Zimmerman again.

I mean. Still hot. Margo Zimmerman is objectively hot.

"UM," Chloe-who's-convinced-she's-Serena calls from across the room. "Blair Waldorf! Get your butt over here! We're taking a selfie."

Margo rolls her eyes to me at *Blair Waldorf*, then heads back over to her friends.

I laugh because hey! I get that reference. And then I watch her walk away, because whatever, I'm not in the closet and Margo Zimmerman is *hot*, but when I turn around, Charlie's staring at me with this face that I can't even describe. Like somewhere between concern and disgust and disbelief.

"Uh, Abs?" she says. "You okay?"

"Yeah," I say, shifting the baseball bat on my shoulder. "Are you okay?"

"I think what she's trying to say—" Adriana starts.

"Margo's *straight*," Charlie finishes. "What are you *doing*?"

"We're friends," I say. Like how I just interacted with her is how regular platonic straight girl friends act.

"You're friends?" she says. "That's new."

"Yeah," I say, "it is. She's helping me in AP US, remember? She's cool, and not just like, capital-C cool. Actually cool."

"You might be cool or whatever," Charlie says, "but you were flirting with her."

I shrug, like it's not a big deal, except oh god it's definitely a big deal; what *am* I doing? "Okay, but did you see her in that outfit?"

"I did," she says. "But that doesn't make her not straight. In fact, I think dressing up as someone from *Gossip Girl* makes her *more* straight."

I want to argue, but I don't know how to without outing Margo, and I won't do that. So I just say, "What, I'm not allowed to flirt with a pretty girl?"

"You're allowed to do whatever you want," Adriana cuts in. "Just—we don't want to see you hurt. Is all. That's all Charlie's trying to say."

I roll my eyes. "Please. Margo Zimmerman is objectively attractive, but she's not my type. Come on, Charles. You know better than that."

She nods and doesn't press the issue. Margo doesn't come up again at all—to us at the party, or in conversation. I think I catch her looking at me a few times, but maybe I'm just imagining it.

That's got to be it.

But I'm not imagining it when she catches my eye in the hallway between classes the next day. I tip my chin up at her in greeting. She gives me a small-fingered wave, something almost shy, like she's not sure how her acknowledging me will go over with the crowd of spectators.

But she's the one who wants to be Gay™, so I text her immediately, even as she walks away, her flat-ironed hair blowing in her wake.

Your greeting could use some work.

I don't get a reply until the end of class: My what?
Your GREETING. It's kind of a bitch to text and navigate the hallways when everyone's got their lockers open, but this is important. This is holding up my end of the bargain. Gays won't recognize you in the wild if you wave at them like a nervous five-year-old.
She writes: excuse me?
And follows up: Gays can't WAVE NOW?
I'm already in my next class, and the bell's going to ring just literally any second, but I can't resist responding. Waving is homophobia, Margo.
I put my phone away.

I don't hear from Margo again that afternoon, but it's not surprising. It was the last class of the day, and then she has only god knows what kind of impressive resume-building afterschool activities. So I go home, and I don't worry about it.
Why would I worry about it?
The house is quiet when I get home, which isn't that unusual.
What is unusual is my parents sitting at the dining room table. Together. There's nothing on the table, not even place mats or the usual week's worth of mail. My stomach falls into my feet.

"Hey, sweetheart," my mom says. She never calls me that unless something terrible is happening. Like when my grandfather died.

My bag's still on my shoulder. My keys are still in my hand. It would be so easy to turn around and walk out and drive away and just keep driving until I ran out of gas.

Dad says, "Can you spare us a minute to talk?"

No. *No*, I want to say. No, because whenever they want to *talk*, everything goes to hell.

I hitch my bag up higher on my shoulder.

"Abbie," Mom says softly. "Sit down, please."

I do, but only technically: my butt is barely touching the chair, hovering almost, ready to launch me back into the hallway and out the front door at a moment's notice.

"Honey, your father and I—" she looks over at my dad, who looks down at his hands "—we've decided that we're better as friends."

I blink. "You're not friends," my mouth says. And then it adds, "You don't even like each other."

"Well, now, Abigail—"

"She's right, Barbara." My dad speaks so softly that it takes my mom and me both a few seconds to register his words. "It's been a long time since this has been...good."

I can't believe I'm sitting here having to listen to this. "Jesus," I say, because I guess my mouth and brain aren't connected anymore, "couldn't y'all get this sorted out before you sat me down?"

"We had," Dad says. "But I guess we didn't take into account how insightful you can be."

"The important part is," Mom says, before I can yell at

them again, "none of this is your fault. We still both love you very much."

I roll my eyes, because I guess my brain isn't controlling anything I do anymore. "Did you download this speech from a *how to tell your elementary schooler you're getting a divorce* site?"

My mom blinks at me. My dad still won't really look at either of us.

Finally, Mom says, "Abigail, just because we're splitting up doesn't mean you can disrespect us."

"Okay." I say it with just the *least* amount of respect I can muster. "So who's moving out? Do I need to start packing? Am I going to have to start meeting boyfriends or girlfriends or whoever and get invited to call them by their first name because they're *so cool*?"

My dad sighs, but my mom is furious. Her face is bright red. "You're grounded."

I look her right in the eye for like, five whole seconds before I respond. And what I respond with is, "No."

And I get up from the table. My bag still on my shoulder, my keys still in my hand.

The sun's so bright it feels like a slap. I'm not thinking. I can't think. And I guess I'm halfway to Charlie's house, so I text her. Hey tell me you're not busy right now please.

I'm turning onto her street when I get her response: Adriana's over, what's up?

I stop. I just. Stop driving. On the side of the little shaded suburban street. And I don't know what to do. I stare at my phone until the screen goes dark, and then for another minute or five or twenty-three or I don't know. All I say is, My parents, because that's all I have to say. Isn't it?

The screen remains the same for so long that I get impatient and start scrolling through my whole inbox for something to do with my fingers and eyes and brain and then I guess I'm opening my conversation with Margo and the last thing I see is Waving is homophobia, Margo. She never replied. And I'm considering texting her again? I guess? After she didn't respond to the last one?

Why do I even care?

I don't know why. I just know that I do.

I just can't be alone right now. I can't be left alone to stew in my thoughts and my *fucking parents* and you know what, yeah, fine, I'm texting Margo again.

Did you get your permission slip signed?

I get a text back fourteen seconds later: What?

And a follow-up: What permission slip? Is this a swimming thing? Or a history thing? Is it a Gay 101 thing.

And then: Shit! I can't find it.

I don't respond immediately because I'm honestly smiling too hard. I can just see her rifling through her pristinely organized backpack, then scanning the syllabus I made, and seeing nothing about permission slips, but not trusting any of it and still panicking.

I mean. She's pretty fun to give shit to.

I reply: We're going on a field trip today. There's no permission slip, I'm just fucking with you.

Oh haha. Well, I'm always up for some education

Margo's house is like, three streets up from Charlie's. It'll take me five minutes, tops. I don't know if I want to give her time to get ready or if I need company immediately.

Who am I kidding? I know what I need.

Great, I'll be there in five

I don't get a prompt response, so I assume she's panic-primping. I head to her house and just wait in the driveway, not even bothering to tell her that I've arrived.

When she comes out and opens the passenger door, I can see her cheeks are pink and the rest of her is in a kind of vague disarray I doubt she'd ever allow herself to display at school. Her hair's in a ponytail, but less a carefully curated style than an *oh shit my hair needs to do something*. She's in leggings and a gray T-shirt knotted off to the side and high-top Converse, and she just looks so effortlessly gay.

"Hey," she says, breathless, and closes the door.

I say, "Looking gay," and put the car in Reverse, throwing my arm across her seat to look out the rear window, and back out of her driveway. Her face is so close to mine that I'm worried about how my *breath* smells, and I hate that. I hate that little spike of anxiety because who gives a shit. I'm not going to kiss her or anything.

Margo looks like she's been slapped. She's staring straight ahead, through the windshield at the closed garage door, her eyes wide and unblinking. Her nostrils flare.

"Mendel's firehouse T-shirt," she says, all tension in the timbre of her voice. "Noted as homosexual. And it's not even plaid."

"It's a man's shirt," I tell her temple, pulling out into the street. I face forward again and Margo's body deflates in what I assume is relief. "And you've tied it off. That's pretty gay."

"See?" she says. "And you laughed at me when I said I needed lessons. Calculus is less intricate than this."

"Yeah," I say, laughing, "you'd need Bill Nye to figure out wearing men's clothes isn't heterosexual. Has it occurred to you that you wanted to wear these gay, gay clothes because you are, in fact, gay?"

She runs her finger across her lower lip. Shrugs. "I wanted to wear them because...they were comfortable."

"Hmm." We're at a red light, and I start scrolling through my music. "Of course they're comfortable. Why do you think I'm wearing what I'm wearing?" (Denim Bermuda shorts, white T-shirt with the sleeves rolled up, bright red high-top Converse.) "I'm *extremely* comfortable right now. But also gay."

"Ah," she says, grinning. "Is comfort also Gay Culture™?"

I pretend to think about it while I find the artist I'm looking for. "Well, being tired is definitely gay, so sure. Comfort is gay culture, and so are naps."

She throws her head back and laughs. I know I've heard her laugh before, but it's different somehow in the close quarters of the car. The acoustics are different. The sound bounces around inside my head like a bell.

I continue, "And so is Lesbian Jesus."

I hit shuffle play on the Hayley Kiyoko artist page and turn the volume up as much as I can while still concentrating on the road.

I guess if I take the long way to Rise & Grind, it's because I wanted more time with Hayley Kiyoko. I find a spot close to the door and put the sun shades in the windshield before I turn the car off and get out.

"Oh," Margo says, looking up at the sign over the door. "Morning Wood! I *love* this place."

I choke on nothing. I mean, I've heard probably all the off-color nicknames for this place, but I guess I never expected to hear any of them out of Margo's mouth. She's always so...prim.

Margo pushes through the door, and in the line, I hear a couple of extremely jock voices I recognize from the halls of S.W. Moody High.

"Shit yeah, I love Wake to a Blowjob."

"Who's not into a little Morngasm, buddy?"

I snort, because I can't not. Margo stiffens a little next to me, and I glance over to see her mouth pulled into a tight line.

"You all right?"

She swallows hard and says, "Fine."

Margo Zimmerman is a shitty liar.

One of them turns around, and his face lights up. "Zimmerman!"

Could high school boys *be* any louder?

Margo sighs and turns around, bright smile painted on her face. "Robbie, Manny."

Her shoulders are up by her ears, anticipation practically visible between them.

Then Manny (who I always thought of as Manuel, so I guess they're nickname-basis friends?) says, "Where you been, you fuckin' heartbreaker?"

Robbie throws his arms around her in a bear hug. "Chad's so boring at parties now, dude. What did you do to him?"

"Oh, Jesus," says Margo, but her muscles are kind of starting to relax.

"You broke him," says Manny, "so I think you owe it to us to come back and liven up the parties again."

Margo rolls her eyes, a genuine smile spreading across her face. "Please, as though I was the life of Saturday nights before."

"Eh," says Robbie. "Close enough." He glances at me. "Uh, Annie, right?"

I shrug and say, "Sure."

"It's Abbie," says Margo.

"Duh," says Manny. "Get your shit together, Robbie."

Margo says, "Honestly, Robbie."

Robbie narrows his eyes, but he can't control the twitch in the corner of his mouth.

"Robbie," says Margo, "seriously, you're next in line. Actually get your shit together."

"Oh. Right. Yeah, right. Well. Don't be a stranger, dude."

Robbie and Manny head up to the counter. What they order are basically milkshakes, like there's not a Sonic two blocks away.

"So," I say to Margo, "this is the educational part of the trip. We've already established that comfort, naps, and being tired is gay."

Robbie and Manny fist-bump their way away from the counter.

Margo says, "Okay?"

I gesture for her to precede me. "Order something gay."

Margo purses her lips and her eyes go wide. She studies the menu like she did my syllabus. "Uh, hi!" She looks at the barista like somehow she can help. "I'll have, well. Just... let me get." She blows out a breath. "Okay. I. Will have. A large vanilla latte." She glances at me. "With...an extra shot of espresso?" Glances at me again. "And also. Almond milk. NO. Oat. Oat milk. No whip." One more glance, then she decides that she can breathe. That a large vanilla latte with an extra shot of espresso and oat milk with no whip is gay. "Yes. That is my order. Thank you."

I take a couple seconds to compose myself because, well. Not laughing, as it turns out, is a lot more work than one might assume.

I lean one elbow on the counter by the register and say, "Kayla, ignore everything she said. Just give us two large iced coffees."

Margo whirls to face me. "Iced coffee? That's IT?"

Kayla—who frequents Willow's Teen Night almost as often as I do—lifts her eyebrows at me like, *So this is your new girl?* And she's not, but there's no way to address it without exposing Margo to the silent conversation and boy, she's not ready for Gay Telepathy.

Kayla says (out loud), "No problem," but her smile is smug and annoying. "Are these together?"

I say, "Yes," at the same time Margo says, "No," and the knowing look on Kayla's face makes me want to simultaneously sink into the floor and smack her.

"Yes," I say again. "Listen, I showed up uninvited so the least I can do is drop three dollars on a coffee, okay?"

Margo wrinkles her nose, then says, "Yes, you know what—you *did* get me out in public looking trollish. You can buy me a coffee."

The thing is, she *doesn't* look trollish. And she should. I would, if I were in her shoes. But I can't tell her that because Kayla. I hate Kayla right now.

I pay for our drinks and let Margo lead the way to a table and I can't help it, the second we sit down, I say, "You don't look trollish."

Her eyebrows pop up and her lips curl up around her straw. She takes a drink and releases the straw, then says, "You're just saying that because you have to. Positive reinforcement for looking so gay."

"Take the compliment," I say. "Taking compliments is gay culture."

Margo narrows her eyes and leans toward me. "Is it?"

"Fuck if I know," I say, laughing. Then Margo is laughing, bright and genuine, and probably the last thing Margo Zimmerman could ever look is *trollish*.

"Well," says Margo, scraping her teeth across her lip, "anyway." And at some point, she must have stopped laughing? Jesus, how long ago did she stop laughing? This thing with my parents has really knocked me sideways. Forget Robbie, I'm the one who can't get my shit together.

"This is your gay lesson," I say. "Iced coffee is gay culture."

She smiles again, leaning forward to take a long sip without lifting her cup. Taking the slowest *joy* in it. "I can accept that." She cocks her head and says, "So now the hard part's over. Phew." She kicks me lightly under the table.

"So what fascinating things did I rudely pull you away from this afternoon?" I want to keep this easy camaraderie going, but I also want to know what she was up to. I'm interested, I guess. In Margo's life.

Or something.

"Oh," she says, "studying. Not even for school. Truly, I live a thrilling, wild life and this was a *real* sacrifice."

"Should I even ask what there is to study for if not school?"

"Horse gestation."

My expression is the facial equivalent of mashing down all the keys on the keyboard at once. "Horse—sure. Okay. Well. You sure know how to party on your day off."

She's laughing again, dragging her finger over her T-shirt collar. "I want to be a large animal vet. I don't just get home from school like, *what fetus can I study next?* But, yeah. That's— that's what I was doing."

"I wish I could believe you," I say, bringing my coffee up to take a drink, "but precedent indicates otherwise."

Instead of responding, Margo waits until the straw is in my mouth and the coffee is in the straw before leaning across the table, grabbing my cup, and *squeezing.*

I pull back as fast as I can but it's not fast enough. I choke on whatever coffee doesn't go on my shirt. I'm laughing, and Margo's laughing, and *oh, no.*

Oh, oh, no.

Margo Zimmerman is *flirting with me.*

"You utter jerk," I say, still laughing, trying to fit the lid back on my cup. "Spilling iced coffee is homophobia."

Margo's eyes sink shut as she takes a long, s-l-o-w drink of her nearly full coffee. When she opens them again, they're positively sparkling. "Gosh, this is *so good.* How's yours? You've got something." She touches her own collar again. "Just there."

Margo Zimmerman is flirting with me, and it's *working.*

"Just—just where?" There's coffee on my hand and I flick it back at Margo. "Oh shit, you seem to have some just—" and I wipe my sticky hand over her face.

She sputters and is actually *giggling*. "Jesus Christ," she says. "The iced coffee has *truly* sunk in. I've learned. So now you tell me. What led to this impromptu gay field trip?"

My smile falls away and Margo's face mirrors it. "Oh shit," she says. "I'm—sorry?"

My heel falls off the chair rung it was perched on. "No, it's—it's fine. I'm fine." I stop, then say, "No, you know what, I'm not fine. My parents were—they're getting divorced and they just told me this afternoon and I thought I'd be fine and I guess I'm not? Fine?" I hadn't meant to say all of that. Any of that. But it's too late now. And Margo doesn't look like she wants to say something. She doesn't look like she wants me to stop talking, either. So I don't.

"I'm not fine. But that's ridiculous. I should be celebrating," I say. "They don't like each other. I don't know if they ever have. All of us are always miserable, and I've been wishing for them to split up since I was like, eight or something, and now they're doing it, and as it turns out, I'm pretty fucking upset and I guess I just needed to not be alone. Or something."

She peers at me and breathes. For a beat. Two. Three.

My phone buzzes in my back pocket, but I can't bring myself to look at it, because what if it's my mom? Shit. I hate this. I hate everything.

"Sorry," I say. I try to prop my foot back up but I miss twice and suddenly I'm on the verge of tears and it makes me so immediately furious that I want to pick up my chair and throw it across this stupid bougie coffee shop. "You don't care about any of that. Sorry to just. I don't know. Puke all that out on you."

"No," she says. "That's not what I was thinking. I was thinking *god, adults are all shitty at being adults, aren't they?* And I was thinking that it sucks. And that I'm sorry. That it sucks."

I don't know what to say. I've never been so glad to have spilled so much coffee, because it puts us that much closer to leaving. I can't handle the way Margo's looking at me—with an intensity I haven't seen from her since *hey, you're gay*. Like I'm the only one in the room. Like I'm the only one anywhere that matters.

"I guess," I say. "Yeah, it sucks."

She says, "Hey—when we're done, do you want to hang out? At my place? Dame Julie Andrews has been asking about you."

Even I notice how long it takes me to answer. I say, "Thanks, but I think I'm okay now. I think I just needed to say it out loud or something and I'm fine now. Tell the Dame I'll see her on Tuesday."

Margo's eyebrows twitch together so briefly I hope I imagined it. She just says, "Okay," and then schools her face into neutrality. She adds, "Did you know that Mary Shelley and Aaron Burr actually met once?"

I smile, and she tells me about this three-hundred-year-old conversation, and everything's fine.

I am a shitty liar.

CHAPTER 15

Margo

Swim practice lets out on Tuesday and Abbie and I just naturally find each other, like we're friends.

Are we friends now?

Is that a thing that's happening here?

It sure seems like it, when we fall into easy step beside each other.

When she gives me shit for absolutely wrecking me at the backstroke and I protest because everyone knows my stroke is the butterfly.

When Julia calls my name from the parking lot and I whip my head around, apparently my hair isn't dry enough because Abbie sort of splutters and says, "Jesus, Zimmerman, watch the hair. You're getting me wet."

"*Getting* you wet? You just got out of the pool. You can't blame me for that."

"I just got *out* of the pool. And then I dried off." I can tell she's trying to suppress a grin and is just utterly failing. "And now this? In this economy?"

I roll my eyes, my own mouth curling up to match hers, and shove her shoulder.

My friends are waiting for me; I made them all postpone their movie so I could come and they agreed to pick me up as a unit. We kind of move as a unit at school, I guess, so this is familiar.

I tip my chin up at Abbie and we part ways so I can go meet them and she can go, well. I don't know. *Troll for bitches* or whatever she does after swim practice.

I adjust the choker I have refastened around my throat post-practice and prance over to meet them. I'm going through the list of *Lesbian Fashion* I compiled from the internet, trying on new stuff that really says "Cheers. M'queers" and today's lewk is *Goth Lesbian*, or as close to it as I could muster. My hair is down and straight, I've got an old scrap of lace I turned into a choker, and I dug out a giant pair of flared black pants with too many pockets that one of Mendel's apparent paramours left in in his closet a few months back.

I stopped after the black nail polish.

Quite frankly, I don't think I'm pulling this off. It's less *My Chemical Romance* and more *My husband locked me in the attic and I may or not be a mournful ghost out for vengeance*. But my friends don't comment on it, which I appreciate. They probably think I'm Going Through Something™. They're not completely wrong.

When I reach them, Aaliyah says, "Thought that swim cap was supposed to keep your hair dry."

"Eh." I shrug. "It doesn't work miracles."

She raises an eyebrow and says, "I'll tell you what a miracle looks like. Or a...strange occurrence. You hanging out with Abbie Sokoloff?"

Chloe asks, "Are you guys friends or something now?"

I shrug again, for lack of a better gesture, and sudden, bizarre panic swells in my chest. I swear, her name comes up and I feel like I'm being interrogated. "Sure, I guess. I mean we've been in swim together for a while, so."

"Huh," says Aaliyah.

"What?" I say.

I don't think she's being judgy; Aaliyah is cool. They're all cool or I wouldn't hang out with them.

She says, "I just didn't know y'all were friendly."

"Does—" Chloe starts, as we approach her car, and Julia makes this almost hissing noise and drags her finger across her swan throat. "What?" I say, furrowing my brow.

"Nothing," says Chloe.

"No, you can't say *nothing* after Julia just mimed a murder."

Julia looks a little sheepish (a lot sheepish; she's absolutely incapable of subtlety).

Chloe purses her lips and leans in close to me, keys still in her hand. I kind of wish she'd spit it out when we're in the car because it's a swamp out here.

She says, "Does *she* know what kind of friendly you are?"

I feel blood rush to my face, my ears. It's quick and painful; it's so hot. "What?" I say. Like I don't know what she means. Like there's any way I wouldn't have picked up on the implication immediately.

"I'm just—it's just that..."

"It's just obvious she was hitting on you," says Aaliyah.

I try to make some kind of noise of protest, and it comes out fake. "I don't—"

"Girl," says Aaliyah. "Y'all were four inches apart and she was looking at you like you were a freaking snack."

I don't know how it's possible that *every* part of me can feel suddenly this hot. How can my blood rush to literally every surface on my body at once?

"She was hitting on you," says Chloe.

"She was not."

Aaliyah just raises that eyebrow again and I cross my arms over my chest.

She wasn't.

Was she?

My throat is practically closing; my pulse is certainly jumping in my veins, which is ridiculous. It's *ridiculous*.

She wasn't flirting with me. Not any more than she would with any of her other friends.

Was she?

I blink at the ground and manage to say, "Just because she's gay, doesn't mean she wants to bang every girl in existence, okay?"

"Jesus," says Julia. "We're not being like, homophobic or something. We're just saying she's obviously into you and you shouldn't lead her on."

I just about choke. It comes out like a scoff. I don't even know what that scoff is supposed to mean. "I'm not leading her on!"

"Well, just be careful," says Aaliyah.

"Unless, you know," Chloe says with a little smirk, "you're

into that." She waggles her pale blonde eyebrows and I just roll my eyes.

I don't say anything. I feel like I should. Like I should tell them I'm gay, and every second I don't is a betrayal. I'm acting like I don't trust them with the deepest parts of myself, but I do. Because none of them has ever given me a single reason not to! And yet...the thought of announcing something as personal, as closely held, as this—it feels impossible.

I should... I should tell them.

And then I can't because GOOD GREAT.

Abbie's car is two down from ours.

And she is standing at her driver's side door, frozen.

She heard everything.

SHIT.

I catch Abbie's eye over top of her Corolla, and she's just... staring at me. Her eyebrows up and her eyes wide, like she's waiting for me to...what? Defend her? Come out to my friends?

What am I supposed to say?

I just hang there for a beat too long, and settle on, "Chloe. Don't be a jerk."

Which causes Aaliyah to follow my eyes to Abbie, and she says, "Shit," which somehow makes everything even more awkward than what I had, up until this instant, assumed was maximum awkward.

Now everyone in the car is looking at her! GOOD! BE FUCKING MARTIANS ABOUT IT!

JESUS CHRIST.

Abbie doesn't just get in her car. She extremely, decisively, 800 percent gets in her car and drives away.

My friends are basically past it by the time we leave the lot, and I can't stop checking my phone, like there's anything she would possibly say.

I am checking my phone all throughout the movie, committing a cardinal cinematic sin.

It does not buzz.

Of course it doesn't.

CHAPTER 16

Abbie

The thing about being publicly queer is that your sexuality and interests and pursuits are always a popular topic of conversation. It doesn't matter that your crushes work the same way as The Straights'; being queer in high school is like living on the wrong side of the fence in a zoo. And I was never really *in* the closet—when we moved here, I already knew I didn't just like boys, and I didn't care who knew. If straight kids don't care who knows they're straight, then why should I have to care who knows I'm bisexual?

In a perfect world, sure. But this isn't a perfect world. It's Florida. We can't even *say* "gay" here. And Margo's circle of friends assuming that I was flirting with her just because I like girls—and not that Margo was flirting with me, because they think she likes boys—is par for the course.

I mean. I *was* flirting with her. But that is entirely beside the point.

The point is that girls who like girls are allowed to have girl friends who aren't girlfriends.

The point is that I should be used to this. I *am* used to this. I've heard it enough times from enough people about enough girls that I had no interest in that it shouldn't even merit a second thought.

But it does. It's been two freaking days and I'm *still* thinking about it. I'm still thinking about how monumentally unfair it is that they get to say those kinds of things about someone they never would have otherwise given the time of day and then just…forget about it. There's no way any of them are still thinking about what they said, and there's no way I can think about anything else.

Because, sure. I was flirting with Margo. I flirt with a lot of people. But she's not my type, and it's not like it would matter if she was. We both know this is a business transaction.

My concentration is shot, and it's not just because I can't stop thinking about…well. Margo. It's also because my parents are yelling so loudly about *something that I can't focus.* So I shove my laptop and history stuff into my bag and walk out the front door without even saying goodbye. It doesn't matter; it's not like they know when I'm home and when I'm not.

I end up at a Starbucks because they have caffeine and Wi-Fi, and I have a test in three days. I've barely gotten my notebook flipped to the correct page when I hear the door open and Charlie's telltale laughter.

Shit. I am *never* going to get anything done.

"Abs!"

"Hey," I say, dragging the syllable out way too long. "Fancy meeting you here."

She slings herself into the chair across from me. "What's up, man?"

"Came here to study," I say. "Can't at home. My parents are. Well. My parents."

"Getting along?"

I sigh. "No. They're finally splitting up, actually."

Charlie blinks. "What? When did this happen?"

"I don't know," I say. "They told me like a week ago?"

"Abbie!" She sounds legitimately offended. I guess I should have told her earlier, but it's too late now. "What the hell, man?"

I shrug. "It's been a long time coming. Guess it didn't shock me."

"Jesus," she mutters.

"You're mad that my parents are getting divorced? That should be more my thing, don't you think?"

"I'm not—*god*—I'm not mad that your parents are splitting up, I'm mad you didn't fucking tell me!"

There are lulls in the conversations around us. "I'm sorry, okay? I've just got kind of a lot going on."

"I would have known that if you'd tell me anything."

"I do, Charlie. Look, I'm sorry. I'm just—I have a history test on Friday, and I'm really stressed out trying to study for it. This class is like the one thing standing between me and getting into FIU and the fuck out of this place. So like, yeah, I guess I'm a little preoccupied at the moment."

Charlie blinks. "That sucks, man. Anything I can do to help?"

Before I can answer, my phone buzzes on the table next to me. It's a text from Margo. I don't pick it up, but when I turn my attention back to Charlie, her eyes are still on my phone.

Is there anything she can do to help? Yeah, maybe get off my dick.

"I don't know what it'd be," I say. "Margo's been helping me study—"

"Ah," Charlie says, *knowingly.*

"I'm sorry, what does that mean?"

"Nothing," she says breezily. "Just curious circumstances, is all."

"Curious circumstances?"

"Sure," she says. "Margo's very pretty and helping you study, and you suddenly don't want to dance with strangers and you *very obviously* flirted with her at that Halloween party."

"I don't know what you're trying to imply."

"That you like her," Charlie says. "Duh?"

My phone buzzes again.

It's Margo. Again.

Charlie looks pointedly at my phone. "You gonna get that?"

I've been desperate to look at it since the first buzz, so I pick it up.

Are we on for tonight?

and.

No big deal if not, just wondering

I say, "Sorry," to Charlie, and tap out a response.

Wouldn't say no. I've been trying to study on my own today, but my brain is total spaghetti and I can't focus on anything.

I've barely got the phone back down before it buzzes again. I grimace.

Charlie says, sounding a little exhausted, "I'm going to go get in line."

"Cool," I say, already unlocking my phone.

Margo's texted, Sometimes my focus sucks, too; I've got a few tricks I could show you whenever you get here?

I reply, Omg I would love that.

She texts, Cool ^_^

I type, Charlie thinks I have a crush on you and maybe she's right, and then delete it all. I type, I'll see you tonight.

She replies, Yeah! It's election of 1800 night.

I say, lol you sure know how to show a girl a good time.

Shit.

But she replies, I learned from the best!

And then I'm just sitting there, staring at my phone, watching the three dots appear and disappear over and over and over, waiting, feeling a little like laughing hysterically because ha ha ha oh my god??

Charlie sits down across from me again and says, "Dude, you okay?"

I have...no idea what I look like, but it's probably something close to *shell-shocked*.

"Yeah," I try to say, and clear my throat; on the second try, it comes out audibly.

Margo Zimmerman is flirting. She's not practicing flirting; she's flirting with me.

"Adriana's on her way," Charlie says, clearly just looking for something to say.

"Cool," is the best I have.

Margo texts, I mean, you're a great teacher and I really appreciate everything you're doing for me.

That…doesn't help.

I reply, Back at you, which is honestly like the conversational equivalent of bisexual finger guns and I want to sink into the floor and die.

"Abbie?"

My head snaps up. I slap my phone back down to the table. "Hey. Hi. What's up?"

"Is that your mom?"

"No, it's Margo."

The way Charlie just blinks at me makes me think I should have lied.

"Abbie."

"What."

"You're going to get hurt."

"I'm fine, Charlie."

She cocks her head so far to the side she looks like an owl. *"Are you?"*

"Yes. Yes! I'm fine! She's just helping me study!"

Her eyebrows go up. "Okay."

My phone buzzes again.

I laugh. Weakly.

Charlie rolls her eyes. "Read the text."

I snatch my phone up, too eager, probably.

Margo's texted, About studying! I'm free all afternoon and evening, so just come whenever you want.

Then: *come over.

Then: the telltale signs of her typing and erasing and typing and erasing and trying to figure out how to extract herself from the awkward position she got herself into.

"You should see your face," Adriana says.

Her voice surprises me so much I actually flinch. "Damn," I say, trying to cover my ass somehow, *anyhow*, "we got to put a bell on you or something."

Charlie slides Adriana a knowing look.

I text Margo, How about in twenty minutes?

She replies immediately: Perfect.

Margo's mom answers the door, holding onto the collar of the chestiest brindle pit bull I've ever seen.

"Abbie?" The dog's pulling at its collar, but in a friendly way, not like an *I want to rip out your throat, you interloper* kind of way. "Sorry, I meant to have the dogs out back when you came. They're all nice, just…"

"A lot," Mendel shouts from somewhere behind her. Then, "Dammit, Julie Andrews!"

"Language, Mendel," Mrs. Zimmerman says off-handedly, wrestling the door open. "You're not afraid of dogs, are you, Abbie?"

"No, ma'am."

"Do you mind if I let Sean Connery go, then?"

I don't even know how to process this when Mendel says, "Mom, he's a *Peer* of the *Realm*."

I say, "Sure?" and. Uh. Sean Connery? Apparently? The dog. Licks my hand. Then runs off back down the hall to Mendel, and I can hear him saying, "Good boy, Sir Sean Connery, good boy."

I love this house. I love everything about it. Even the weird dog names.

"Margo's upstairs in the FROG," Mrs. Zimmerman tells me. "Do you want something to drink before you go up there?"

"There's a mini-fridge up there," Mendel says. "I'm sure Margo's stocked it already. You know how she can be."

"Well-prepared?" Mrs. Zimmerman asks.

"Yes," he says, but it doesn't sound like that's quite what he's saying. "There's probably like a homemade quiche up there, too."

"Mendel," his mom says, sighing. "Go feed the dogs. Abbie, you know where the stairs are?"

"Yes, ma'am," I say again, because I don't know how else to respond to her. She's so...warm. And I'm not emotional about it or anything, but. I mean. I am.

She walks me to the stairs, anyway, and says, "Let me know if you need anything, okay, sweetheart?"

"Sure."

I go upstairs to find Margo on the couch, her legs crossed in front of her. I won't tell her—I don't want to spook her—but she's sitting completely wrong, and I'm honestly a little proud. I'm sure it's only because she knew I was coming, but sitting wrong takes commitment.

Margo looks up when I climb the top step. "Hey," she says, laughing at something that happened before I walked up. Her ponytail swings with her movement, slipping over her shoulder. Her shoulder, which is bare in a black racerback tank top. Her shoulder, which has more defined musculature than we're led to believe The Popular Girl would have.

Her shoulder, which slopes up to her neck, to her jaw, to her—*why am I like this?*

"Hey," I say, because I don't know, she probably caught me staring at her neck. Like a weird gay vampire. "I didn't know your dog was a Peer of the Realm."

She smirks. "Ah, you met Dame Helen Mirren?"

"I—no? Sir Sean Connery. I can't believe I just—are all your pets? Peers? Of the Realm?"

"Yes," she says, faking offense. "You've met them. They're *regal*. I should have known it was Sean. Dame Helen Mirren is shy."

I'm not sure what I'm supposed to say to that, and I don't know if it's because of the dogs' names, or because of just this whole delightfully chaotic house, or because of Margo's freaking shoulders in that freaking top.

So I guess I say, "Don't let Mendel hear you call him Sean. He seems really adamant about that dog's peerage."

"Don't even get him started on the royal baby." I raise my eyebrows and Margo says, "I'm messing with you. Mendel doesn't give a crap about royalty. He's a communist."

I blink. "I don't know if you're joking or not."

Margo does some flawless awkward bisexual finger guns. "Speaking of systems of economics and running countries..." She gestures to the meticulously laid out floor of history in front of her. Like that was the smoothest segue.

Sure. Of course. I hitch my bag higher on my shoulder. "Are we on the floor or on the couch?"

She shrugs, and my eyes cut to her shoulders again. "Wherever you want."

We start on the floor, but within about twenty minutes, my

butt just falls completely asleep. ("Drawbacks of the FROG," Margo says, "no carpet pad.") We move to the couch, and we're facing each other, our backs pressed against the couch arms, our books between us, and she's taking so much joy in the incredible precedent Washington set by not running for a third term that it actually makes me smile. I try to keep it under wraps, and I think I succeed, but there's just something about watching someone *really enjoy* what they're doing that makes them, I don't know. Beautiful.

Margo's relaxed a lot since that first session at her kitchen table. She's relaxed a lot in general. She only sometimes seems like that girl who waited for me at the top of the pool ladder. She's explained everything in the assigned section, in a way that makes sense to me and sticks in my head, in less than an hour. And suddenly, the thought of the exam on Friday doesn't make me want to curl up in a ball anymore.

Margo pulls her phone out and says, "Well, we knocked this out. So I don't know if you have a hot date or something, but if you wanted to hang out and I don't know. Watch a movie? We could probably make that happen."

"Yeah," I say, and she starts typing on her phone. "I mean. No hot date. No date at all. Just this. This isn't a date. I don't have a crush on you. I mean. A movie! Let's watch one. Sorry. Jesus. No, maybe I should go."

Margo looks up at me, eyebrows practically in her hairline. Then she says, "No. No, stay." She punctuates this with her hand on my ankle and I wish I hadn't pushed these goddamn joggers up over my calves because then I wouldn't have to feel her *hand* on my *skin*. On my leg, of all places. She's telling me to stay and her hand is on my leg, even though I just shouted about how I didn't have a crush on her and this night is not going the way I predicted.

"Listen," says Margo, fingers still resting on my leg. "I, uh, the crush thing?"

Oh. G-d. How am I supposed to handle this? My entire heart is in my throat because I don't know what I'm supposed to say when she says what she's definitely going to say. Or probably. Or. I don't know.

I'm sweating, I think, and my tongue is numb for some reason and my heart is beating so fast I honestly feel a little nauseated and oh, my god, is this what it's like to be Margo Zimmerman?

Okay. I'll just—I'll tell her the truth. I'll tell her I've had a really good time hanging out with her and teaching her about being gay, and even learning history, but she's just. Not my type.

But Margo beats me to it and says, "I just—I know you heard what my friends said the other day. I should have said something about it earlier and I didn't and I'm sorry. They're assholes. Well. They're not. They're just... They were being weird and insensitive. It's just... Yeah, I'm sorry. I know that's not what this is. I know you don't *have a crush on me*. Okay? Are we okay?"

My mouth says, "Yeah."

She takes her hand off my leg. Rearranges herself on the couch. I'm just. Kind of staring at her.

I know, *Margo*. I know that's not what this is.

She asks, "What do you want to watch?"

And I have to figure out how to talk again. I have to figure out how to sit on this couch.

Face forward, Sokoloff.

She says, "Something gay. What's a gay movie I should have seen?"

I open my mouth to respond, and Mendel thunders up the stairs. Well. Mendel walks normally. Sean Connery—*Sir* Sean Connery—thunders up the stairs in front of him.

Mendel's holding a giant bowl of popcorn in one hand and a water bottle in the other. Margo says, "Thank youuuu," and I presume that's what the text was about?

Mendel grins, wide and a little goofy, and takes a swig of the water.

Sir Sean Connery huffs and Margo says, in the most baritone, intensely Scottish accent she can muster, *"Just the way your mother likes it, Trebek."*

Mendel actually spits out the water laughing.

I'm laughing, too, but I don't know if it's more at Margo doing a terrible Sean Connery impression or at Mendel's spit take, but thank god I'm laughing and not just word-vomiting all over the couch.

He recovers, wipes the water from his chin and brushes it from his Communists Have No Class shirt, and says, "You win. You always do." He tips his chin at me, hands Margo the bowl, and hops over the back of the couch, legs everywhere, missing Margo's head by a few inches.

"G-d," Margo mutters, and when he mimics her ("Godddddddd-duhhhhhhhh"), she smacks him in the back of the head.

It doesn't faze him, and he settles down between us and reaches into the bowl on Margo's lap. "So," he says, and tosses a giant handful of popcorn into his mouth, "what are we watching?"

"*But I'm A Cheerleader,*" I blurt, because I don't know what else to say. There aren't a lot of queer girl movies, and even fewer that aren't just like, soft lens and directed by aging French straight men. Bonus: this one doesn't have, like, egregious on-screen sex.

Not that I'm not down for that. Just not. Here. With Margo. And Mendel.

He reaches over Margo to grab the remote from the couch arm and finds a program where it's streaming. He reads the description and says, "Well. I don't think I'm the intended audience for this particular film." He grabs another handful of popcorn before levering up off the couch and turning to face Margo for long enough that I'm sure he's sibling-communicating *something* to her, but I can't see it through the back of his head. "Ladies," he says to us. "Mr. Connery."

And he and the dog disappear down the stairs.

Margo's face is as red as Mendel's politics.

I ask, "You okay?"

She says, "Yeah. Just, you know. Choked on some popcorn."

The movie's starting, and Margo gets up and turns off the lights, and when she sits down again, it's right next to me. Not so close we're touching, but when she folds her legs up under her, we almost do.

She says, "Popcorn?"

And all I can do is say yes. Because that's why she sat next to me. To share the popcorn.

She says, "Oh, you know what," and then just hands me the bowl and gets up again. And no, I don't know what. What is it that I should know? I haven't eaten any of this popcorn and I don't think I could possibly because my stomach feels like a wet rag. I feel like I just got off a roller coaster and I don't know why.

Margo comes back with a fluffy blanket, so big it's dragging on the ground. Is she proposing we—

"Listen," she says, "the window unit up here is absurdly efficient, and if we turn it off, it takes like seventeen years to cool this room off again because the insulation sucks so we just keep a blanket up here in case we get cold."

I know she's not asking a question, because it's her house, and her FROG, and her damn blanket. But I think she actually is; I think she's asking if I'd mind sharing the blanket with her.

Why wouldn't I? Girls who like girls have girl friends who aren't girlfriends. Girl friends do this shit all the time. I've done this with Charlie a ton, and we've never fooled around. Or even been tempted. So two girls who like girls sharing a blanket in a dark room while watching a movie about girls who like girls is completely and totally regular and normal.

The blanket is over us. It's big, but not so big that Margo doesn't have to scoot just close enough to me that her knees are touching my thigh. I'm glad I'm not wearing shorts. I'm glad she's not wearing shorts. I'm still holding this stupid bowl of popcorn and Margo keeps reaching her stupid hand into it. Her fingers are distracting me from the movie.

The movement. Of her fingers. In the bowl of popcorn. It's noisy.

Jesus Christ.

Halfway through the movie, she pulls the tie out of her hair and it falls around her shoulders. Suddenly, I'm surrounded by the scent of her shampoo, I guess—coconut. It's better than the sticky smell of the popcorn butter. It's better than…a lot of things. It's extremely good.

I want to touch her hair, I guess? When did I become a person who wants to touch Margo Zimmerman's hair?

I mean, I don't touch it. I'm not a fucking weirdo. But I'm not even really watching the movie and I'm glad it wasn't on the syllabus because then Margo would expect, like, a quiz or something, and to be honest, I haven't watched this movie in like three years so I don't remember nuance. I'm not great at nuance, anyway, and I can't pay attention to nuance with Margo Zimmerman's *perfect* knee pressed against my *thigh* and her *perfect* hair smelling like *coconut* and her *perfect* laugh brightening the whole goddamn *room*.

The movie ends and Margo leaves the television on. As a light source, I guess. But we're just sitting there, in the dark, and I swear she moves closer to me but I don't know, man. Maybe I'm imagining it. Maybe I'm…maybe I'm *wishing* she did.

Margo plants her hand next to her hip and ha, oh god what is happening? But she just turns.

No. She doesn't *just* turn. She shifts her entire body so she's facing me, and her bent knee is lying on my thigh under this blanket and no, no, nope.

I fumble with the blanket, getting caught in the damn thing in my rush to pull it off me. "Well," I say, and my voice is, wow, *awfully* high-pitched, "I have to go. It's. A school night. I'm just. Thank you for the popcorn and the history and I'll probably show myself out unless you've got like, the knights of the round table guarding the front door. Pets, I mean. Named for. Jesus."

Stop talking, Sokoloff.

She laughs, and says, "No, not even a disciple—"

I laugh, too hard, probably, and just cut her off. "Okay, well. Thanks. I'll see you at school or whatever bye."

I *flee.*

I get an 83 on the election of 1800. That's my highest score yet.

Margo Zimmerman
Queer 101
For: Abbie Sokoloff

On A Queer Historical Figure

I've always had a thing for Julie D'Aubigny.

You've probably never heard of her, because no one has ever heard of her, because Julie was too busy kicking men's asses and seducing women to have been allowed to be included in history books.

Anyway, I guess I've been obsessed with her since I was a kid. I probably should have known, honestly, that I was gayer than not when all the other sixth graders were doing essays on Abraham Lincoln and Martin Luther King Jr., and Jesus, and I was busy absolutely fawning over this bisexual sword fighter from the 1700s.

I always wanted to be her.

Or well...do *something* about and/or with her.

Anyway, you should know that she was a sword fighter who absolutely DEFINED the phrase "steal your girl." Once, she went to a ball, dressed up like a man, and kissed a ton of girls, and the men hated it and challenged her to a sword fight, and she beat EVERY SINGLE ONE OF THEM. Three men at once!

She had this love affair with a guy she beat in combat. They hated each other, fought, then wound up banging it out for like a million years.

Maybe the best Julie story is that she was dating this girl?

And the girls' parents caught her and flipped out, and sent her to a convent. So Julie literally joined the order, stole a dead body, burned the CONVENT DOWN, and snuck her girlfriend out.

They broke up like two weeks later.

Is she not the most incredible person you've ever heard of?

Is she not an utter INSPIRATION? Just to live like that. Breezing your way through life with a sword, being whoever you want, dressing however you want, completely...completely free of control.

What a nightmare. Or... I don't know. An ideal life.

Maybe to be queer in a time like that, you had to be completely radical.

Maybe to be queer now, you have to be... I don't know.

What I know is that it's a crime that Julie D'Aubigny isn't the first person we learn about in European history, because she had the audacity to have sex with women.

See, and you thought I was going to dig up some dirt on Mary Shelley or Aaron Burr, didn't you?

CHAPTER 17

Margo

The next Wednesday, I walk into Room A24 at 3:55 p.m., and Abbie doesn't even let me sit.

She's leaning up against her desk, and she straightens when I move for mine. "Nope. No lectures today. You're learning to queer in the wild."

I blink, stomach suddenly twisting into a knot. "What?"

"Come on. I'm driving."

Then we're in Abbie's car and she won't tell me where we're going. Which is fine, I guess. Who cares? It's not like I need to know. It's not like *control* is a thing I care about. Ha. It's just that I like to have notice when things are going to happen, like when someone will show up to my house or if we're having dinner before the movie or after, and also where we're eating and if I for some reason have to order something different than I usually do. Thanks, autism brain!

Spontaneity is for other people, people like Abbie, apparently, which definitely explains why my pulse hops up about

10 bpm being around her, and why being in the car with her sends it up another fifty. We're going somewhere! But where! Am I dressed appropriately? I'm going for cottagecore, so: my hair is wavy, my makeup is natural, and my dress is floral and ephemeral and perfectly twirly.

I was built to frolic in a wheat field and post sponsored content about it on Instagram. But are we *going* to a lesbian wheat field? Am I going to have to meet new people? Make small talk? Who knows!

I am too autistic for this shit. AT LEAST TELL ME WHICH MASK I NEED TO PUT ON.

I want, *desperately*, to ask her where we're going, but I'm trying to be cool, as if that, too, is a thing that occurs naturally, so I guess I just stare out the window. Trying to guess where we're going.

Autistically.

Girl in Red is blasting through the car's old speakers because "Melissa Etheridge is for Gen X and Tegan and Sara are for millennials. But Girl in Red—Girl in Red is for us."

Twenty minutes later, we pull into Ocala Skate Park.

I have flowers in my hair.

I don't even unbuckle. I say, "Abbie. I do not skateboard."

"Nobody's asking you to," she says. "But this place is like a watering hole on the gay savanna."

"Okay," I say. "All right. But I swear to god, if you try to get me to stand wrong on a skateboard—"

"Goofy-foot."

"Gesundheit, and don't try to tell me that doing an ollie is gay culture…"

"It's not *not* gay culture." She reaches over and unbuckles my seat belt and her fingers brush the outside of my thigh through the thin fabric of my dress.

There goes another 50,000 bpm.

This…freaking *anxiety*.

Or something.

I shove my door open so hard I about fall out of it, but she's not looking (I don't think) because she's crossing around to her trunk.

She pulls a worn skateboard out of it, and tucks it under her arm, tilting her head toward the park. "Come on."

I groan and follow her.

The particular sound of wheels on cement gets louder the closer we get, and I don't know how many of these people are gay, but there's sure a lot of them. It's a *very different crowd* than I'm used to hanging out with. *The baggy jeans and baggier Anarchy T-shirts and snapbacks and weed* kind of crowd.

I look… I look like a Puritan Vietnam War protestor in a skate park.

WHATEVER.

I look fine.

I feel very fine.

I smile brightly—so comfortably fine—at Abbie. "So. What's the plan, professor?"

"Well," she says, "I was kind of thinking about skating."

I stand there in complete silence for four full seconds, which doesn't sound like a lot. But as a reaction time, in skate park silence, it is, in fact, a lot.

"Cool," I say. "Yeah, cool, yeah. Go and skate, obviously." My hand is in my hair. "In this skate park." My mouth is going to start hurting soon if I continue smiling this aggressively genuinely. "GREAT." It's supposed to come out, "Great! :)"

It does not.

She adjusts the board under her arm and tilts her head. "You're friends with everyone. Don't tell me you're afraid of this crowd." As she finishes, someone with a long low ponytail and in a baggy Ramones T-shirt and high-top Vans and fitted jeans that are sagged just enough to be Making A Gender Statement comes up to her, and they greet each other with a sort of handshake/bro hug hybrid. "Margo, this is Jordan. Jordan, Margo Zimmerman."

Jordan tips their chin at me and downs whatever is left of their Monster energy drink in a single swig. "You skate, Margo Zimmerman?"

I consider tipping my chin back at them but opt not to attempt it. "I extremely do not." I laugh and their mouth curls. "Here for moral support," I say, cocking my head at Abbie. "Or something."

Jordan glances at Abbie, and Abbie sort of rolls her eyes. Jordan tosses their can in the trash, drops their board on the ground, and takes off.

"Jordan can be a lot," Abbie says, and I'm not sure if it's an apology.

I shrug and glance around the cement park, wondering when exactly Abbie's gonna take off and leave me to fend for myself. Not that I'm scared of this crowd...

I'm not scared of this crowd, god.

I AM friends with everyone.

There's at least four kids here in beanies. In eighty degree weather!

I don't know why that matters.

The point is I'm not scared.

Of this crowd.

I shoot Abbie a look that there's no way she can interpret because she's not in my head, and follow her into the semi-crowd. She introduces me to a few more people—whose names all run together in a nervous blur—and eventually just kind of says, "Well," and dips into the bowl.

Cool.

I'm alone.

There's not even anywhere to sit except on the concrete.

I breathe.

People here are in their cliques, like they always are, because who wants to talk to strangers, I guess.

I know I look completely awkward, out of place.

Of course I do.

But this is about being gay in the wild.

I sit. I try to signal, through this, that I am a Homosexual™, and I do succeed in sitting a little awkwardly (the way I would have instinctively sat, anyway, I think; who knew?) but not in drawing any fellow queers to me.

For a few long minutes, I wind up just…watching Abbie skate.

She looks effortless. I mean, she always looks effortless, like she can completely relax into anything worth doing. But she's fluid on that board, and my eyes are trailing the liquid movement from one jump to the other, the gap in her men's white V-neck when she crouches to distribute her weight just the right way. My gaze is tracing the lines of her throat and jaw when she laughs, grabbing her backward snapback when it about flies off her head and Jordan gives her shit for it.

She glances over at me, and my throat *knots*, and I blink away.

This...was not what she meant by being gay in the wild.

Jesus Christ, Zimmerman, she straight up *told you* she didn't like you the other night.

So freaking...stop.

I do.

I stop.

I stand way too fast, just about giving myself a head rush, and I march up to the first girl I see. She's cute, as tall as I am, not someone I have to slouch six inches just to look in the eye. She's got a half-shaved head and black shiny hair and a cool septum piercing, and I say, "Hey. Come here often?"

Oh god.

No.

WELL. IT'S TOO LATE NOW good god.

She blinks at me. "It's...the only skate park in like twenty miles."

I say, "Uh." Stand with Big Dick Energy. I relax. The way Abbie would relax. Except there's no wall behind me, so I end up just kind of slouching, which I hate, so I guess instead I'm not relaxing. It probably is.

I know it is because I'm totally doing it.

"Yes," I say. "Yup. Ha ha. That's why I myself come here."

She arches an eyebrow at me.

I choke out, "Often."

Another girl sidles up to her, and I shoot her some bisexual finger guns.

And I leave.

I just go back to my earlier spot; that is my territory now. My empty, empty gay territory.

I'm focused so hard on sitting and recognizing who might be gay and who's not and slouching the proper amount that I can't even begin to relax.

I'm so focused and stressed and *embarrassed* that I don't notice when someone's shadow falls over me.

Not until she says, in a kind of fake-deep voice, "Come here often?"

I groan and glance up and she smiles. She's got warm brown skin and a warmer grin. Rings on every finger. Abbie introduced me to her earlier. Izzy, I think? Whoever she is, I want to sink into the pavement. But there's probably not a literal sinkhole right here (probably!) so I guess that's out of the question. I just put my face in my hands and hope that conveys all the intricacies of what I'm feeling.

I hear her sit next to me and she says, "Let me…get you a drink." Something cold and hard bumps my knee. I consent to pick my head up, and she's holding out a Mountain Dew for me, and I laugh and take it from her.

"What a crash and burn," I say, watching the skaters. I don't know if this is easing my embarrassment or making it worse.

"That queer girl life, man," she says. "Girls are impossible to talk to. Margo, right?"

Suddenly, it's clear. She's not making it worse. I make eye contact with her, because that's what I have to do. My smile, for the first time this afternoon, is relaxed. "Yeah," I say. "Yeah, Margo Zimmerman."

"I'm Izzy."

"I know." It comes out defensively, and I kind of wince at my own tone.

But she doesn't even acknowledge it, bless her. She just says, "You're Abbie's friend," almost like a question.

I nod and look for Abbie in all the slopes and edges below. Izzy cocks her head, following my gaze, and kind of smiles in this too-sparkly way and I know what she's thinking and I...don't correct it.

It's been a weird afternoon.

But this is nice.

It's nice—probably too nice—when Abbie pulls up out of the bowl and finds me, cheeks flushed from the heat and the skating, the joy of it all over her face.

Izzy doesn't seem to see her until she's almost on us, then does that chin-tip thing that I swear to god I'll master one day. Abbie's breathing hard, sweat trailing down her face and jaw and throat.

"Hey," she says, and drops the board next to us and plops down on it. Her knees come up to her armpits, and she's just sort of rolling side to side. She's so...so fucking *pretty*. Like, her face, yes. The rest of her, yes. But also the energy just rolling off her. It's distracting, it's always distracting, and I swallow it down.

She doesn't like me, and I need to not get wrapped up in a bunch of thoughts that won't lead anywhere.

"I made a friend," I say proudly, and Izzy's laugh bubbles out of her.

Abbie says, "There's no accounting for taste," and Izzy punches her in the arm. Abbie dramatically tumbles off the skateboard, lying on her back on the concrete, laughing. And Izzy's laughing.

And I'm laughing.

For the first time since summer, I think I'm actually comfortable?

Holy crap. I'm not… It's not a lie. I'm really, actually *not* afraid of this crowd.

We hang out in the suffocating heat for longer than I'd planned, probably longer than either of us planned. But it all felt so natural, is the thing. Until we're all sticky with sweat and I'm really regretting walking home in this dress because I know my thighs are going to chafe. It's just… Well, I didn't want to leave.

What a twist.

I get home just before the sun sets to find my parents cuddling on the couch, watching something from the '90s, something that *reminds them of when they were young.*

I smile, because it's nice that they still actually like to hang out.

I don't want to think about them doing anything *else* but it's nice that, like, two kids later, they still cuddle on the couch. That they still like to touch each other.

My mom hears me come in, I guess, and she says, "Hey, baby. How was the…the thing. Whatever thing you were doing?"

"The thing was good," I say. I slip off my shoes and lean over the back of the couch. *Robin Hood: Men in Tights.* That sounds right.

Prince John eyes the giant pig on the table in front of him

and says, "Ugh. *Treyf*," and my dad quotes it along with him and my mom laughs too hard to have seen this a thousand times.

I laugh, too; it's a highly underrated line.

Then I'm in my head.

The thing, I think, *was good.*

The thing, I think, *is that a queer girl I didn't even know said "that queer girl life" to me, like I was one of them. And she just knew. And I am. I am.*

I say, over *Robin Hood*, "I'm—I'm gay."

My mom kind of tilts her head, and my dad tilts his toward her, just as subtly.

Just a little.

He reaches for the remote.

And the screen freezes.

"What?" he says.

I blow out a breath, and I walk out into the living room and stand in front of them. I've said it now; it's nice, not having to work up to it. But they're staring at me expectantly and they're cool, I'm sure they'll be cool. They've always been cool. They've gone to protests for queer rights and my mom has commented happily more than once on the couple of gender-neutral bathrooms in our synagogue.

And they're fine with Mendel! He's been telling them offhandedly about the handsomest boys—and the prettiest girls—in his class since he was six, officially announcing the day after his Bar Mitzvah that he was queer and that they had to be cool with it because he was an adult now and could do what he wanted.

There was...some negotiation over the second half of the statement. But not the first.

And they were cool when he told them he was poly a couple years back. I believe Dad said, "You're taking this communism thing a little far now, aren't you, kid?" And that was it.

So I'm not actually worried, but also I am? Because sometimes...sometimes people are cool about everyone else's kids and weird about their own, or cool with gay boys but not gay girls, or cool with being gay but not trans, and I'm sure that's not my parents but...what if.

I don't know.

I look at the ceiling, then back at them.

I see Mendel in the hall, leaning against the wall in the shadows. He looks at me and smiles.

And I say, more clearly, more resolutely, to my parents, "I'm gay. I'm just... I don't know what else to say. I'm gay."

There is total silence in the room.

Then my mom says, "Oh, thank G-d."

I blink. "What?"

My dad sighs, like he's relieved. "Margo. Sweetheart. You have *terrible* taste in boys."

Suddenly, I'm laughing, like a whole life's worth of tension has been wrapped up in me forever and now it's just gone. I say, "What about Chad!" like I'm offended or something.

And Mom and Dad say together, "We HATED CHAD."

Mendel steps into the room. "We hated Chad," he confirms. "Chad's a cop."

Dad furrows his brow and says, "Chad's...still in high school."

I want to cry.

I don't.

I steal Dad's popcorn.

I watch *Robin Hood: Men in Tights* homosexually.

Which, as it turns out, is the same as watching it hetero-sexually or bisexually or any other kind of sexually.

I laugh just as hard at "IT'S AN EVERLAST," and Mom snorts at all the medium funniest parts and everything about tonight is absolutely, anticlimactically normal.

I go to bed.

And I sleep like the gay, gay dead.

CHAPTER 18

Abbie

When I show up at Margo's house for the War of 1812, her dad answers the door, no dogs in sight.

"Hey," he says, a big genuine smile on his face, "come on in. Margo's in the shower, but she should be down in a few minutes."

Good. I get to think about Margo in the shower *and* be alone with her parents. Cool. Everything is cool.

"Can I get you something to drink?"

"I'm okay," I say, because I don't know what else to say.

"Well, if you change your mind." He turns and is halfway out of the vestibule before he realizes I'm not following him. "Come in," he says. "Pretend like you like us, at least."

My face gets hot, and I feel ridiculous, like I've forgotten how to human. "Sure. Yeah." I follow him into the living room, where Margo's mom is curled up in an armchair with a book on her lap and a cat on the headrest behind her.

"Abbie's here," Mr. Zimmerman announces.

Mrs. Zimmerman marks her page and shuts the book.

"Hey," she says. Her smile seems extra wide, like she's got an amusing secret. "How are your classes?"

I blink. "Fine," I say, because what else am I supposed to say? I can't remember the last time my parents asked me, their own child, about school. "Margo's helped me a lot in this history class. And you guys are really generous to let us do it here."

And then I'm blushing, because I said *do it* and I didn't mean do *it*, I meant *study*, but it doesn't matter because I can't correct myself now because these are parents and get your shit together, Sokoloff.

"It's no problem at all," Mr. Zimmerman says. "We like having people around."

"We're glad you get along so well," her mom says.

"I mean. Same." I swallow, and I'm still standing in the doorway to the living room, my bag on my shoulder. "Sure makes studying easier."

Easier, harder. Potato, potahto.

Mr. Zimmerman perches one leg on the arm of the chair his wife is sitting in, his hand settling somewhere between her shoulder and the back of her neck. I literally cannot even imagine my parents doing this, and I'm glad I don't have to want to anymore. She looks up at him and smiles, and he smiles back, and man, is someone cutting onions in here? My throat is tight and dry, and I'm so jealous of Margo and Mendel I can barely think.

The cat behind Mrs. Zimmerman's head stands up and stretches, arching its back, and leaps onto the floor.

"I guess you've only met the dogs," she says, then nods

toward the cat sauntering out of the room. "That's Sir Anthony Hopkins."

I—

"The dogs are in their kennels," Mr. Zimmerman says. "It's Mendel's turn to host the union meeting tonight."

Margo appears behind me, smelling like coconut, as always, and oh no, I've made a huge mistake. Her hair is damp and wavy and she's wearing an oversized T-shirt and shorts and that's. That's it.

"Is he hosting it in the FROG—" she starts.

Then an extremely loud and off-key, "SOLIDARITY FOREEEEEVER," floats down from the stairs. Which answers *that* question.

"Yes," Mrs. Zimmerman says, and Margo laughs.

Margo says, "Sounds like Zack made it tonight. That voice is difficult to forget."

"Would you say," her dad says, pausing dramatically, "it's a little...*wobbly?*"

Margo groans, and it's clear I'm the only one here who doesn't get the joke. It's so clear Margo says, "It's a nickname for IWW—no, you know what, it's not worth it."

Her dad's snickering, but her mom just smiles indulgently and says, "The communists have taken the FROG, and we're having a date night out here, so you have to be somewhere else."

"Or not," Mr. Zimmerman says. "But we *are* thinking about maybe kissing, so..."

"Jesus, Dad." Margo turns to me and says, "We're going to my room." She grabs my elbow and drags me down the hall. When we're out of earshot, she says, "You have to forgive my parents. They're…well. Parents."

"I love your parents," I say before I can stop myself. But I don't care, because I do love her parents. Her parents and her brother and all their ridiculously named pets and the chaos and dad jokes and all of it. I can't even remember the last time my own house felt inviting, even to me.

She turns back to glance at me, smiling a little, and says, "They're all right." Like she knows they're way better than all right.

Margo leads me to her bedroom, which is, predictably, immaculate and organized within an inch of its life. The walls are a pretty periwinkle, white curtains on the windows, all of it coordinating perfectly with the fat royal purple and white stripes of her bedspread. Fairy lights are strung across her headboard and coiled across the back of her desk. Everything is hyper-coordinated in true Margo Zimmerman fashion, except for the posters on her walls.

They don't make any sense in the space. They're so… *Science*. Diagrams of horse and cow anatomy, down to the smallest detail. Like stuff straight out of a textbook. Hell, knowing Margo, they might be. I wouldn't put it past her to scan the images and blow them up just so she can surround herself with *knowledge*.

It's intimidating; she really knows what she wants, down to the neurological systems of the animals she wants to help, and I'm over here, failing a history class and not even sure if I'll get into college. No wonder FIU is trying to rescind my acceptance—between Margo Zimmerman and me, I know which one should get a place in the lecture hall.

"Well," she says, sweeping her hand through the air, "this is where the magic happens."

Her voice surprises me. I guess I kind of fell down a distracted rabbit hole, but I think I recover okay. "You forgot the awkward bisexual finger guns," I tell her. "What a perfect opportunity, totally missed."

She wrinkles her nose and says, "Good thing I'm not bisexual," then rummages in her backpack. The stuff isn't already laid out for studying like it usually is. She's just a little frazzled, a little behind.

It's probably nothing.

"So," I say, "where are we sitting?"

Her gaze sweeps over the room and clears her throat. "Floor's as good a place as any."

I plop down with my back against the foot of her bed and pull my books out. "Your posters," I say, since she's still arranging and rearranging her stuff, "they're, uh. Interesting. A little gruesome for all this purple."

"Oh." She looks up at her wall, like she's surprised they're there. When she looks back at me, her face is a little pink. "I'm into horses, I guess." She gestures down at her Live Oak Stables shirt and says, "When I'm not student-counciling or history-tutoring or swimming, you can find me mucking horse shit out of stalls. In the summer. Margo Zimmerman, Horse Girl. Tell no one."

I don't know why this surprises me, but it does. No, I do know why: Margo Zimmerman is too femme to be elbow-deep in a horse. I'm wrong, obviously, but we all have some biases to unpack.

"There's a difference between a Horse Girl and a horsewoman and you know it," I tell her. "Horse Girls don't spend their summers shoveling shit."

"And horsewomen," she says, "get doctorate degrees." She winks.

"Ones like you, anyway." People say a lot of things about a lot of things, but I don't believe anyone like I believe Margo Zimmerman. She'll do what she wants to do, without a doubt. If she wants to be a vet, she'll be a vet. And good for her.

And if I'm being honest, I'm pretty jealous of that kind of certainty. I've wanted to be eighty-seven different things when I grow up, from astronaut to Supreme Court justice to professional figure skater, but I've never figured out what I want to do. I mean, I will. Probably. Eventually.

I just can't do it here. I'll scream.

She settles down next to me on the floor and we spend the next two hours (of which I spend too much time reining Margo's enthusiastic historical tangents in, to be honest) talking about the War of 1812 and the Treaty of Ghent and how much of an asshole Andrew Jackson was.

Margo introduces me to her sugar glider, who is actually real and actually named Sir Michael Caine, and okay I definitely thought it was a joke but only because "sugar glider" cannot be a real Earth animal.

And then it's after ten and the house is quiet. I think Mendel's friends are all gone, and the parental date night seems to have concluded in a much less stressful way than my parents' date nights historically have.

The thought of going home right now, to whichever parent is there, in whatever emotional state they've wrapped themselves up in, seems impossible. Not undesirable; *impossible*.

Like if I tried to walk through my front door, some magical unexplained force in the world would keep me out, like the door had been painted with lamb's blood and I'm the Angel of Death.

But I can't decide if it's because I can't imagine walking into my own house, or if I can't imagine walking out of Margo's.

So that's the thing, I guess: I want to stay. I want an excuse, any excuse, to stay longer.

Good thing she's. You know. Not my type.

She's putting her books away, her back to me, in those damn shorts, and I don't know how to prolong the night. She'd tell me to leave if she wanted me to leave, right? It's not like she's one to beat around the bush.

The words are out before I even know they're coming. "Have you kissed a girl yet?"

She freezes. She's still looking at her backpack, slowly zipping it up, when she says, "One. Over the summer." She clears her throat and says, "Uh, it was spin the bottle so I don't know how much it really counts."

I don't know if she's still doing anything over there, but she's definitely not looking at me. Which isn't that unusual, I guess. She used to look at me. Back when she was yelling at me in the pool about being gay, but now she doesn't. I don't know, maybe she knows me too well now. She saw me, and decided what she saw was too much, and I don't know. Join the club.

I say, "Ah." I hope it doesn't sound to her like a deflating balloon. So I just: "It's different. From kissing boys, I mean."

I can actually hear it when she swallows. "How. How exactly?"

Wait—oh no. Congrats, Sokoloff. You've played yourself.

"Well," I say, determined to not make a *complete* ass of my-self, "girls are usually better at it. For one."

"Should I be taking notes?" Then she does look at me, to smirk. Margo never *smirks*.

"I imagine you'd have gathered that yourself." I can barely breathe and it's my own fault. "Don't know there's much to take notes on."

She glances at her bag and settles back down next to me, bare knee brushing against my thigh. Is she closer than she was?

No. No. I'm losing my mind. I'm staring straight forward because if I turn my head, it'll be too much, and I can't. I can't do that.

I can't find out that she's not looking at me.

She says, "My notebook's irretrievably buried, anyway."

"It's not something you can really—" and I have to stop and swallow around the lump of nerves in my throat, because, ha, she's definitely closer "—like. Explain. With words."

She just breathes for a second, then turns her face. Jesus, the tip of her nose nearly brushes my cheek. "Did you...could you—" She breathes one more time and I feel it on my skin. "Do you want to show me?"

I look down at my lap. "Uh. Yeah." I rub my thumb and forefinger together, like that's going to alleviate literally any tension at all.

I say, "I can do that."

I finally, finally make myself turn my head—and it's absurd, how nervous this makes me, as if I haven't kissed girls before, as if I haven't done more than just *kiss* on bedroom floors— and she's so close, if I move at all, we'll be pressed together.

So. I move.

I put my hand on her neck and my mouth on hers and it takes no time at all for her mouth to open and for mine to mirror it and Jesus *Christ*, I'm kissing Margo Zimmerman. Her hands are in my hair and on my waist and everywhere all at once, and I feel her teeth scrape my lip and her fingers tighten on my hips and she's pulling me into her lap and I let her because why wouldn't I?

Her legs are bare under mine and I've never been so bummed to not be wearing shorts. But it's okay, because there's so much of her to touch, soft and hard and everything between.

I guess it doesn't matter if she's my type or not.

Then there's a knock on the door and I'm so surprised I almost yelp.

Mr. Zimmerman's voice comes through the door. "Knock-knock."

Fuck, *fuck*, fuck. I clamber out of Margo's lap—I WAS STRADDLING MARGO ZIMMERMAN?—and when I look over at her, her face is furious for a split second before she says, sweetly, "Come in."

Her dad eases the door open. "How's the studying going?"

"Great," she says, her face somehow completely neutral. I don't even want to know what mine looks like. "Just. Great."

"It's almost ten thirty," he says.

"Sure," she says. "Abbie's just—she was just going."

"Yep," I say, like he needs the extra assurance. "I was just. Going. And—yep."

"All right," he says. "Well, have a good night, Abbie." He leaves, very pointedly not shutting the door behind him.

"Let me, uh…" Margo tucks her hair behind her ear and takes half a second to kind of laugh. "Let me walk you to the door."

Sure. Yeah. A totally regular thing for regular, regular friends to do.

I just shove everything into my bag and shoot up off the floor. Margo leads the way and I am extremely, definitely not looking at her legs in those shorts.

We stop at the front door. Margo awkwardly just…hovers. She leans forward like she's going to hug me, which is weird because we've definitely never hugged before, and then thinks better of it and raises her hand like maybe we're going to high five?

I just?

Then she sticks her hand out resolutely.

And, well. I shake it.

I shake hands with Margo Zimmerman.

Her tongue was *just* in my mouth. Why wouldn't we shake hands?

"Okay," I say. "Well. I guess I'm going."

"Okay," she responds. "Well. Bye."

I open the door and go through it and I feel like some kind of robot. The door shuts behind me and the porch light goes on and I just stand there for a second, until the moths and flying night critters annoy me into moving.

It takes me until I reach my car to realize I've left my keys inside. I stare at my traitorous locked car. I try the handle. No dice.

I google the walking directions home. Two hours is too

long. Just go back inside, Sokoloff. It's not like it'll be the weirdest thing that's happened tonight.

On the other hand, I've always wanted to be able to hot-wire a car. But I'd still need to get in, and I don't think I have anything sharp or heavy enough to break the window, and—

Go. Inside.

Christ.

I walk back to the door. I want to die.

I knock.

Somewhere inside, a bloodhound loses her shit.

I mutter, "G-d, shut *up*, Julie Andrews."

Mendel opens the door wide, and leans on the doorframe, his grin like a cat who just ate a farm full of canaries. "Abs," he says. "Back so soon?"

"Mendel," I say primly. "I seem to have left my keys here."

"Oh?" he says. "Where?"

I clear my throat. "Margo's room."

"Ah. Well. I can go grab them for you, or you can head back there. If you want." If he were grinning any wider, his face would split in literal half.

"I'll go," I say. "Thank you."

He pushes off the doorframe to make room for me to walk past him just as Margo comes down the hallway.

I swallow. I'm still standing on the Shalom Sweet Home welcome mat and I'm staring at Margo and she's staring at me and Mendel's just standing there, looking back and forth between us, arms folded, that infuriating Cheshire Cat grin still on his face.

"Hey," Margo says. "You left your keys."

"I did."

Mendel rubs a hand over his mouth. I hate him. I hate everyone here.

I say, "Did you—"

"Oh," she says. "Yes. Here." She holds them out at arm's length but doesn't come any closer to me. We're still like a foot apart.

I clear my throat and step into the foyer and take the keys from her, careful not to touch her hand. "Thanks."

"You're welcome."

Mendel's mouth twitches. This time, when his hand goes to his lips, it stays there.

"Well," I say, and clear my throat again. "Thanks."

"You're welcome."

And I just. Turn around. And walk out.

The door shuts behind me, and I can hear Mendel's laughter through the door, and you know what? Same.

We're ridiculous.

Nothing to be done for it now, though.

I drop my keys twice while trying to get in my car and when I finally make it inside, I lean my head against the steering wheel. What a fucking nightmare.

What a fucking dream.

My dad's sleeping on the couch when I get home, grainy black-and-white war footage on the TV. I don't know where my mom is, but I can't bring myself to care. Sure, they're getting divorced, but their sleeping arrangements have been as erratic as always. I can't remember ever feeling weird about one parent or another sleeping on the couch or the guest room. So it's anyone's guess if she banished him to the couch tonight, or if he just fell asleep watching yet another World War II documentary.

I close myself in my room, drop my bag on the floor, and lean against the door.

Everything was simpler before Margo Zimmerman. More boring, probably, but definitely easier. When I'm with her, I overthink everything. I've never done that before. With any gender. It was always easy—a bright smile or a curling smirk, making myself look smaller or making myself look bigger. A casual hand on the arm, a warm breath of a whisper.

But Margo has turned everything sideways. She shifts from all nerves to all confidence like the tide, and I don't know how to interpret or predict it.

She *pulled me into her lap.* That's not the same Margo Zimmerman that arranges and rearranges her pencils on her desk, or the same Margo Zimmerman that almost fell out of her chair trying to sit wrongly enough. Like as soon as kissing was on the table, she switched gears and became this whole other person.

A person I'm really. Really. Into.

To be fair, it seems like I'm pretty into the neurotic pencil-arranger, too.

I thought about that kiss all the way home, and I'm still thinking about it when I brush my teeth and when I wash my face and when I slide under the covers. I'm still thinking about her bare legs in those shorts, and the way her hands tightened on me, and the way her teeth scraped over my lip, and the way she responded to *me*, to my hands and my mouth and—

And I'm still thinking about it when I roll over onto my side and pull my nightstand drawer open. My vibrator is small and bright green, maybe the size of a tube of lipstick. It doesn't have any bells and whistles, just a soft tip and three speeds that pretty reliably get the job done.

I'm so wound up, and what I want to do is think about anything else. I always feel kind of weird thinking about a specific person, especially if it's someone I know and someone I'm not dating. And I'm not dating Margo Zimmerman. We have a business relationship, and that's all.

So it would be really weird of me to think about the dip of her waist and the muscles in her thighs when I switch the vibrator on, and it would be even weirder of me to think about the sweep of her tongue and the press of her hips when I slip it between my legs.

I want to think about something else, about faceless perfect humans that are doing exactly what I want, about celebrities I'll never meet and definitely never bang.

But I can't. I try, but I can't. I'm thinking about Margo and her big eyes and her shiny hair and her strong shoulders and long legs, and I'm thinking about how her lips would feel on my neck, how her teeth would feel there, how her breasts would fit in my hands, how her fingers would feel between my legs. If she'd be conscientious or wild.

I want to think about anyone else, but Margo just Margos her way into my brain and soon I'm too close to the edge to feel guilt or remorse or anything but fucking Margo Zimmerman. My back arches and that sweet champagne fizz rushes through me and I have to bite my own hand to keep from making enough noise to wake the neighborhood.

And then I do it again. And a third time. And I'm so exhausted I pass out with the vibrator still in my hand.

CHAPTER 19

Margo

I am hanging at Jamal's house, because it's Sunday, and on Sundays I hang at Jamal's house. This Sunday is a little different than usual, by which I mean that usually we hang out alone, but sometimes (today) he asks me to bring my hot friends over. So today, Jamal isn't pushing to play video games, because he's trying very hard to impress Julia, and "let me show you my skills at *Mario Kart*" is not exactly a primo pick-up strategy.

I'll tell you what is: let me show you my horses. I'll give you a literal pony.

So we're outside, and Julia is absolutely lit up touching Best Friend Black Horse's muzzle. None of us is planning to ride today, not in what we're wearing. Julia's in heels (not that she *cares* how her legs look, not like she *cares* what Jamal thinks of her legs. Please. She *cares* in heels that high), Aaliyah and Chloe are in cheer uniforms because they came from an extra weekend practice, and I'm fully made up, and in a miniskirt, because hey, lipstick lesbian *is* a thing. Abbie totally said so. So, like I said, not here to ride. Jamal is. We're here to watch.

Julia is certainly here to watch.

"Can I feed him?" she asks, eyes sparkling.

Jamal leans in when he says, "Sure," all smooth like he's asking her if she comes here often.

"What's his name?" she says, and Jamal shoots me a look, then opens his mouth to lie. He's going to say the horse is named something cool like NIGHTMARE or CHAINSAW or CHUCK FUCKING NORRIS and I can't let Best Friend Black Horse be disrespected like that so I say, "Best Friend Black Horse."

Julia and Chloe both choke.

"I'm sorry," says Aaliyah. "What?"

"Best... Best Friend Black Horse," Jamal mumbles. If looks could kill, I would be dead.

Julia takes a minute, hand on the massive animal's muzzle, a smile curving her mouth.

"I was a kid," Jamal says.

"Well," says Julia, "that's about the cutest damn thing I've ever heard."

And now she's charmed, which means Jamal has like 900 percent higher odds of getting that phone number, and he is *welcome.*

I KNOW GIRLS, JAMAL.

I know girls.

What I should be doing right now is helping brush the horses, getting close enough to them that maybe I can literally *ever* conquer my fear and get on one.

What horsewoman was ever too afraid to ride a horse?

Not me.

I'm not afraid.

It's not that I'm afraid; it's just that I'm...not totally prepared.

And I'm not totally paying attention.

I'm thinking about girls and everything I know about them and I'm thinking about Abbie Sokoloff's tongue in my mouth. I'm thinking about the dip and knot in my stomach when I managed to choke out, "Did you want to show me?" and the press of her hips into my stomach when she wrapped her legs around me, the softness of her thighs, her lip between my teeth.

Jesus.

I pull at my collar.

I don't know what any of this means except that it shouldn't mean much. It was instructive and even though I know—I *know*—she was into it that moment, she's not into *me*.

But I can't stop thinking about it.

I haven't stopped thinking about it since, and now here I am, dangerously still thinking about it, obsessing about it, when I'm supposed to be thinking about my friends. About these horses. About my future, kind of. Well, horse-wise.

I actually jump when Aaliyah touches my elbow and says, "Earth to Margo?"

"Oh, hmm? What? Sorry."

Her eyebrow arches and she says, "Catch you in the middle of something?"

"No, sorry just. Spaced out."

She narrows her eyes—Aaliyah has always been eminently

readable, because of her eyes. "Mmm-hmm," she says. "We're going out to watch Jamal ride. Julia might even hop on."

"Yeah, I bet she might," I say, smirking.

"She should. That boy is fine."

"Oh, no arguments."

"I can't believe *you* haven't," she says.

Suddenly, my pulse is racing and my throat is closing. I don't have a response that isn't a lie. That doesn't feel almost like a betrayal.

I don't say anything. I just follow her outside.

We all lean against the split rail that borders the pen, watching Jamal work his magic with Whiskey.

"That horse," I say, "is a son of a bitch."

Julia laughs, eyes glued to Jamal. She's always been drawn to risk. Where I have my whole vet life planned out and Aaliyah has a scholarship to the ag school, and Chloe just kind of has no idea what she wants beyond this year, Julia wants to be a pilot. She got her pilot's license before she could drive (and she drives like every road is Fury Road). She wants to live her life in the air, where humans shouldn't go. I can see the way she lights up watching Jamal conquer something totally different, something he probably shouldn't ride.

She says, "If I were to ask him out, what would you say?"

Jamal glances at her as he pulls Whiskey into a trot, just to make sure she's looking, and she's looking at me, so his face falls a little. I'd feel bad, but this is very much for his benefit.

"I'd say go for it."

"You sure?" says Julia. "I know you guys hang out all the time, and I always kind of wondered if—"

"No," I say. "Nothing ever happened with us and nothing ever will."

I say it too resolutely, I think, because sudden concern flickers in her eyes.

Chloe says, "Well, is there something, like, wrong with him, or?"

"No."

I watch him ride. I feel the rough wood over the bones in my arm, scratching at my skin. The light breeze blowing humid air over me so suddenly it feels like it's rained. I feel this moment, before I tell them. And I stand in it, just for a second.

Because I think maybe I'm done hiding.

Maybe I want them to know.

Not that I was exactly *hiding* before, just that...well. No one knew.

But now it's not just Mendel. It's not just Jamal. It's not just my parents. It's not just Abbie. It's people. It's enough people, and I kissed a girl last week and I *loved* it and I've learned how to exist in this space as this person. I don't know everything. I don't know half of what I want to know. But I think... I think I'm ready for this to be a thing I am.

No.

I know.

I say, "I'm gay, Chloe."

Chloe blinks. "What?"

"I'm..." I look at Chloe, then Aaliyah, then Julia. They're all staring at me and it feels like a lot. "I'm gay. I'm gay. I'm just...well, that's it."

Julia says, "Well, that's... god, how long?"

"Forever, probably," I say. "But I didn't really know when

I was with Chad. Or any of the other guys. If that's what you're asking. I don't know, maybe I should have told you guys earlier, but…"

Suddenly, Aaliyah's arms are around my neck and she says, "I love you, babe."

And I say, "No homo?"

She laughs into my hair and says, "Nah. But I love you."

Chloe claps her hand over her mouth and says, "Oh my god, the stuff I said about you and Abbie. Oh my god, I'm such an asshole."

Julia says, "Shit. Shit, I'm sorry if I said anything. I don't care, we don't care."

"No." I shake my head. "It's…it's okay. You didn't say anything super bad."

"So *were* you flirting with her, then?" says Julia. "And we were just being complete jerks about it?"

I want to say no.

I don't say no.

Jamal and Whiskey sail through the air, and I cock my head toward the pen. "Jamal's gunning for you, man. I distract you from this, he'll divorce me."

Julia laughs and welcomes the excuse to watch him.

Chloe sidles up to me and sticks close for the rest of the day, like she's trying to proximity me into not being mad at her, and making sure I'm not, which I'm not.

No one presses me for an answer about Abbie.

Which, thank G-d.

Because I don't… I don't think I have one.

CHAPTER 20

Abbie

It's after ten o'clock on Sunday night and I'm still feeling weird and kind of gross about masturbating, like, *to* Margo. Which makes it even more awkward when she texts me. Her name pops up on my phone and the first thing I think is *oh god she knows*.

But she doesn't. There's no way she could.

Get it together, Sokoloff.

She hasn't texted, *YOU FUCKING PERVERT.* What she's actually texted is, So hey. I came out to all my friends today.

And, Well not EVERY SINGLE ONE of them. But the main ones. You know. The ones that matter.

I swallow down the giant lump in my throat and reply, Mazel tov! How'd it go?

Good. Everyone was cool. Every single human I've told has been cool so far, so I'm like waiting for the other shoe to drop.

I don't know where to go from here, because all I can think about is what an asshole I've been. So I just say, I'm so glad.

She doesn't respond immediately, so I put the phone down and pick up the *Spider-Man* graphic novel I was reading before she texted me. Twenty minutes later, my phone buzzes again.

It's Margo. Margo, who has sent me a picture of Chris Hemsworth and Tessa Thompson. Jesus.

I reply, Christ I am so bisexual, because where do I look?

A minute later, she responds, Wait, bisexual?

My stomach drops about seventeen feet, through my whole body and down into the foundation of the house. Fuck. *Fuck.*

When I agreed to go to the eighth grade dance with Stu Feeney, Charlie didn't talk to me for a week. She told me it was because she was so surprised, she wasn't sure how to approach the situation, because, as she eventually said, *But Abs, I thought you were* gay.

We'd been friends for long enough that we eventually got past it—me gently rejecting Stu's follow-up advances probably helped—but I never forgot the betrayal she felt all because I liked a *boy.*

And the betrayal I felt at her reaction.

One of the perks of being openly bisexual in high school is, theoretically, everyone knows you're bisexual, with all the positive and mostly negative trappings that go with it. It's at least half the reason I've got a reputation for getting around. And of all the people to give me shit for being bisexual, I thought *teach me everything about queer culture* Margo Zimmerman wouldn't be one of them.

But I'm just. Pretty tired. So I reply, I thought everybody knew.

She says, Oh, you've just said you were gay so many times?

No, Margo, *you've* said I'm gay so many times. And I just…

haven't corrected her. Because she didn't say lesbian, she said gay. Which I am. Sort of.

I should give her the benefit of the doubt. I agreed to teach her, sure, but I guess I didn't realize how little information she was starting with. I guess I didn't realize that unless I explicitly said it, she wasn't going to get it. I guess I didn't realize leaving it out could blow up in my face.

And, to be honest, I hope that's all this is. I hope this is just my typical level of oversight. It's just that I've dealt with so many intensely biphobic lesbians—and biphobic bisexuals, and biphobic heterosexuals—and I really thought Margo wasn't one of them.

I hope she isn't, anyway.

Besides, I've been openly bisexual since the eighth grade. I thought she knew, is the thing, because I thought everyone knew. Everyone knows I'm not just into girls. Everyone remembers that I went on dates with two of the three openly nonbinary people in our grade because it was, for some reason, a huge deal.

And Margo The Lesbian has dated boys. So I guess? It's an understandable mistake?

Except I'm tired and mad and embarrassed and maybe feeling a tiny bit passive aggressive, so I say, Here's a free lesson: "gay" isn't just homosexual.

She doesn't respond for long enough that I can really settle into my anger, and I'm two sentences into a dissertation on why I think this generation has reclaimed "gay" when her picture flashes up on my screen.

She's calling me. At least she's not FaceTiming me, I guess. "Hey."

Margo says, "I'm sorry."

I sigh.

"I didn't mean it like...like *OH GROSS NOT A BISEXUAL. NOT A GIRL WHO HAS KNOWN THE TOUCH OF A MAN.* I've dated boys. You know I've dated boys. I just meant... I just meant that you've said you were gay like a million times, and I've said you were gay a million times, and I was just. Confused. It's okay if you're bi. Not that you need me to say it's okay. Or something. Fuck. Jesus. Am I making this worse?"

She says again, "Fuck. Jesus."

"All right," I say, "so here's the thing about what just happened. Biphobia is pretty rampant in the lesbian community, and I've been turned down by more than my share of lesbians because I've been theoretically tainted by dick. Even though they don't know whether or not I've ever actually touched one, because it's none of their business. And, to be honest, it's not really any of yours, either."

"No. No, it's totally not and I don't think it is. I don't care."

"Well, thank you for that," I snap. I open my mouth to say something else, but god. I might be too mad to let her know how mad I am. I'm just so fucking *tired* of this shit. Like there's something wrong with me because I'm not monosexual.

"For what?" she says. "Agreeing with you?"

"For not caring!"

"I don't care! If you've touched a dick! Why would that matter to me? You just told me it was none of my business and I'm agreeing with you that it's none of my business."

I run my hand over my face. "Never mind," I mutter. "It doesn't matter."

She's quiet for a second. "I think it does matter."

"Why?" My voice cracks, just enough that I feel it and I hate it. "It's not like we're dating."

"You're not allowed to matter to me because you're my *friend*?"

Jesus. Why are my eyes burning? Why is this hitting me so hard? It's not like she's the only person who thinks I matter. Who thinks who I am and what I am matters. I don't know how to respond to that, so I say, "Margo, I don't know how to respond to that."

She says, "Okay."

There's silence on the other end for a while. For long enough that I am reminded why the phone sucks as a mode of communication.

Then she says, "Are you mad, still? Don't lie about it if you are. I want to know."

"I don't know if I am. I don't know what I am, except just tired." I take a deep breath. "No. I'm not. I'm just—I don't know. Pretty gun-shy. I guess. Everyone gives bisexuals shit about being bisexual, including other bisexuals. Because no matter what, you're doing it wrong. You're transphobic, or you'll fuck anything that's breathing, or whatever. There's no right or good way to be bi and it's just pretty exhausting. Is all."

"That's…well. That sucks." She doesn't expound on it. She's more interested in listening than talking, I think, opening panic-apology notwithstanding.

"Yeah." I lie back on my bed and cover my eyes with one hand. "Sorry for being an asshole. It's just—I don't know. A Pavlovian response or something."

"Sorry for Pavloving you into an impromptu gay culture lesson at eleven o'clock on a Sunday night."

That makes me smile. For the first time in what feels like hours. "No, you're not."

She laughs. "You're right. I hope I'm keeping you from something super important."

"I'll have you know you are," I say. "The Green Goblin just kidnapped Aunt May."

"Oh no. Not Aunt May—hasn't Peter Parker been through enough?"

"And yet he's still the friendly neighborhood Spider-Man."

She laughs, and somehow we go from Peter Parker to entomology to the house next to Margo's that she's pretty sure is haunted, and then it's two o'clock in the morning and we both have to get up for school tomorrow but we're both just sort of existing at each other, the silences between conversations longer than the conversations.

"Dude," I say, yawning, "I gotta go. I'm going to fall asleep."

"I think I've already fallen asleep like four times."

"Glad to know you like me for my riveting conversation."

Sleep is laced through her laugh. "Shut *up*."

"Go to bed, you degenerate. I'll see you at the pool, bright and early."

She says, "*You're* a degenerate."

"It's true," I say. "I'm a slutty, slutty bi."

She laughs one more time, a little softer, a little throatier than before, and I'm pretty sure she passes out again before ending the call.

CHAPTER 21

Margo

I've never been to Abbie's house, and it's never struck me as odd until this moment—that we always meet at mine. Her place is nice, nice in about the same way that mine is. Pretty, trimmed lawn and a fence and an interior that matches. The carpet is new enough not to be stained with living yet, and there's art on the walls.

It's nice.

It's comfortable.

It's so *quiet*.

There's a difference between quiet and empty, and this house is both.

I mean, they don't have any animals, royal or otherwise, so that's probably the biggest contributing factor—that and the fact that it's just literally empty; her parents aren't home.

If they were, I don't think we'd be sitting face-to-face on her living room floor, about to dive into *this* topic, of all things.

I don't think Abbie would have said, "Queer sex," so loud.

If it weren't empty in here.

But well.

It's sure EMPTY in here.

"Sex isn't just putting a penis in a vagina," she says.

"Oh, thank you, Captain Obvious. Now I know that I, a lesbian, do not have to die a virgin."

"Virginity is just the commodification of female reproduction."

"You've been dying to say that somewhere besides TikTok, haven't you?"

"Shut up." But she's smiling, so I don't completely panic. "I'm saying this because I know you know, but it never hurts to hear, out loud, that sex and virginity is viewed through a heteronormative lens, and that's bullshit. Now, heteronormative is—"

I cut her off because she's being a jerk on purpose and it's making me smile but also: "I know what heteronormative means, thank-you-very-much."

She smirks. At least she doesn't have a chalkboard behind her.

"Stop stalling and tell me what you know about sex." I smile when I say it, aiming for something between cheeky and flirty, but it's not because I'm feeling cheeky or flirty—it's because this room is like twelve degrees too hot with Abbie talking about sex and she's so freaking pretty and I'm not so unaware of my own face that I can't tell I'm blushing furiously.

Alone. In this empty house.

Talking about sex.

After she—we kissed. I don't know who started it, but I

haven't been able to think about anything but that kiss since it happened. That kiss is my new special interest.

But right now, I am confident.

I am cool.

Man, I am absolutely—I am neither of those things. I am having a tiny heart attack. And I hope to god she can't tell.

She wags her eyebrows and says, "Please, Margo, we don't have all night."

I'm not confident.

I'm not cool.

I choke.

"Okay, so, first of all, who's the boy and who's the girl is something you're going to hear about lesbians, but that's not a thing. Queer relationships can't be defined by the same terms as heteronormative relationships. And even then, the idea of masculine being dominant and feminine being submissive is bullshit, no matter what genitals are present in the equation."

I don't know why taking notes on this makes me feel so much nerdier than taking notes on anything else. But here we are.

I'm taking notes.

I'm feeling pretty nerdy about it.

I'm also really freaking glad to be able to stare at the notebook because it means I do not have to look at Abbie.

I cannot. Look at Abbie right now. It's too much, and she's too much, and I really need to be focusing on what she's saying here, and I can't do that while I'm looking at her. For... for a lot of reasons. Not just the reasons I'm usually bad at eye contact.

"Okay," I tell my notebook. "I'm with you."

"The thing about what sex is or isn't is really up to the people having it," she says. "Some people define sex as having had an orgasm, or genital contact, or tenderly interlocking fingers while John Mayer sings about your body being a wonderland."

"Well, hold on," I say, looking up from my notes—but not at her; the joke should have been enough to cut some tension but it hasn't, so I just let my gaze rest on the seam where ceiling meets wall and kind of pinball back and forth because I'm thinking, this is what people do when they're thinking, right? They don't stare deeply into beautiful girls' eyes while they try to work some concept out? I guess? "Does the latter count as sex if there are no candles gently flickering in the room?"

"Listen, the only way I'd count it as fucking is if I smashed the device playing the John Mayer song."

I say, mostly to ward off what I know is going to be a nervous cackle if I don't get it under control, "Well, Abbie, do girls actually *fuck*? Because I hear all we can do is *make love*."

"I guess it depends on who you ask, Margo. I'd venture to say that we as an inclusive gender contain multitudes and are capable of having whatever kind of sex we want." She smirks and says, "I myself prefer fucking."

I laugh, and I know I'm blushing again. I can feel it on my face. Because now I'm thinking about Abbie fucking. And not just generally.

Extremely. Specifically.

I scrape my teeth over my lip. "Well, thank god, because I hate John Mayer."

Then I realize what I said, or what it *sounded* like I said. I think I was going for: it's a good thing girls can do sexing how they want, and we don't have to be soft and romantic and laid gently upon rose petals in order to come. But what it sounded like was: *Thank god you like to fuck, Abbie, because that's what I like.*

Is that what I meant to say? I make myself look at her, because it's been so long since I have, and I don't want her to think I'm being weird or something, even though HA HA HA I'm being SO WEIRD with my eyeballs and I know it!

This is absurd, because I'm good at this. I'm good at making people feel relaxed and welcome and happy and paid attention to, but I don't know how to do it around Abbie, and it feels disingenuous, anyway, and JESUS I don't know, I'm still kind of stuck on "Abbie fucking"? I guess?

Her eyebrows are dangerously close to her hairline. "Margo, he's an excellent blues guitarist. It's not all gently drawing the back of your hand down someone's cheek, you know. I bet John Mayer can fuck, too."

"John Mayer doesn't fuck; he slow dances."

She snorts. "I think we've lost the thread here. The point is, sex is what you define it as. Don't let someone else tell you what does and doesn't count. And, listen—you're pretty headstrong, but no one talks about this so I'm going to—don't let anyone of any gender bully or coerce or force you into doing anything you don't want to do. Consent knows no bounds. You don't have to have a penis to be a rapist."

I swallow hard. "Yeah. Yes, you're—you're right. I didn't even really think about that, I guess. Yeah."

All of this is suddenly making me nervous, and I don't think it's the consent stuff. She's right. It's important and that doesn't make me nervous.

What makes me nervous, for some bizarre reason, is not having a definitive black-and-white *and this is the moment you have officially had sex, you gay. Congaytulations.*

There's so much riding on that moment. On… I don't know. On virginity, or whatever. People sure tell you that, anyway. And suddenly having the definition taken and knowing that I just need to…decide for myself?

I don't know if I'm unsettled or if that's freeing.

I don't know.

I want to organize my pencils.

I organize my pencils.

I'm still organizing them when she says, "Any questions so far?"

"No, not—not yet."

"Cool," she says. "I assume you know about condoms?"

"Duh."

"Dental dams?"

I want to say, "Yes, duh," and then google it. But I don't. I'm not good at not knowing things, but friendships are built on honesty, so I make myself say, "Not really."

What *not really* means is no, I've literally never heard the term.

Thank god I have this notebook to look at.

She just says, "So dental dams are rectangular pieces of latex you use for oral sex. They're made out of the same stuff as male condoms, and in fact, if you want to have a safe dinner out and all you have are male condoms, you can just cut it from opening to tip and use that."

My pencil slips briefly at *safe dinner out*, my god.

"Dental dams. Condoms. Okay."

I am trying so hard, so very, very hard, but I have to put my pencil down, have to do something with my hands or my body or something so I don't literally explode. I know I came to her to teach me, which means I don't know information, but something about this, this is making me feel. I don't know. Small. Or...young.

Embarrassed.

I tap my fingers 1-2-3-4-4-3-2-1, and it helps.

"Pro tip," Abbie says, "if you have to go the DIY route, non-lubricated condoms are best. So when you've got your piece of latex, you just cover the vulva in question, and go to town. Any questions?"

"Yeah, actually," I say, though my head is kind of screaming, NO ACTUALLY, because hearing Abbie talk about sex in this much detail has obviously been murdering me, but I realize now that hearing her talk about it *clinically* in this much detail is murdering me in a completely different way. You don't talk about sex like this, like a medical professional, to someone you want to have it with.

Which is fine.

Of course it's... Of course it's fine.

I say, ignoring that completely, or trying to, "Why do you keep saying male condoms?"

"Male condoms are the kind you're probably familiar with, the kind that go on penises, male or otherwise," she says. "The other kind is a female condom, even though it was originally developed for anal sex. They're more expensive than male condoms, because of course they are, and instead of fitting snugly on a penis, they are inserted and secured in the orifice to be penetrated."

Orifice.

To be.

Penetrated.

Someone please penetrate my neck with a knife.

"ALL RIGHT," I say. "GOOD. COOL. I feel educated on this." I am drumming my fingertips on the carpet. I cannot stop, and more importantly, I will not.

"You okay?" she asks. "You need something to drink, or...?"

"No. I mean, yes, I'm okay. No, I don't need a drink. I can talk about sex and orifice penetration, thank you, Abbie."

"Good, because unless you have any more questions about safe cunnilingus, we'll move on to finger banging."

I'm no longer red because of words like *orifice*.

I'm back to square one. Which is: red because Abbie Sokoloff is sitting in her living room with me about to educate me on *finger banging*.

Jesus, why did I think this would be a good idea?

YOU'RE GAY.

Congrats, me. I did this to myself.

"Safety and hygiene is important even when you're not rubbing mucous membranes together, so if you want to put your fingers into a vagina or an anus, you'll want to have clean hands."

I look at my hands, which are pristine, thank you.

Abbie's eyebrows go up. "Oh, and, uh. You're going to want to cut your fingernails."

"What?" I stare at her.

"Look, if you're going to be putting your fingers into areas of delicate tissue, you've got to be careful about, like. Injuring the other person. So you can wear gloves or you can cut your nails. At least, you know, the ones you plan on putting in people."

"Oh." I stare at my fingers. The cool, not at all, *I can't breathe* thing about this line of discussion is that Abbie is not talking about people's fingers in people; she's talking about mine. She's looking at mine. I wish that my nails were magically short. "I can... Yeah, I can cut them. I'll cut them."

I guess I'm shaking a little, because I—I almost want to *leave*. Objectively, this is all great information! But once it became *Margo's fingers* and *Margo's sex*, it became overwhelming. It became too personal, like, *profoundly* personal, and I can feel the intimacy on my *skin* and it's too bright and too loud and too *much*, just much too fucking much.

I gotta—I gotta do *something* here. Tapping doesn't work. Shaking my head doesn't work. I want to climb out of my skin but that's biologically impossible, so I just—

Fuck it. I flap. I flap my hands like I'm shaking water from them, and it's enough, it's finally the correct thing to get my head back in order. I don't know why stimming works, how a physical action can have such a monumental effect on my mind. But it does, so it doesn't matter why. I flap, and I don't look at Abbie while I do it, and it keeps me from having to literally leave the room.

When I stop, my hands are ringing like bells, and I feel a hundred times better—except the part where I just did my stimmiest stim in front of this girl who's teaching me about sex, this girl I really want to kiss again, and I guess I just hope I haven't completely shot myself in the foot.

I want to know all of this. I need to know all of this and I don't know how the hell else I would have figured it out. But there's this whole other level of stuff that I don't know that I want to ask Abbie about, because it's not like she can really tell me. And it's not like I can say, *Wanna show me?* again.

I find myself saying out loud, "I'm just... I'm *nervous* about all of this."

"Well, yeah," she says. "Of course you are. It's sex. Sex is terrifying, dude. It can be great and it can be terrible and it changes everything. Don't feel weird about being nervous. Listen, I know—" She stops, and for the first time that evening, she looks uncomfortable. She swallows and runs her hand back through her hair. "I know I've got a reputation. And it's—I don't know. It is what it is. But for what it's worth, most of what I just told you I know because I looked it up. Not because anyone told me. Because no one talks about queer sex beyond like, scissoring. And that's not realistic. So don't worry about it. I got most of my education from Scarleteen and Planned Parenthood. No shame."

"Yeah." I say, but what I'm thinking is in the realm of: how on earth are you totally cool with what just happened? How are you treating that like it was nothing? Just. Yes, my question is: WHAT?

But she just keeps looking at me expectantly.

I stare at the carpet and it's not really surprising to me that I've gotten a little closer to her. I'm gravitating toward her, I'm sure I am. "*Don't worry about it* is not easy for me."

Her mouth drops open. "Whaaaaaat? That comes as a complete surprise. I refer to you to my friends as Margo the Chill."

A laugh bubbles out of me and I shove her shoulder. I know

I'm looking for excuses to touch her; I know exactly what I'm doing and Jesus, I should not.

I say, "I'm..." And I look up at the ceiling. "I haven't done what I would call sex. But I've given like, hand jobs. And penises are pretty simple, is the thing. So I'm worried. I'm worried I'm gonna like... I'm worried I'm going to get with a girl and she's gonna be like, *NOPE. NOPE, NOPE, NOPE. YOU ARE BAD AT THIS, MARGO ZIMMERMAN. GOOD AT KNOWING KNOWLEDGE BUT BAD AT SEX. Please get your neatly trimmed nails out of me.*"

I have said this to a girl I am now pretty irrevocably sure I myself want to put my neatly trimmed nails into.

To a girl I am...pretty irrevocably sure I... I like. Or. Or something.

And now, for my next trick, I will disappear into the carpet.

"Sorry if this is too forward," she says, and my throat closes up. "But I know you pretty well, I think, and if I know anything about you, it's that you pay attention. And the thing about being a good lay is you just have to *pay attention*. If you do a thing, and your partner makes a positive noise—they're pretty easy to identify, I promise—then do the thing again. If they make a negative noise, don't do the thing again." She kind of backhands my knee, a very casual touch. The most casual touch. "You'll be fine, man."

It is casual, but not to my rushing pulse, my breath, my skin.

Because I am paying too much attention to Abbie Sokoloff.

I'm... I've been paying attention.

For a long time.

I guess that's all we're covering tonight because Abbie floats the idea of watching a movie, and we wind up on the couch, under a blanket again, yeah, sure, okay.

I say, "Are your parents going to care that I'm here?"

She shrugs one shoulder. "Why would they?"

I say, "Well. I don't know."

"They don't care that I'm here, so I doubt my having company will change anything."

She doesn't look at me when she says that; she just turns the television on. The gayest thing she can find is the Kristen Stewart *Charlie's Angels*, which, YUP.

What she said about her parents is still kind of lingering in my brain, and I don't know what possesses me to do this, if I'm crossing a line, if I have completely lost my whole entire mind, but I kind of just...lay my head on her shoulder?

Because I don't really know what to say.

And maybe neither of us wants me to say anything.

She doesn't make me move.

Kristen Stewart has a freaking undercut on the screen.

And I am not paying attention.

CHAPTER 22

Abbie

It's been a long time since I've been out to horse country, but that's where Margo's friend Jamal lives. And that's where I'm going. On Sunday. To invade. Because this is what they do every Sunday—video games and pizza—and now I'm going to be there and it's not going to be awkward.

Sure. Of course it's not.

Because Jamal Tahan, most forgettable right fielder on the S.W. Moody baseball team, is as intimidatingly attractive as he is mediocre in the outfield. Basically, any human who's attracted to boys has had a crush on Jamal. The only thing that saved Margo from the rumor mill was her serial seemingly heterosexual monogamy.

And when I say *any human who's attracted to boys*, yes. I mean me.

Because, I mean. Goddamn. Jamal Tahan can absolutely get it.

So sure, sitting in the living room with MARGO ZIMMERMAN and JAMAL TAHAN will be totally fine and normal and regular and my palms are absolutely not sweating shut up.

Not to mention that the whole ride over here I had a little feeling in the back of my head that I'd forgotten something—not an unusual feeling, if I'm being honest—but I couldn't remember for the life of me what it was.

The Tahan residence is certainly not as big as it could be. The family owns tons of land and breeds Arabians, for god's sake. It's nice, and definitely bigger than mine, but it doesn't seem like their entryway will be just a literal corridor of gold or that I'll find his mom like, twirling diamond necklaces with her fork like it's spaghetti or something.

It's big enough (and they're canonically rich enough) that I'm afraid if I ring the doorbell, some old dude in a suit will answer and I won't know how to handle that, so I text Margo instead.

Hey

I'm here

Where do I go there's too many doors

I leave the car running while I wait for an answer, which is also pretty nerve-wracking, because what if somebody calls the cops on the stranger lurking in their car outside?

Ha yeah that's a VERY REAL STRUGGLE at the Tahans'. We're out back in the stables.

I can't help but read that in like, an aggressively posh British accent, even though I know pretty freaking well what Margo actually sounds like.

Oh sure

The stables

I'll just ask Reginald how to get there

She replies: Please. They fired Reginald; it's Jeeves now.

Super. I don't know how to respond.

Thankfully, she adds, Let me just come out and get you.

I don't bother to say anything because I'm sure she's already on her homosexually fast way here. So I shut the car off and get out and then realize that maybe I'm not supposed to park here? Jesus, this is stressful.

I greet her (because I'm cool) with, "Can I park here?"

"Oh my god, Abbie. It's Jamal's house. Not the Queen's. Yes. You're fine."

And then I look at her. She's...filthy. Margo Zimmerman is covered in dirt and...

"Is that *shit*?"

Margo kind of laughs and looks down at herself. She says, "Well. Yup, seems like it's shit."

"Have I entered some kind of parallel universe, where Margo Zimmerman goes barefaced and has shit on her boots?"

She's a little pink and I don't know if that's from the outdoor labor or well. The shit. She says, "I told you I was a horsewoman. This comes with the territory."

I blow a long breath out. "Well, I guess I thought it was more like, riding them, or—"

Jamal says, "Well, yes, *usually* that is what horsewomaning entails. MARGO." I didn't even hear him walk up.

What a bisexual nightmare.

"Hey," I say, in a way that I hope is cool, and not because I want to bang Jamal (because I don't), but because Jamal exists in that specific high school league that is *so far* out of my own that it's weird to acknowledge that he even sees me.

"Hey. Abbie, right?"

"Hey, yeah, Abbie. Yeah. Hey. You have. A great house. Probably. I haven't been inside."

I think my face is going to burst into actual flames, because 1) I don't get like this around people, and 2) I am making an absolute ass of myself in front of Margo and I want to sink into the ground and die.

And yet, I want to stay, because if I don't stay, I have to go home. Where my divorcing parents are still coexisting in the same space and it's terrible all the time.

Jamal just shrugs and says, "Well, let's fix that. Come in," and cocks his head toward door number 93757294.

He says, "So you're the other half of the inner circle, then? You gotta be. Margo doesn't just bring people over—not in those." He gestures toward her filthy clothes.

Margo chokes next to me. "That's like *Top Tier Human* level," he continues. "I'm almost jealous."

I cut a sharp look in his direction, but he's already walking away, leading us into the house. He's right—I can't believe Margo would let *anyone* see her the way she is now. Like, she needs a *shower*. Reginald definitely would have made her take those boots off at the door.

Jamal gives us the world's laziest house tour, only technically announcing what rooms we're walking past until we get to *the important room, the room where the magic happens.*

It's not his bedroom, thank god.

Margo says, "Think you two can survive without me? Because I am stealing your shower."

Jamal says, "Please. *Please* steal my shower."

Margo rolls her eyes, mouth curling up, and says to me, "You good?"

"Yep!" I say a lot more brightly than I mean to. Jesus. I never say *yep*.

But she walks off and I watch her just long enough that when I turn around to act like I was totally not watching her walk off, Jamal gives me this look like, *I caught you*.

I defiantly hold his gaze.

He shrugs one shoulder and says, "I tried to tell her that her ass looks good in Carhartts. She doesn't believe me."

If I'd been drinking something, I would have spit it out.

"So, uh," I say, resolutely changing the subject, "you're the right fielder, right?"

"Yeah," he says. He turns his TV on and settles on the couch. "And you're a swimmer."

"I am." I look around at the half-dozen framed movie posters around the room. It takes me a second, but I recognize the pattern—they're all Harrison Ford films. What a niche. I'm desperate for conversation, for anything, so I say, "So, uh. How did you and Margo meet?"

And then immediately want to punch myself in the face.

He doesn't actually turn to look at me; he's still messing with the controller. But I see his brow furrow at the question, for *just* long enough to really unmistakably say, *Yes, Abbie. That was a weird question.*

He says, "Uh. I don't know. School?"

"Cool, cool, cool, cool, cool." We just don't speak the

same language and that's fine, I can definitely do this for fifteen more minutes. "Hey, uh. Where's your? Bathroom? I just need to—I don't need to tell you that. I just. I need to use it. Please. Sorry."

He finally does look at me. "Well, don't use *my* bathroom. Margo's in there."

I laugh. Too high-pitched. I hate everything in my life because now I'm picturing Margo in the shower and Jesus Christ, he definitely knows that I'm picturing Margo in the shower and I actually hate everything *more* now.

"Or, I mean, do, I don't care. But if you'd like a backup option, the guest bathroom is down the hall, third door on your left."

"Thanks," I say over my shoulder as I flee.

The bathroom is regular, absolutely normal, a toilet and a sink and a guest towel on a ring on the wall. But I'm not here to pee—I'm here to burn some of the Margo-less minutes away from Jamal because this is my actual nightmare situation: me, Abbie Sokoloff, being stuck in a room with someone who is so many high school castes higher than me that I literally cannot see them from where I stand.

So what I do is grip the sides of the sink and stare myself hard in the face and say, "All right, Sokoloff, get your shit together and go talk to that human who is just a regular human. You're a human. He's a human. It's fine. Get your shit together and go."

If I'm being honest, it takes a couple minutes for that sentiment to sink in, and when it does, immediately on its heels is, *Oh no I've taken too long in the bathroom, I'm going to be the person who shit in Jamal Tahan's house eight seconds after walking into it.*

I don't *run* back down the hallway, but I do my gayest best.

"Hey," I say breathlessly when I get back. "I just—I mean, whew, there's a lot of doors, am I right?"

Jamal's mouth twitches up and then he says, "Abbie?"

"Jamal." I try to say it jauntily, like of course I belong here in his giant horse-breeder house and I. I give him. Awkward bisexual finger guns.

Help.

He looks, to his credit, like he's trying really, *really* hard not to let that twitch form into a full laugh. But he loses, and just does it the once. Just a single, kind of breathy, *what in the hell* "Ha." He says, "Dude. Do you play video games?"

There's no way his friends won't know about this interaction like, immediately after I leave, so I just fucking lean in because what else can I do.

"Yeah," I say. "Some. What do you have?"

"Like, everything. Sit down, man. Pick whatever you want."

I sit. On the same couch as him, but not next to him. And I—relax? All right. I've relaxed. Sure. Okay. "Do you have *Gears*? I mean, I don't have it, and I suck at it, but. It's fun."

He grins. "*Gears of War*? Okay, yeah, I knew I liked you, Sokoloff." And scrolls to the game.

I don't know how long we've been playing when Margo comes out on a cloud of Old Spice and plops down between us on the couch.

"Your friend is murdering me," I say, and Jamal laughs.

"We're on the same team," he says, "and you know. We're winning, so that's what matters."

"Well," she says, "hand me a controller."

He does, and she proceeds to whip both our asses.

★ ★ ★

It's later than I thought it would be when I leave Jamal's house. Margo has to make curfew, and instead of making Jamal take her home, I selflessly offer to do it. She smiles as she takes me up on it and my insides kind of curl up like a cat.

The ride back is comfortable, easy, both of us laughing at some shit Jamal said. She waves as she shuts my car door, and she runs up the driveway to her house and waves again, and I wait until she's inside before I put the car back in gear and drive away.

Despite the complete disaster the first few minutes alone with Jamal were, I feel *good*. I feel good about having spent the majority of the day with Margo, about seeing her in a way that virtually no one else ever does.

And not for nothing, she stimmed in front of me a few days ago. I mean, we all do it, leg-shaking or finger-tapping or whatever, but she like, went for it and wasn't embarrassed about it. There's a difference between private and public stims, I guess, and what she did, sitting on my living room floor while I talked about sex, was definitely a private one.

Jamal was right. I guess I'm in Margo Zimmerman's inner circle.

Wild, how much I like it.

The car's quiet after my rowdy day, after the laughter on the way to Margo's house, and I feel like I need to fill it.

I call Charlie.

She answers, which I guess I'm a little surprised by. It's pretty late, though; Adriana wouldn't be over now.

"Hey!" I say brightly.

Her answering, "Hey" is a lot warier, like she's waiting for the other shoe to drop.

"Listen, man," I say, "I just had one of the most surreal days of my entire life. I played video games all afternoon at Jamal Tahan's house."

A beat of silence. "Jamal Tahan," she says. "I—wow."

My brow twitches; I can feel it. "What do you mean, *wow*?"

"I mean, *that's* what you were doing instead of at the movies with us?"

"Oh." Shit. *Shit*. "That was today?"

"*Yes*, Abbie, that was *today*."

"Sorry, dude. I totally forgot."

"It's fine."

It's clearly not fine.

"So," she says, her tone still acid-etched, "Jamal Tahan?"

"Yeah, he's Margo's best friend, and—"

"Oh, sure, right. Margo. Margo Zimmerman. I got you."

Something in her tone makes my muscles clench. "Charlie?"

"Yeah, Abs?"

"Is there something you want to say to me?"

"No," and then immediately, "Yes. Yeah. You know you're going to get your heart broken, right?"

I blink. "What?"

"This is going to end badly for you. I just—I don't want to see you get hurt."

"What are you talking about? Margo and I are friends, Charlie."

"She's *straight*."

I...don't know how to respond to that.

"Abbie? She's straight, right?"

"I don't *like* her."

"Oh my god," Charlie breathes. "She's not straight."

"Jesus, Charlie, that isn't what I said, and it doesn't fucking matter, okay? We're friends. Cope."

"*Cope?* All you do is talk about Margo—when you're not blowing us off to hang out with Margo and her *super cool* friends, and you're telling me to *cope?*"

"I'm allowed to have other friends."

"I'm not telling you you're not," Charlie says. "I'm not a complete asshole."

I roll my eyes but manage to keep my mouth shut.

"Margo Zimmerman can't be gay," she says, almost to herself. "That is the craziest shit I have ever heard."

"Well, I guess you're right!" I say. I'm sitting in my driveway, in my car, yelling at my best friend, I guess. "You're the authority on other people's sexualities, so if you say Margo Zimmerman's straight, she definitely must be."

"Look at her, for god's sake."

That lands harder than anything else, because that's exactly what I would have said a month ago if anyone besides Margo herself had told me she was gay. And I feel like a real asshole.

"I've looked at her, Charlie."

She snorts. "I bet you have."

"You know what, first of all, fuck you. Second of all, how dare you say that? Because she wears dresses and gets pedicures, that there's no way she can be gay? That's fucked up, Charlie, and you *know* it."

"Fine," she says, her voice hard, "she's gay. Just like she was an anime girl in seventh grade, and a punk in ninth grade, and Student Council President in eleventh grade. Now she's gay. Okay. But when she moves on to the next aesthetic and leaves you heartbroken, you know I'll be the one who's there to pick up the pieces and put you back together."

"A phase." My voice has gone completely flat, and that's how I know I'm furious. "A *phase*. Do you know how many people have told me my being gay is a phase?"

"You're not gay." Charlie laughs, but there's an edge to it I don't like. "You're not gay, Abbie."

"You know what I mean."

"Yeah, I know you're not gay."

I press my hand to my face. "Can you please—"

"Is that why you're spending so much time with her? What are you doing, giving her lessons on how to kiss girls?"

My face heats. "I'm pretty sure somebody like Margo Zimmerman knows how to kiss."

"*Wow*."

"Charlie—"

"Something's going on with you," Charlie says, a little more gently. "Listen, I know she's hot. I've seen her. But you've got a thing for her, and you're just—spending so much time with that nutjob is making you as crazy as she is."

Her words bounce around my car and I stare at the phone. I don't know how to respond to that. How do you tell your best friend she's being an absolute garbage bag?

Apparently with, "Margo's autistic, you garbage bag," and a stab to the little red circle that ends the call. And just like that, Charlie's gone.

Charlie's *gone*.

She calls me back after I get inside, and I don't answer. She texts me, Abs, pick up, and I don't respond.

Until I do.

I text her back.

I say,

There's a lot of things you said that can be filed under "asshole" but only one that needs to be filed under "bad fucking person" and I think you know exactly what it is. So what you can do is leave me alone until you get your shit together and apologize to me for saying that about one of my friends.

I say,

I'm sorry you're mad I have a friend who doesn't fit into our incestuous gay-girl clique but listen, we're graduating this year, and I'm going to make other friends, and you're going to make other friends, and we're all going to grow as people. But before that happens, you better figure out what made you say what you said to me and decide if your too-cool judgmental gayness is worth ending our friendship over.

She says, I just wanted to understand.

I say, FIGURE. IT. OUT.

And I turn my phone off.

And I go to bed.

I wake up in the morning to a voice mail from Charlie, time-stamped 3:56 a.m.

"Abbie, listen. I'm—I'm really sorry. I didn't realize you felt. I don't know. That way about Margo. Not that there's a wrong or bad way to feel about Margo! I'm glad you've found someone you can. I don't know. Anyway. She's not a nutjob, and I shouldn't have said that. And she dresses so femme, and I don't know, I guess I just never thought she was your type. I'm just—I'm jealous of your time, I guess, because you're always with her and I don't ever see you anymore. And you're right, we're graduating, and I'm going to miss you and I'm sorry I'm an asshole and—I don't know. I love you, and you're my best friend, and I want this to be okay. I'm sorry."

I text Charlie: Thank you for your apology.

She replies almost immediately. So we're okay???

I look at the screen, at the years of text message history.

And I say, No.

Three dots appear. Disappear. Appear. Disappear. Appear. Abs, Jesus, I'm so sorry.

I know, I reply. But you better sit down with yourself and figure out your beef with femme girls. And why bisexual girls aren't gay enough.

I don't think that!

I have a history test to ace this week, and I definitely don't have any more time to waste on this argument.

So I just say, Okay, Charlie. I'll see you in school.

And that's. That's the end of it.

CHAPTER 23

Margo

I am in Forever 21.

By myself.

And you know what I'm not looking at? The snapbacks. The plaid. The...well, I *am* looking at the Converse. Those are great shoes.

I realized this morning that I hadn't actually been shopping since I'd started taking lessons from Abbie, and that's just so bizarre for me.

And please. There's no way I'm skipping Black Friday of all days.

Mendel doesn't believe in the blatant consumerism of *my* Lord's Day ("no gods, no masters" and all that) so he let me take his car. Bless.

I left with his vehicle and told him to enjoy eating the rich or whatever he'd be doing at home, and he told me the rich were treyf.

So now, here I am in my bustling happy place in the mall

and I'm thumbing through clothes and I don't want to cry. I have tried everything. Over the past couple months, I have sorted through every single member of the cast of *Scooby Doo* on the lesbian fashion spectrum. I've tried Velma and Shaggy and Daphne and Fred and several villainous ghosts, and you know what?

You know *what?*

I want these little lace shorts, and a spaghetti strap tank, and this freaking adorable yellow mini dress that I think makes my boobs look as great as it does my complexion. I love everything I'm purchasing to put on my body and I love the way my body looks in all of it and I love the way *I* look in all of it.

I love the way I feel in all of it.

I love.

The way I feel.

I walk out of there with a slightly decreased bank account and slightly increased level of serotonin and I am calm. I am…at peace.

With shopping.

I don't care; it doesn't matter if people would find that a little shallow.

I'm happy.

Bless Mendel for letting me borrow his car and take this little self-evaluative journey.

I get home and hang his keys on the key ring, then dump all my bags on my bed and slip into the matching set of pajamas I just purchased, because they're the prettiest teal and they're some Forever 21 version of silk and they beg to be worn. It's only 2:00 p.m., but I have been up since 3:00 a.m., so hell yes I am putting on the pajamas.

I head to the living room, and instead of coming face-to-face with the nothing I was expecting, I come face-to-face with Mendel.

He is descending the stairs that lead to the FROG, shirtless and buttoning his jeans. "Oh," he says. "You're, uh, home early."

Jesus Christ.

I can't stop the expression that comes over my face, or maybe I could have if I tried, but I didn't. I'm sure the frown looks almost comical in its depth. I just say, in a voice that matches my face, "Mendel."

He looks at me.

I look back at him.

He looks at me.

He zips his zipper.

Zzzwwwtthhhiiiipppp.

I say, "MENDEL."

He says, "YOU'RE HOME EARLY."

I run my hand through my hair and glance back down the hall trying to think of anything, just. Anything besides which one of my brother's socialist friends is up there right now. The jury's out; I can't even narrow it down by gender. It could be literally anyone.

"Gross," I say. "Gross, gross, gross. Gross."

"Margo, you take that back. There is nothing gross about the physical expression of love."

"JESUS CHRIST."

"I see you're not ready for this talk yet."

He comes down the last couple steps, then stares into the kitchen and sort of…shuffle-steps toward it. Like a space alien.

He is hiding his back. Why the hell would he be hiding his *back*?

No, you know what? I don't want to know.

"I came down for a drink of water," he calls and I just stand there, gaze bouncing between Mendel and the shut door.

"Okay."

"Had I known you were here, I would have *definitely* put on a shirt."

The water comes on.

I groan.

He comes back out of the kitchen, back still facing the wall.

"Well," he says, "Sister. Sibling. Closest on the planet to my DNA. This is where I leave you."

I'm so busy puzzling over his choice to walk up the steps while still facing me that I don't realize until he's gone that he was balancing three glasses of water.

By the time I force myself to interact with Mendel again, I'm sitting on the couch, watching *Indiana Jones* (a promise I made to Jamal; he threatened to friend divorce me when he realized I hadn't seen them) when Mendel comes in and plops down on the couch next to me. I say, "UGH."

He waggles his eyebrows. "Well, I'm sorry I had an interesting afternoon."

"Please," I say. "Like whatever debauchery went on upstairs was that out of the ordinary for you."

"Well, I'm sorry I had a Tuesday afternoon."

"It's Friday."

He rolls his eyes, at which point I clock that he was making a joke. Right.

I groan again and shove him and he laughs and kicks a foot up on the ottoman. Just the one, just hanging off enough to make it clear that Mendel can't sit straight to save his life.

"How many people are you even banging, man?" I say.

He shrugs. "You really don't want the answer to that question."

"No. No, you're right. I do not."

He's smirking when he flips on the TV, but keeps it muted. He scrolls through three streaming services he "communally subscribes to" with his friends and it's truly astounding how even with three streaming services, there's nothing on.

"Don't be a dick," he says, even though he's being good-natured about it. "Polyamory is kickass and more people should try it."

I say, "I don't want to think about my brother having sex. That's what I'm being a dick about. I don't care about the polyamory stuff. What else did you call it?"

"Ethical non-monogamy?"

"Yes! Ethical non-monogamy."

"Aw," he says. "I'm touched. You were listening."

"So you're polyamorous and/or ethically non-monogamous, and...bisexual, right?"

"Pansexual. I guess I've never used the word with you."

I frown. "So that means...what? You want to bang everyone?"

Mendel says, "No. G-d, not *everyone*."

I cock my head and he says, "Capitalists."

I say, "Jesus."

Then his mouth curls and he says, "Well. No *relationships* with capitalists."

I blow out a breath.

"Cops," he says. "Republicans."

"Mendel."

"Anti-vaxxers. Climate change deniers."

"Oh my god."

"People who talk on speaker phone in the middle of Starbucks and they take up the table next to the outlet but they don't even have a laptop and you're like, *bitch, you don't even need that outlet! I'm at eight percent!*"

"That sounds like one specific person."

"Whom I would *never* fuck."

I'm laughing and Mendel actually looks riled remembering the Starbucks person; he takes a second to come down from it.

"I'd fuck whatever gender," he says finally. "That's what I mean. Gender is propaganda, probably."

I chuckle and lean my head back on the couch. "Spoken like a true agender human," I say. Mendel refers to himself as genderqueer, nonbinary, agender, in basically equal measure. He doesn't really give a shit about brother or sister or sibling or pronouns; a few of his friends are nonbinary and care very much about their own pronouns and titles, and Mendel, in turn, cares a lot about *that*. And so do I. I think he personally just doesn't give much of a shit about any of it for himself.

I say, "Honestly, I can wrap my head around the pan thing more than the polyamory, I think."

"Well," he says, "sounds right. People are weird about communism."

"What?"

"Deciding there's enough of you to go *around*, little sister."

"Nooooooo," I say.

He says, "Seriously, people are weird about it. Like monogamy makes so much goddamn sense. Like people are a monogamous species who don't just make each other miserable half the time and get monogamously divorced every day! And *I'm* the weird one for coming up with an arrangement in which everyone is happy."

"Well," I say, "when you put it that way."

"Really, *reallyyyyyy* happy, Margo."

"No. Please don't put it *that* way."

He cackles.

I stare at the silent TV, and say, "This is the future liberals want?"

He says, "Leftists, Margo. This is the future *leftists* want."

We eventually settle on *She-Ra* and Mendel's so pleased glancing up at that stupid FROG every now and then and *I'm* so pleased every time I catch a glimpse of these pretty teal pajamas and humans are just.

We are extremely effing unexpected.

Margo Zimmerman
Queer 101
For: Abbie Sokoloff

On Being Queer

I think I hate plaid.

Not on other people; other people can really make it work, and it's maybe objectively the gayest pattern out there.

But it makes me feel like a lumberjack, and I am just *not* a lumberjack, Abbie.

I hate plaid and I *like* straightening my hair and putting on makeup and wearing heels.

I walk fast, though.

I sit wrong; I think I've always sat just a little wrong.

I've been learning all this stuff about queer culture and how to be gay and I swear I could write a whole thesis now, with everything I've learned from you and everything that I am. But...god, how do I even put this.

Maybe the REAL queerness was the gay we made along the way.

I don't know what I'm saying.

It's four in the morning.

Maybe iced coffee is queer culture.

Maybe anxiety is queer culture.

Maybe it's freaking lumberjack plaid.

Maybe it's all of those things and none of them, and is that what you were trying to tell me? That I could like girls, or boys and girls, or boys and girls and enbies, or not have a gender, or want sex or not want sex, or only have ever kissed boys and never girls, or only love high heels and straight girl makeup, and STILL. BE QUEER?

Is that what you're saying?

Maybe it's what I'm saying.

Maybe I'm saying that I know who I am.

I'm fucking gay, Abbie, I'm fucking queer, and in a couple hours, I guess I'll see you at school in my gay, queer, flat-ironed ponytail.

CHAPTER 24

Abbie

I ace the Monroe Doctrine test.

Well. I don't *ace* it. But I get an eighty-nine on it, which is the highest grade I've gotten in that class to date, and it's more than 89 percent Margo's doing. I'm so thrilled that I want to run into my house and wave the test in the air, shouting to my parents about how proud they should be of me. I want to stick it on the refrigerator door with my mom's Taylor Swift magnet. I want bragging rights.

But I won't get them. I know my parents don't care about my test scores, good or bad. They're too busy not making any decisions about how they're going to progress with this divorce.

A car I don't recognize is sitting in the middle of the driveway when I get home, so I can't even pull up next to it. I have to park in the street at my own house. Whatever. I head in, my test tucked safely in my backpack, my mouth safely closed. There's no telling who the car belongs to.

Fortunately, it's not my complete nightmare scenario—it's no one's new significant other they've decided to take for a test drive on the couch.

My mom and dad are both sitting in the living room with a woman a few years older than my mother, her blond hair in a perfect chin-length helmet.

"Sweetheart," my mom says.

Great.

"Heyyyyyyy," I say, hiking my backpack up higher on my shoulder, because whatever's happening, I hate it! "What's up?"

What I hate even more is the absurd desire to pull my test out and show it to my parents.

"This is Sheila," Dad says. "She's going to be putting our house on the market."

Well. At least she's not, like, the woman who's going to help them fix their marriage. By like, being their third or something.

"Oh," is all I manage to say. "Well. Okay. When?"

"We're going to have an inspection done, and do some fixing up," Mom says. "Hopefully by spring."

"Oh," I say again.

"It's a pleasure to meet you, Abbie," Sheila says, standing and offering me her hand. But not a real handshake, one of those little half ones, where she's basically offering her knuckles up to be kissed.

It's a *hand*shake, Sheila, not a *finger*shake.

Her nails are long and squared off and fake, fake, fake.

"Okay," I say. "I got an eighty-nine on my history test."

Sheila blinks, and my dad's the only one who manages to give enough of a shit to say, "That's great, honey."

"Yeah," I say. "Great. I'm going to go. To my room."

I'm halfway down the hall before my mom calls my name,

and hurries after me. "You got something from FIU," she says, and hands me an envelope.

This…can't be good.

"Thanks," I mumble, and I shut myself in my room and rip the envelope open and scan the contents and—

Jesus.

Christ.

They've rescinded their offer of admission.

They've *rescinded* their *offer* of *admission*, because of my grades this semester, which, JESUS, yes, they've been bad, but they're getting better! I got an eighty-nine on the Monroe Doctrine test! I'm within five points of the average I need, but I guess they don't know that, because some douche behind a desk in Miami looked at a spreadsheet and decided I don't matter, nothing of mine matters.

G-d, what am I supposed to do about this?

What am I going to tell *Margo*?

I'm not going to tell Margo anything right now, because I've had a bad fucking day, and my parents are selling the house and who knows what they'll expect me to do when that happens, like where am I supposed to live? I'm eighteen, so it's not like anyone will fight for custody. But I'm still in high school; renting an apartment is out of the question.

Great. Great. Good. Everything is fine.

I just. It's just that everything is bad.

It's just that this eighty-nine doesn't matter, and I guess that guy at FIU was right and nothing I want matters, and my parents didn't bother to tell me about the house before having the conversation with the Realtor, and my college decided I wasn't good enough, and what am I going to do after I graduate? I don't have anywhere else to go and I can't find a job that will let me rent an apartment with only a high school diploma—Jesus, if I even get one of those—and. AND. Everything. Ev. Ry. Thing. Is bad.

I sit heavily in my desk chair and spin in a circle, staring at the ceiling.

Then I think, *fuck it.*

I take the test out of my backpack, *89* and *I'm so proud of you!* scribbled in green at the top, and I slap it against the corkboard over my desk and stab it with a pin.

The test wasn't the only thing that came out of my bag. I guess I'm just too pissed to have fine motor skills and Margo's essays come tumbling out, too.

Margo's gay essays.

I haven't read them. I mean, of course I haven't. I never really thought she'd write them—not when I wrote up the syllabus, anyway. But now that I *know* Margo, of course she did.

I haven't read them, but I guess I'm reading them now.

She titled the first one "How I Knew I Was Gay," and formatted it like it's for a real class instead of just me being an asshole to her and/or hitting on her for an hour or two at a time.

In the next one, she wrote about Julie D'Aubigny, eighteenth-century French bisexual icon.

Then she wrote about being queer, and about her queerness, and that her heels and makeup and hair straightener doesn't make her less queer, and she's right. Of course she's right. She's not my type, and it doesn't matter, because I am so into Margo Zimmerman that I don't even know how to deal with it. She's like, all three answers to Fuck/Marry/Kill. Something about her actually writing whole-ass essays for a class that doesn't even exist, asserting herself in 12-point Times New Roman, for me, *to me*, injects steel into my spine.

I wrench my laptop open and punch out *how do I get my admission reinstated* and start scrolling through the results. I'm furious and panicking but I can't freeze in fear. I won't.

I may not get everything I want, but I'll get something.

I text Margo: Hey, clear your calendar. Tomorrow night is Teen Night at Willow.

CHAPTER 25

Margo

Mendel is back from his last forty-eight hours at the firehouse, and typically what he wants to do immediately following two days of work is sleep.

Typically, I allow him this.

Tonight, he walks in, tips his chin up at me in a kind of greeting/dismissal, and I say, "Mendel," and my voice cracks.

He gets this look on his face like, *Shit*, and I can see him considering.

Considering what is a stronger driver: sleep, immediately, or aiding his sister in her clear time of need.

I hope, I *hope* he's feeling altruistic.

Because I'm completely losing my mind.

Mendel closes his eyes and rolls his shoulders, and he says, "What's up, little sister?"

"I just…"

"Wait," he says. "You know what—let me snag a shower. It'll wake me up. Make some coffee or something."

I want to talk to him right at this very second, but I'm also terrified of saying what I need to say out loud, so a shower sounds good.

Coffee sounds good.

I think, in great, focused detail, about the coffee, about the steps in the process—fill the kettle, turn it on, wait-wait-wait-wait, scoop the coffee, pour the water, stir, squish, wait-wait-wait. I think about the science of it, why a French press is objectively superior to a drip coffee in every way, because of how the oils get pulled into the water.

If I think about that, if I focus *hard* on it, then I don't have to think about Abbie.

I don't have to think about her knee pressed into mine, and the silk of her hair against my face when I laid my head on her shoulder. I don't have to think about her absolutely owning every room she saunters into, dragging my attention to her. I don't have to think about every joke of mine she laughs at like I've earned it. Like I've been dying to earn it. I don't have to think about how her face looked talking about her parents, like she was cracking herself open for me. I don't have to think. About kissing her in my room.

And her just...running out of the house.

I don't have to think. About her flat-out telling me she didn't like me.

And this whole spiral started with her texting me about going to Willow, and what that means is that I'm about to graduate from Queer 101, and what *that* means is that this business relationship is over. What happens after that? Abbie and I are friends, I think. I think? I don't know. I'm friends with everyone, but quite frankly, I don't exactly have the best radar as to when I'm wrong about that. So I'm just left here *wanting* to be right about Abbie and *wanting* to believe that tomorrow isn't the end of it.

But wanting doesn't mean much, does it? Not really.

I focus back on the coffee. That way I don't have to think about how tomorrow I'm going to go pick up a girl. A girl who is not Abbie.

I don't have to.

I can think. About the coffee.

Mendel takes a little too long in the shower before walking out into the hall in bare feet and sweats, and he grabs a mug from the counter. "Come on," he says, nodding to me and then to Sir Sean Connery, who lopes out with us onto the front porch.

I settle into the porch swing.

I immediately relax by about twenty degrees.

My feet are tucked up under me, and I'm clutching my mug with both hands.

Mendel sprawls out on his three-quarters of the swing, long legs stretched on the porch in front of us, arm slung over the back. He says, "What's going on?"

I shrug. "It's not a huge deal."

Mendel takes a slow sip of his coffee. He drinks it black, which I think is an affront to humanity and also his stomach lining. Mine is basically creamer with a dash of caffeine.

"Well if that's the case," he says, "I'm gonna crash for the night."

"No, wait."

He says, "Mmm-hmm," and drinks again.

"It's—Abbie. Abbie Sokoloff."

Mendel laughs. "As opposed to the four other Abbies you bring over on a regular basis, yeah."

"I think…god, I think I'm in love with her, Mendel." I'm not looking at him because focusing on the words I'm saying, the impossible feelings I'm trying so hard to handle, is difficult enough. And Mendel isn't someone I need to appease with the appropriate amount of looking at him. We love each other, and we understand each other, and so I don't have to. I can let myself look away.

Mendel waits a moment before he speaks. "Mazel tov," he says.

"No," I say. I'm not doing anything with my body and I have to do something with my body before my body rattles apart, so I tip my head to rest it on the back of the swing and count the slats on the porch ceiling. "No, this is not tov."

He says, "Ugh."

"She's not into me."

"Nah, there's no way that's true."

There's eight ceiling planks overhead. I just go back and forth over them like a Ping-Pong ball. Eight each way. "You wanna bet?"

"Have you seen you guys together? She doesn't get more than a foot away from you. Or take her eyes off you even for long enough to appreciate these *astounding* guns."

I can see him flex from the corner of my eye as he says *astounding guns* with the kind of reverence Chad would have used talking about the chassis of his truck. The whole thing is so absurd I have to laugh, even though saying *I love her* and *she's not into me* felt like scraping a layer off my skin.

It hurts.

Way more than I thought it would.

"She told me," I say. "She straight up told me she didn't like me, Mendel. I don't think it gets any clearer than that."

"I don't know if you know this…" he says, and I finally look up at him.

"Know what?"

"But there's this thing that some people do, called *lying*."

"Ugh." Back to the ceiling planks.

"It's bullshit," he says. "I'm telling you she likes you."

"And I'm telling you you're wrong. It's fine. It's *fine*. It's regular. Everyone has to deal with this nightmare at some point or another. I'm just crazy about this girl who's not—"

And then I start crying.

I just lose it right there on the porch, in front of G-d, Mendel, the fireflies, and Sean Connery. I close my eyes and curl forward and I guess Mendel takes my coffee from me because it doesn't end up burning my thighs. He may not be convinced I'm right, that Abbie's not head over heels into me, but it doesn't matter because he puts his arms around me and lets me cry because this *hurts*, it fucking *hurts* and he knows it.

It doesn't make me feel better, exactly.

But it doesn't make me feel worse.

Well, okay. Maybe it does help.

Because by the time I've dehydrated myself, I at least have the presence of mind to be able to sniff out, "How's the revolution coming?"

He snickers and draws his finger across his throat. "Oh, *everyone's* getting the block."

"Good. Timeline?"

"Six months at most."

"Well, I'll gather all my bread and roses."

He pats my head. "That's not a thing."

"It will be," I say. "When the revolution comes."

"Jesus," he laughs. "I'm going to bed. You gonna be okay?"

My phone buzzes in my back pocket and I pull it out to look at it.

Mendel doesn't wait for me to answer; he says, "Who's that? At this hour? The indignity."

"Uh." I blink down at the screen. "Abbie."

Mendel makes maybe a half effort to hide his curling smirk. He says, "Goodniiiiight."

And leaves me there.

CHAPTER 26

Abbie

I pull up to Margo's house five minutes early. I'm in suspenders and slacks and Halsey's blaring out of the speakers and I am *ready*. I text her to let her know I'm here, and she comes out the front door almost immediately, like she'd been waiting in the vestibule for me to arrive.

It's dark enough that I can't see her properly until she crosses in front of my headlights, and Jesus shitting Christ. She's in this emerald green, long-sleeved, cold-shoulder dress, where her shoulders are gloriously, impractically bare, the fabric hugging her body all the way down to its hem. And thighs for days, because "all the way down to its hem" isn't nearly as long as it sounds, and thank god for that. Her hair's up in a sleek ponytail and her makeup is perfect. She looks *incredible*. She looks so good I've just forgotten how to speak.

She bounces into the passenger seat, smiling, and when she buckles herself in, she gives me a pretty thorough up-

and-down, from my perfectly knotted Oxford to my too-bright Converse half hidden by the center console.

I don't know why I'd been worried about this.

"You ready?" I ask.

"Born ready."

I give her half a smile, put the car in gear, and we go. I'm sure I'm going to know a bunch of people at Willow tonight, and that's fine, but I don't really care. I'm not going for them. Not this time.

This time, I'm going for Margo.

We get inside, and I spot Charlie and Adriana at one of the high tables halfway down the bar. After what she said to me, the idea of hanging out with Charlie all night is not the most appealing. On the other hand, she needs to know that I'm right about Margo, and more importantly, that *Margo* is right about Margo. So I grab her elbow and shout, "Come on." We wind our way through the crowd and after we exchange awkward hellos with Charlie and Adriana, I ask Margo what she wants to drink.

"Cherry Coke," she yells.

I give her a thumbs-up and head to the bar. While I'm waiting, I fiddle with the knot in my tie and watch the three of them talk. Mostly I'm watching Margo, mostly because I can't stop.

But when I come back with Cherry Coke and water, something's changed. Margo's, I don't know, subdued, maybe, and Adriana's not making eye contact with anyone, and Charlie says, "Hey, you remember that girl you danced with last time? What was her name?"

Margo's eyes are bright and fake and she's looking anywhere but at me.

I say, "Erin."

Charlie smirks and says, "She's here again, and she's been checking you out. You should go dance with her. You know. Blow off some steam."

My whole body stiffens, and I'm so furious I don't even know how to respond.

But I don't have to, because Margo finishes her drink and says, with a forced smile, "All right. You go dance. I have surveyed the land. And I think I'm ready to graduate."

And then she—

Walks away?

I don't. I don't know? What just happened?

I shout, "What the fuck?"

Charlie's brow furrows. "Who are you even talking to?"

I throw my hands up. "I don't know! Nobody. Anybody!"

"Uh, my dude? We're at a gay club. She's probably going to go find someone to dance with. Which is what you should do."

I laugh. "No," I manage. "No, absolutely not."

Adriana's face is filled with pity, of all things, and she says, "Abs, maybe she didn't come here for you."

I turn on Charlie. "What the fuck did you say to her?"

She blinks. "What? Nothing! I—"

"It wasn't nothing," I snap. I open my mouth to say something else, but Charlie's eyes flick over my shoulder and I turn, and I see Margo. Leaning, with her back against the wall. One be-Chucked foot propped up behind her. And there's this, I don't know, this other girl. Leaning over her. Her hand on the wall by Margo's head. And Margo's laughing, tipping her chin up to this girl, closing the space between them.

Man, she works fast.

I mean, of course she does. She's the most beautiful girl here.

And Margo—kisses her.

She just kisses some other girl.

Right…right in front of me.

Charlie puts her hand on my arm. "I tried to tell you, Abs."

I say, "No," and throw it off, and I stalk straight across the dance floor, because that's the shortest distance between our two points, loosening my tie, unbuttoning my collar because it's choking me—because that's why I can't breathe, sure—and by the time I get over there, they've come up for air, and Margo's smiling and blushing.

Well, she is until she sees me. Once she does, she almost falls off the wall. I guess my face must sure look like something. The other girl turns to me—and what do you know, the other girl is Sydney Arroyo—her face set to ask me what the hell it is I think I'm doing.

"Hey," I shout. I'm not talking to Sydney; I'm talking to Margo. "Hey. I need to talk to you. Now."

CHAPTER 27

Margo

Abbie looks like she is about to commit literal murder.

Maybe?

Murder, or... I don't know. Maybe she wanted me to pay for the Cherry Coke?

Or maybe she's going to take Sydney out to the parking lot and ask her to, "Hit me. As hard. As you can."

Or—

My pulse was already hopping pretty impressively because well. Making out. And Sydney is hot. But now my heart is about to actually strangle me. And it's probably *only* 110 percent because Abbie's like, literally coming apart, her tie askew and her top button undone and when did that happen? Did that all happen while I was here? With Sydney?

Should I ask her that? Except I can't stop looking at her tie and her hands and her unruly hair and all I can say is, "Uh." My foot slips completely off the wall. "Okay. Yeah, okay."

Abbie's expression does not shift.

I glance up at Sydney, who was a really good kisser, by the way, and intend to say something that makes any kind of sense or leaves her with the assumption that I'll be back or…anything that might quell the potential weirdness of seeing each other at Student Council since this meeting of the mouths has gone unexpectedly awry. But what comes out is: "I'll just—thanks for the—well."

And I let Abbie lead me to the bathroom.

She pulls me inside the single-person bathroom and kicks the door closed behind us, because I guess letting it fall closed like a normal person wasn't fast enough. For her to…say whatever it is she needs to say.

She turns the lock, and I say, "Jesus Christ, Abbie, what—"

And then her hands are on my shoulders, and I'm stumbling back into the wall. She curls her fingers around the back of my neck and—

G-d.

She's kissing me.

Abbie is kissing me and not because I asked her to teach me anything? It takes me a full two seconds to even figure out how to react because going from *this girl who is not into me is PISSED* to *well wait hold on her tongue is in my mouth, allow me to reconfigure* to *well. I think she was lying. About the not liking me* is kind of a whirlwind.

But well.

I figure out how to react.

I slide my hands down her waist to pull her hips into me and I *kiss her back*. Like we never left my room.

Her hands, and her gayly trimmed nails, are slipping up over my dress, curving over my breasts, and I almost think she's *surprised* by it. Because her breath hitches. She makes this little sound in the back of her throat when I kiss her, like she hasn't done this a million times with other people. Like, I don't know. She's nervous.

About me.

What the hell. Me, who's so clueless that I had to hire someone to teach me to be gay, for god's sake, I'm the reason Abbie Sokoloff can't keep her breath under control. Is it possible that kissing me is making her feel like it's making *me* feel? Like I'm drowning, like I can't figure out how to make it from one breath to the next, like I can't even *think*.

But what I can do is push her suspenders off her shoulders, so they're hanging down over her hips. Jesus Christ. She scrapes her teeth over my jaw, and I pull back just for half a second, to look down at her, and she's flushed, hand sliding back down to my waist.

"Hey," she says, a smirk curling one corner of her mouth, "you should probably go tell your friend you're leaving."

I legitimately bluster out a laugh. I'm so freaking flustered. Or. Well. *Something.* The important thing is that my mouth is laughing, but my finger is curled in Abbie's belt loop.

She says, "Tell her you're leaving with me."

Heat flares in my stomach and I choke out, "Yeah, I'm not planning on telling her anything."

Abbie's smile slides a little higher, a little less even, and we head back out into the club. She doesn't bother to pull her suspenders back up.

I don't look for Sydney, and Abbie doesn't look for Charlie; we look for the goddamn *exit.*

CHAPTER 28

Abbie

Margo Zimmerman tastes like Cherry Coke. I'm speeding and I don't care because I need to get us somewhere with a closing door that's not a public bathroom. I'm speeding and Margo's hand is on my thigh.

I pull up in the driveway and I guess I hit the brakes pretty hard because the car sort of jolts when I put it into Park. I don't even know if either of my parents are home but honestly I don't care. The adrenaline must really be messing with me because I drop my house keys twice before I manage to get the front door unlocked. Margo has the good grace to only laugh the second time.

Inside, the house is dark, so I feel like, sure, maybe I can do this, and I press Margo against the front door and kiss her again because honestly, how am I supposed to not? She kisses me back like she wants to spend the rest of the night right here in the vestibule, but I finally make myself break away and grab her hand, except I miss and grab her wrist and I don't care, I'm dragging her back to my room.

I slam the door, I guess, but when I reach for Margo again, she takes a half step back.

I don't even consider being offended; I just sort of appreciate the moment to take a whole actual breath.

She runs a hand over her mouth. "Are your parents home?"

I say, "I don't give a fuck."

Margo smirks and grabs my tie, winds it around her wrist, and drags me toward her.

I let her.

She kisses me, slower but no less desperately than before, her hands sliding up my waist. They're moving, but they're also shaking, like every motion is punctuated with a question mark.

But she stops again, kind of laughing, and smooths her hands back over her hair. "Seriously," she says. "Are your parents home?"

She's stopped, but she hasn't moved away. I say, "I don't think they are, but I don't know for sure. Do you want me to text them, or…?"

Margo laughs again, but this time it's nervous. It's that specific *I'm Cool, Didn't You Know* panic laugh she has. "No," she says. "No, you don't need to. It's totally fine. I'm sure they're not home." She glances back at my shut door, like she'd be able to see them through the wood.

I pull my phone out of my back pocket and hold it up to show her, then text my mom and dad both the same message: Where are you?

We just stand there, waiting for their responses. Margo's

looking around my room, absorbing all the nothing on the walls. The regular beige carpet on the floor and regular blue blanket on the bed and the regular plastic Venetian blinds on the window.

My phone buzzes. Spending the night at Sharons.

"One parent down," I say. "Mom's not coming home. Why do you have that look on your face?"

"Look? I don't have a look. On my face. Or." She glances away again, and I know she's going to want to talk about this later, about why I'm so nonchalant about my disaster family dynamic.

Another buzz. Wing night.

"My dad won't be home for several hours," I say. "Is that all right?"

"Yeah." That nervous timbre in her voice pitches a little lower, the smile on her face spreading slowly. Relaxed almost, but...not quite. She's still shaking a little. "Yeah. That's, uh... very all right."

I reach for her hand again, but I don't take it, just slide my fingers up her arm, over her shoulder. "How about this? Is this all right?"

She says, "Yeah. Yep."

My fingers drag across the slant of her collarbone, to the hollow of her throat. "This?"

I can barely hear the "Mmhmm."

My hand travels up the length of her neck. "And this?" She nods. My fingers find the elastic holding up her perfect ponytail and give it enough of a tug to show my intention. "How about this?"

"Okay."

Our faces are so close I can feel her breath on my skin. So close I can see the unevenness of her perfect liquid liner.

I don't kiss her. I slide the elastic down the length of her ponytail and let that perfectly straightened auburn hair sweep down over her shoulders. It smells like coconut. I drop the elastic on the floor and push my fingers into her hair at the nape of her neck and *then* I kiss her. She makes this little sound in the back of her throat that curls my fingers in her hair and then she gasps and shit, that's not playing fair.

Somehow we end up on my bed and I'm straddling her hips and Margo's hands don't feel so timid anymore. They're not even trembling as they pull on my tie to unknot it.

Or, I don't know, maybe we're both just shaking at the same vibration now.

She unbuttons the top button of my shirt and says, "Is this all right?"

My laugh is weak because I know what she's doing, rhetorically, but also, Jesus, I know what she's *doing* and—"Yes. Extremely."

She makes quick work of my buttons and I sit up and pull my shirt off and drop it over the side of the bed. The way she's looking at me, like I'm the only person in the world—and for all intents and purposes right now, I am—her hair all splayed across my pillow, it's just. A lot.

But not enough.

I scoot backward on my knees until I'm over her bare thighs and hook my thumbs in the hem of her dress, one on the outside of each leg. "All right?"

"Jesus. Yes." She laughs and half sits up, moving to help

me with her sleeves, about knocking me in the head with her elbow.

She laughs harder. "I'd be lying if I said you were the first girl I'd almost injured helping me out of this dress."

I'm laughing, too, because this is fucking ridiculous. "Just—hold on. Don't help."

"I *am* holding on. These sleeves are not loose. What do you want me to do with my hands?"

"Boy, that's not how I thought that particular question would go," I say. "Make your hands regular. In your sleeves. Like they were earlier tonight, when you were fully clothed."

"Abbie. I don't know how to break this to you," she says, pulling her hands to their previous, regular positions, "I'm still fully clothed."

"Don't rub it in. Here. Sit up." She does and I pull on the dress until it gets stuck on her boobs, and I am Hashtag Blessed. "Margo, goddammit, get your stupid, amazing dress off."

"Oh shit," she says. "This...this hidden zipper. I always forget about it." Her voice is kind of muffled because she has a whole-ass dress around her face. "I got it. Wait. Help me with the hook and eye. Come here."

"Come here? Margo, I'm literally sitting on you. Where is this stupid zipper?"

"I've *got* the zipper, Abbie, god. It's the hook and eye. In my dress over my head, come *here*. In my dress."

"Look, if anyone's coming in your dress, it's you."

I hear a muffled snort of laughter through the fabric.

"So the closure is inside? Like, by your face?"

"Yes!"

Somehow I get both my hands in there and after too many minutes of struggling, I get the stupid hook unhooked and the stupid dress undressed. The fabric pops off her like a champagne cork and I almost fall backward. Margo, for her part, is flushed, her hair an absolute disaster, leaning her elbows on her knees while she catches her breath.

In her matching robin's egg bra and underwear.

She seems to realize it about two seconds after I do, and makes an elaborate effort to arrange herself into a sexier pose, and it just makes me laugh harder.

I, too, am in my bra. What a pair we are.

"I'm sorry," says Margo. "That fabric is just *notoriously* difficult to shed. You wanna know why?"

"Is it like, polyester or something?"

"No, no. It's just...girlfriend material." She flashes me the biggest, cheesiest smile that will fit on her face. I let my head fall back in fake disgust and groan, and she says, "Listen, Sokoloff. After all the effort you went through to get me naked, are you gonna do something with it, or...?"

My eyebrows pop up, and I cross back to the bed in two strides and climb on top of her, pushing her off her elbows and onto her back. "I plan to do plenty, Zimmerman." I kiss her again and our teeth click together and it doesn't even matter. I kiss my way down her throat, and I can feel her moan vibrate against my mouth. My hands find the front closure of her bra and pop it open, and I push the straps off her shoulders. The smile I give her must be hungrier than I intended because she swallows hard enough that I can *see* it.

I lean down again, dragging my mouth down her chest to her nipple. I suck it into my mouth, and her back arches, and one of her hands grabs my hair and pushes me harder against her. I take the hint and scrape my teeth over her skin, over her nipple, hard enough to make her jerk against me.

Margo's whispered, "Shit," makes me bolder, makes me think I'm doing it right. And I want to do it *right*.

One hand stays near my mouth, and the other is on her thigh—*fuck*, her thighs are great—and it slides up and up and up and it brushes the lace edge of her underwear and I say, "Okay?"

"Yes."

Thank god. I slide my hand inside her underwear and I can feel her wetness against my fingers and the backs of my knuckles. Her hand is still gripping my hair and I can't see what I'm doing, but I don't need to. The way she moves against me, the way her breath hitches and rasps gives me all the direction I need. When she comes, her thighs squeeze my wrist and her voice catches as it slides down the register.

I don't stop; why would I? I make her come again before I give her a break.

And with a little direction, Margo returns the favor. More than once.

CHAPTER 29

Margo

Well, holy shit.

I just had sex.

With a girl.

Well, not just with a girl. With *the* girl.

Jesus, I just had sex with *Abbie*.

I'm lying here next to her, in her room. In her bed. With just…zero clothes on. And I don't know, I kind of can't stop laughing.

I'm on some kind of endorphin high or something. Whatever it is, I feel *very, very good*.

I say, "Well. I'm so glad I didn't wear anything under my graduation gown."

Abbie doesn't respond, just starts humming "Pomp and Circumstance" under her breath but doesn't get very far before we're both laughing, and I push her hard enough that she kind of rocks away, and instead of returning to her original position, she drapes herself over me and I guess I have naked Abbie Sokoloff just. Draped over me.

My mouth curls and I say, "What matters here is that I leave Queer 101 with an A."

"Well, Margo," she says, "you didn't."

I can feel it when my eyes go from half shut and relaxed to the size of a Pixar ingenue's.

Jesus. I *didn't*? Get an A? Because I would think that the literal four times—

"—plus," she's saying but I think I didn't hear it.

"What?"

"More of an A-plus," she says. "I hate to break it to you, Zimmerman, but you kind of ruined the curve."

I laugh again, out of sheer relief. Anxiety is *good*. And cool, now I'm blushing.

Everywhere.

"Yeah?" I say. "Well just...cancel the rest of your classes, then, I guess."

"What a shame. I had such a nice time teaching you."

"Mutual. Well. Not teaching you. Learning. Studenting? My god." I swear I ruin my own life. I roll my eyes at me and just kiss her again.

She laughs and kisses me back but breaks away sooner than I'd like—I don't freak out, I don't—and says, "I gotta go to the bathroom. I'll be right back."

Good thing I wasn't freaking out.

She comes back out of the bathroom, still naked—Jesus—and says, "You know, Margo, I don't think I was really fair to you."

I furrow my brow, and she makes her way toward the light switch by the door.

"It was your first time, and, well—" She flicks the light

off, leaving us in dim yellow lamplight. "I didn't even play any John Mayer."

I literally snort.

"So let me fix that for you." She picks up her phone from where she dropped it on her desk and pokes it.

The opening bars...are definitely not "Slow Dancing in a Burning Room." I don't recognize it at all until I hear Andy Samberg. Bragging. About just having had sex.

"Jesus Christ, Abbie." But I can't stop laughing.

Abbie crosses the room to me, arms spread like *you're fucking welcome*, and jumps back onto the bed and I grab her and kiss her and she laughs into my mouth and kisses me back and at some point, we go from making out to *Lonely Island* to lying there in lamplight. And at some point, I go from lying awake on her arm to well...lying asleep there.

I wake up to her standing at the foot of the bed, throwing on her clothes.

I sleepily say, "Spoil sport," and grin.

"My dad's home."

Her voice is oddly flat, almost like it doesn't belong to her, and if a person can actually literally trip from a lying-down position, that's what I do.

"WHAT?" I say. "FUCK." Then I realize that I'm swearing because her dad is home so I hiss, more quietly, "What? Fuck." And I'm searching for my clothes, which seems useless because hahaha like I can get back into THAT dress in thirty seconds.

Abbie's totally dressed now, and she reads my mind, I guess, because she tosses me a pair of shorts and a T-shirt, and I don't really have the time to sink into the specific charm of *I'm wearing Abbie's T-shirt* but I do devote it a solid half second.

She says, "It's fine. He won't care that you're here. Just try to look... I don't know. Less freshly fucked."

I choke. And now I'm blushing again. Good, blushing from my forehead to my feet is definitely less fucky.

He knocks. "You awake?"

When Abbie opens the door, I'm standing by the bed with my arms folded across my chest, trying to look casual.

She says, "Yeah, I'm awake." In a tone I would never use with my parents.

I shift so I'm leaning against the bed with one hand. Like this is somehow more natural.

He clears his throat. "I see. Just wanted to let you know I'm home." He kind of cranes his neck a little so he can see me better. "Hey, good to see you again. Don't stay up all night, okay?"

Abbie says, "Okay," and doesn't wait for him to respond before shutting the door in his face.

Good to see you again?

Good to see you. Again.

He's never even met me.

Suddenly, I'm... I guess I'm mad.

Yeah, god I'm *mad*.

Not because he doesn't know who I am but pretends he does; I don't care. But because he really doesn't pay attention to Abbie. Neither of them do. And they should.

Why wouldn't they? Why wouldn't they *want* to pay attention to her?

I sure fucking do, and I literally don't understand how this could be...anyone's default around Abbie.

I swallow hard, digging my fingers into my palms.

When Abbie turns to me again, I barely recognize her. There's something on her face I've never seen before—not directed at me, anyway. This expression matches her *reputation*, not the actual human Abigail Sokoloff. The single cocked eyebrow, the defiantly lifted chin, the twenty-five degree head tilt.

Then it hits me: this is *her* masking.

And when she says, "You wanna spend the night?" it's like being propositioned by a stranger.

"I... Listen, of course I want to—"

"Cool." Her eyes sweep over me like I'm not even here. Like I'm any girl anywhere and it doesn't matter who. I hate it. "You know, you look pretty good in my shirt. I can only think of one place better it would look."

I finish what I was trying to say: "But, no."

I can see it land exactly how I wanted it to, and all told, she recovers pretty well. "No?"

My phone buzzes on the carpet. It's gotta be one of my parents. And yeah, no shit; it's like 1:00 a.m.

I ignore it. "Abbie," I say. "While I do think you're right, this shirt *would* look great on your floor, and yeah, I'm kind of dying to get back into that bed with you, but it's not going to fix anything right now. So, like...no."

Her face shifts back into that total neutrality of when she was talking to her dad. She has so much armor, and I thought we were past that. I took mine off; why is she putting hers back on? "Congratulations, Margo Zimmerman, you graduated. You fucked a girl. That's what you wanted. And now you're done, I guess. Why don't you go home to your perfect fucking family and get on with your life?"

Her voice cracks at *perfect fucking family*, and I feel like... like I've gotten the wind knocked out of me.

It takes me too long to recover because my chest actually hurts.

And in the time I'm figuring out how to breathe, I analyze it.

She doesn't...she doesn't want me to go home. And she knows, she *knows* she's not just a girl I fucked. This...

I breathe.

This is not about us.

I tell her.

"That's bullshit," I say. "No, that's fucking bullshit, Abbie. And you know it."

"Which part?" she snaps. "The part where you wanted to fuck a girl, or the part where you did?"

My phone buzzes. Again. I ignore it. Again.

I say, "The part where you pretend I'm not in love with you because you're mad at someone who is definitely not me." Oh my god, did I just say that out loud? Yeah. I did. You know what, yes. I did. Okay.

"You're—" She shoves her hands into her hair and curls them into tight fists before saying, "Margo, please, you don't even want to fuck me again."

"That's not what this is about."

"Is it because my dad's here?" She spreads her arms, to indicate her dad, her house, her whole entire home life. "He doesn't care. He's never cared about anyone I've brought home. Why would he start now?"

I swallow down the immediate jealousy that she obviously wanted me to feel. I choke past the fact that she didn't say she loved me back, that she basically told me I was lying about it—I'll work through it later, probably. But now it's a challenge. And I'm not going to be diverted by all the other *people she's brought home*; okay, well. I'm diverted for like four seconds.

But then, I'm focused again.

I blow out a breath. "Abbie."

My phone buzzes twice in rapid succession and I swear to god I'm going to throw it out the window.

"Are you just going to let your fucking phone buzz all night?"

"YES, ABBIE."

That knocks her off-balance just enough that I hope she can really hear what I'm saying. "Your dad's an asshole, man. And so's your mom. Your parents. Are assholes. Why are you taking this out on me?"

"I'm not." It's a denial, sure, but it's not aggressive. It's not 80 percent accusation like everything else she's said to me in the last five minutes. "I'm not," she says again, a little heat creeping back in. "And I know my parents are assholes. You don't have to tell me that. I also know that I'm conveniently the gayest girl you know, and—"

And my fucking phone buzzes again. And again. And again; it's an actual call. I practically growl when I have to march across the room and pick it up. "God*DAMMIT*," I say, and I see *Mom* flash across the screen before I throw the fucking thing into Abbie's closet and slam the door shut.

"I'm sorry," I say, whirling back to her, crossing the room again, and staring her in the face. "You were saying."

Sometimes a person can stutter without saying a word.

That's what Abbie's face is doing right now. Like she can't believe someone, *anyone* is prioritizing her. And I'm mad, and heartbroken, and *mad*.

She doesn't look at me when she says, "What did Charlie say to you? At Willow?" It's a question, technically, but there's no inflection. She sounds empty. Exhausted. Defeated.

I say, "Nothing. It doesn't matter."

"Nothing? Or it doesn't matter?"

"Abbie. Come on." Honestly, I just…don't want to tell her. I don't want to say it out loud.

"Jesus, Margo." She looks at me, like, *really* looks at me, and I can't look away. She says, "Don't do this to me."

I feel it in my chest. In my *everything*. And that's what makes me say, "She just—she told me you weren't interested. And that…" I take a second. I don't know why *I* feel guilty saying this to her. "That she was watching out for me? Because if anything happened, you know. Between us. That that's just how you blow off steam."

Her eyes close and if I didn't know better, I'd think she was warding off tears. "Yeah, that seems right."

I am not a violent person. But fury rushes through me; I want to physically hurt Charlie. Right in her face. I say, "Why do you let her do this to you?"

Abbie shrugs and says, "I'm just. I don't know. Pretty lonely." Her voice breaks right at the end, and when it does, she opens her eyes, but she doesn't look at me. She turns her whole face away from me.

I want… I don't know what the hell I want. I want to touch her. I want to hit her best friend. I want to hit her dad. Jesus, the list is sure growing.

I just… god, I'm sad. What I want to do is fix it and I don't know how.

I can feel it on my skin, watching her be sad. And lonely. In the dark.

Because everyone is an ASSHOLE.

CHRIST.

"It just sucks, I guess." She's still not looking at me. "Charlie started dating Adriana, and sort of. I don't know. Something changed. She changed. And like—your parents are so great, and you have Mendel, and all your ridiculous pets, and I have. Nobody. I guess. I don't know. It's stupid." She rubs a knuckle over her cheek, and I think she's crying?

All I say is, "It's not stupid. And you have me."

"It *is* stupid," she says hotly. "Needing people is stupid. Look at my parents. They needed each other. And where has that gotten any of us? They hate each other now, and they're selling the house and moving to different places, which could be anywhere, and what am I supposed to do? Spend my last semester of high school with a bunch of strangers? And then when I do graduate, I don't know what's going to happen, because my acceptance got revoked, and—" Her mouth snaps shut, almost audibly. Like she said one too many things.

I don't know what to say.

I don't know what to do.

I'm frozen halfway between touching her and giving her space and looking for something wise to say and…

I say instead, "What do you need? What do you need from me right here, right now?"

She doesn't answer me, just covers her face and sobs once, really hard. She shakes her head, like *no, I don't need anything,* and I know I've already called bullshit once this evening, but I guess I'm doing it again. I close the distance between us and wrap my arms around her and she doesn't hesitate, she pulls me against her and buries her face in my shoulder and finally, finally just. Lets go.

She doesn't cry against me for that long, really.

There's just only so long a person can lose it before they're too physically exhausted to lose it anymore. No matter how much their life is falling apart. And the kind of crying Abbie is doing, well. Like I said. She can't do it for that long.

She slides out of my arms and breathes for a second, and I say, "Hold on."

I leave her room. I go to the kitchen.

Her dad is there, and he looks up at me like a dumbass deer in the headlights. I say, flatly, "Where are your cups?"

He clears his throat. "Uh, cabinet to the right of the fridge."

I don't answer. I just stalk across the kitchen like somehow my feet on the tile will let him know that I hate him.

That I just. *Hate* him.

I pause briefly by the knife block.

Then I go for the cabinet by the fridge and get the glass.

The clink of ice cubes, the trickle of water from the fridge fill the silence.

I stare at the full glass of water, then I turn around and say, "By the way? We've literally never met."

And I go back to Abbie's room and shut the door behind me.

I cross the room to where she's sitting on the bed, and I probably still look a little *paused briefly by the knife block* when I hand her the glass and say, "Here, have this."

"Thanks." Her voice is still too small and it makes me

simultaneously softer and harder. Our fingers brush as she takes the glass from me and I sit down next to her, shoulder to shoulder and hip to hip. I don't say anything while she drinks, and when she's done, I take the glass from her and set it on the floor by my feet.

Abbie says, "Thanks. For the water. And for…you know. Putting up with me."

I say, "I'm not just putting up with you." I'm shaking when I decide to say this for the second time. Because god, what kind of masochist… "I'm in love with you. I wasn't… I meant it. When I told you earlier. I'm in love with you."

She puts her head on my shoulder and says, "You should go home." I know what she means: I should go before I reach maximum parental punishment.

It should cut a little, maybe, that she doesn't technically say it back, I guess.

But it doesn't.

Because with her head on my shoulder and her side pressed against mine, every muscle in her body relaxing into me—her "you should go home" is as good as her saying it.

I know her.

And I know that.

And so it doesn't hurt at all.

I say, quietly, "I will."

Eventually.

CHAPTER 30

Abbie

The next Thursday, I have an appointment with the guidance counselor, Mr. Lewis. The internet has told me it's not completely unheard of for admission that's been revoked to be offered again, if sufficient improvement is shown where it hadn't before. But there's a big gap between Google search results and real life.

Mr. Lewis's office is decorated in about as close to religious propaganda as you can get in a public school: *Take a leap of faith*, one poster advises. Another reminds me that there are seven days in a week, and *someday* is not one of them. No secular *hang in there* kitten for him.

"Have a seat, Abbie," he says. "Gretchen said you're here about your AP US History class?"

"Sort of," I say. "Florida International revoked my admission because my grade in that class is killing my GPA, but I got some help and I've brought it up to passing, so I was wondering if you could help me, like, apply for readmission? Or what the process is?"

He blows out a hard breath. "I'm not sure, Abbie."

"You're not sure you can help me, or you're not sure what the process is?"

"I'm not sure I can help." He remains impressively cool, but he probably gets a lot more teenagers a lot more sullen than me coming in here.

Either way, it's hard to keep from snapping at him that it's his freaking *job* to know. "Well," I finally say, "is it something you can help me look into?"

"I'm not sure how successful we'd be."

I point at one of the posters on the wall. "'Being negative only makes a difficult journey more difficult,'" I read, and then I crack. "If it's not your job to help me navigate this, then what is?"

"Miss Sokoloff," he says stiffly, "there is no reason to take that tone with me."

"Sorry," I say non-apologetically. "But, in my defense, there's no reason for you to blow me off."

"It is something we can look into," he says, "but I'm being honest with you when I say I doubt very much that it will be successful."

"They admitted me once," I say. "The one thing they took issue with has been fixed. There's no reason to think they wouldn't admit me again."

He opens his mouth again, but I can tell by the look on his face that he's not going to say anything positive, so I just stand up and walk out.

It's not until the next day that I have a chance to talk to my history teacher, Mr. Cameron. After class, I tell Margo to go on ahead, and I linger in the classroom until everyone's filed out.

He looks up from the papers on his desk and sees me standing there awkwardly. "Hey, Abbie. What can I do for you?"

"I have a weird question," I say.

He sits back in his chair, his full attention on me now. "Shoot."

I swallow. "My grade."

"I'm really proud of you," he says. "It's improved so much from where it was. Did I hear you were getting extra help?"

"Yeah," I say. "From Margo Zimmerman."

He nods. "A good choice."

I can feel my cheeks getting warm and I hate it, so I press forward. "Yeah. Well. Okay. So—I got early acceptance to Florida International University over the summer. Except then my grade in here tanked. And they threatened to revoke my acceptance. And I guess I didn't get it up enough, or in time or whatever, so they actually revoked it. And I really want to go, I need to go more than anything, and I don't know how to fix this."

He's nodding, his brow furrowed in thought. "Have you talked to Mr. Lewis?"

"Yeah." Somehow I manage not to roll my eyes. "He was... not helpful. He didn't seem to think there was a way. Anyway, I thought since this was my only problem class, and you're the one who's like, actually calculating my grade, maybe there was something you could do? To help?"

He's quiet for a few seconds. "Let me look into it. You said Florida International?"

"Yeah."

"Sure. Let me see. I can't guarantee you anything, but I'll look into it."

Something inside my chest unknots. "Thank you so much."

"One more thing," he says. "I don't want to be presumptuous, or nosy, but do you know why this was the only class you had trouble in?"

I shake my head.

"You might want to think about that," he says. "Especially since I run my AP classes more like college courses than high school ones. If something about it is giving you trouble, you might want to see if you can find out what it is and address it before you get to real college. You know what I'm saying?"

He's right. Of course. I don't want anything else to stress about, but now I've got a little ice pick in my brain telling me I won't be good at any college class and why am I even bothering trying for readmission?

I swallow hard and nod.

"Don't let it freak you out," he says. "It's just something to think about. Okay?"

"Okay."

"And I'll see what I can find out from FIU, okay?"

I nod again. "Okay. Thank you so much. I really appreciate it."

"You're welcome." He smiles. "Now get out. This is my free period."

I thank him again and get out. I'm already googling *problems focusing* before I even reach my locker. The most common answer is ADHD.

Shit.

I'm picking Margo up that night to go to a movie, but she's not ready when I get there. Mr. Zimmerman answers the door and says, "Abbie, just the person we wanted to see."

Always great to hear *that* from your girlfriend's parents.

(*Girlfriend*. Still getting used to that word. Margo got used to it…literally immediately.)

I follow him into the living room, where Margo's mom is already sitting, an open book on her lap, as usual. She closes it and smiles when I come in.

Margo's parents being happy to see me won't ever not hit me right in the feels.

"Margo should be down in just a couple minutes," her mom says, "but there's something we wanted to talk to you about before she does." She looks over at Mr. Zimmerman, who nods.

"Margo told us about your parents," he says.

I want to sink into the couch and never come out, which is absurd, because my parents are the assholes, not me. I don't need to be ashamed or embarrassed or anything like that.

"And, listen," Mrs. Zimmerman says, "we've moved Margo and Mendel around a lot, and we know how important it is to be with your friends for the big events—"

"Like graduation," Mr. Zimmerman interjects.

Margo's mom smiles. "Like graduation. So, if your parents are going to be moving away from here, I want you to know that you can stay with us. We've got that extra room over the garage and it's not a big deal at all."

I think? There are tears in my eyes?

"We're not going to charge you rent or anything," Mr. Zimmerman says. "Mendel wouldn't let us rest if we did."

From the kitchen, I hear, "Liquidate our landlords!"

"We're not your landlords," Mr. Zimmerman calls back. "We're your parents."

"You're not too old to be grounded," Mrs. Zimmerman adds.

He saunters in, eating an apple. "Yes, I am," he says, smirking. "I'm a heroic first responder, Mom. You can't ground me."

Mrs. Zimmerman sighs, but it slips out through a smile.

Margo walks into the living room. "Hey," she says. "You're not threatening my girlfriend with a shotgun or some other weird *macho dad* thing, are you?"

"No," Mr. Zimmerman says. "We were just telling her about our graduation offer."

"What's the graduation offer?" Mendel asks.

"That Abbie can stay here if her parents move out of town," Margo says, cheeks reddening a little.

"You're moving in *already*?" Mendel blows out a long sigh, like he's exhausted by the whole interaction. "Jesus. Fuckin' *lesbians*."

Margo groan-laughs, and I just throw my hands in the air. She says, "Abbie's not a lesbian, Mendel."

"Jesus, Mendel," Mrs. Zimmerman says, trying not to laugh, "just—go to your room."

"Mom—"

"No. This is my house, and I swear to G-d, Mendel, if you say *one thing* about private property—"

"Fine, I'm going." He lodges the apple between his teeth and pulls a thin rolled-up paperback from his back pocket, then takes a bite as he removes the apple. "It's all right, I had some reading to do, anyway." He brandishes the book and opens it to the first page. "Chapter One—Bourgeois and Proletarians."

"GO." Mr. Zimmerman's laughing almost too hard to get the syllable out.

Mendel disappears from the room, cackling.

"So," Margo says pointedly, "we're leaving."

"Sure," her dad says. "Abbie, just let us know, okay?"

"Absolutely. I will. Thank you so much."

"You're welcome, sweetheart," Mrs. Zimmerman says. "Now go have fun. Be back before midnight, please."

"You don't have to take that shit from your oppressors!" Mendel shouts from down the hall.

"Mendel," Mr. Zimmerman says, and at the same time as his wife, "LANGUAGE."

CHAPTER 31

Margo

I hate this.

I hate this, I hate this, I hate this, I hate—

"Margo."

"WHAT."

Jamal's hands go to my shoulders and he leans over my back to talk into my ear. "I'm not telling you to ride a Bengal tiger. You wuss."

I narrow my eyes and stomp on his foot.

"Jesus Christ!" he says, and he hops back, leaving me to stand there with my arch nemesis. Well, my Everest. It's not like a horse ever murdered my family or something. It's more like...just quite literally something to climb.

"I'm not a wuss."

"That's Best Friend Black Horse, Margo. He's like a thousand years old."

I click my nails together, but it's not as satisfying without my manicure. They just bump; they don't *click*.

I force out an exhale.

"Why are you so afraid of this?"

"It's just..." I say. "It's just..."

And I don't know. I don't know how to use my words. I don't know how to convey why I'm so afraid, so absolutely *terrified* of this animal I have devoted my life thus far to studying. That I want to devote my life after high school to fixing.

I have diagrams of animals this size plastered all over my room. I know how exactly a cow chews its cud. I know how to get a stuck lamb out of the birth canal while giving both it and its mother the best chance at surviving the process. I know the pressure at which a horse's heart pumps blood through its body and exactly how many times that heart should beat per minute and what kind of change means happiness and what kind means distress.

I know everything I can know without veterinary school. And yet.

I can't freaking sit on a horse's back without immediately wanting to swan dive right off.

People don't realize how giant a horse seems when you're right up next to one. How uncontrollable. Horses are majestic and powerful and beautiful, but they're not cars. They're animals. They can't completely, 100 percent be controlled.

It's a risk.

One that catches in my throat every time I think about it.

"What if I fall?" I say.

"You're wearing a helmet."

"I have a bunch of other body parts."

He says flatly, "I have football pads. Do you want those?"

I roll my eyes and flip him off and he says, "Margo. I'm not going to let you get hurt."

I blink. I stare up at this massive animal in front of me and I touch my fingers to his muzzle. I do love this horse. I trust him as much as a person should trust an animal. The Tahans got him as a rescue and he took to Jamal immediately. And Jamal, who up until that point had been more interested in LEGOs than livestock, wouldn't stay away from him. They caught him more than once sleeping in the stall.

They're like, bonded.

And I love him, too.

But that's not enough; it doesn't feel like enough.

I want to think about anything, anything else.

I say, "I'm dating Abbie Sokoloff."

Jamal says, *"What?"*

And I turn around. "I'm dating her. We're dating. We're together. I'm like, in love with her or something but I don't care. I'm not even freaked out by it."

His mouth tips up and he folds his arms across his chest. "If you can come on to someone like *Abbie Sokoloff,* you can absolutely ride this horse."

I was trying to distract him with details of my personal life.

It, of course, did not work.

Well, maybe I was trying to distract myself.

Or maybe the two go together in my *PLEASE HAND ME CONTROL, I HATE NOT HAVING IT* mess of a brain.

I didn't have control over her.

I don't have control over Best Friend Black Horse.

And shit, is there anything, *anything* scarier than that?

I think about the first time I officially called her *my girl-*

friend, and she choked on nothing and said it back. Two full weeks later. And I smile.

Then I'm laughing.

I can Be Out And Gay And Femme and all these terrifying things but I can't GET on a damn HORSE?

No.

No, absolutely not.

Come on, Zimmerman.

This is *nothing*.

"Okay," I say. "Okay, okay." I hop back and forth from one foot to the other and flap my hands because it helps. "All right, I'm going to do it. I'm doing it, Jamal."

"So do it!" His eyes are sparkling.

I slide my hands up Best Friend Black Horse's back and grab for the reins. I jam my foot into the stirrup and flex my thigh, ready to spring up into the saddle. And panic hits me like a hammer to the ribs. Sudden tears spring to my eyes because I can't breathe. "I can't do it," I squeak.

Jamal is behind me again, all comfort and solidity. "I won't let you fall," he says.

I breathe.

I *breathe*.

I.

B-r-e-a-t-h-e.

I get on the horse.

CHAPTER 32

Abbie

Today is the day.

Today is the day I get to tell my parents I'm leaving their house, no matter what FIU says. My stomach is roiling. I've never felt so gross about feeling so happy. My hair is still damp from the twelve laps I swam in an attempt to get this manic energy out before I got home. I just wanted to be somewhere I felt like I belonged, and Margo had Student Council after school today, and I know I shouldn't, but I still feel weird about going to her house when she's not there. They've literally invited me to live with them, but like—I guess I'm afraid that if I take them up on it, they're all going to point and laugh and tell each other they can't believe I fell for it, ha ha ha.

Which obviously wouldn't happen.

And yet.

Both of my parents' cars are in the driveway, which I find a little weird, since they've separated. Mom's been sleeping at Sharon's, but it doesn't seem like she's moved anything out yet. Dad hasn't packed, either, for that matter. That's the thing about moving: there's always crap everywhere. Everything gets fourteen times messier until suddenly it's all gone and all that's left on the floor are dust bunnies and dead mosquito hawks that you somehow missed the last time you vacuumed.

It's been weeks since they told me they were putting the house on the market, and since Mom started staying with Sharon, and everything still looks normal. No tubes of spackle ready to fix picture frame holes, no rolls of packing tape, no old newspaper for wrapping plates.

No boxes.

They're sitting on the love seat in the living room, huddled over a tablet. Mom says, "Zesty."

Dad's silent for a second, and then, "Hey, nice! Three guesses. It took me five today."

And the way they look at each other is…

Like they don't know I'm here.

I say, "Hey," except I actually croak it.

They both turn around at the same time. Dad says, "Abbie," as Mom says, "Sweetheart," and now my stomach is roiling for a different reason.

They changed their minds about the divorce. They changed their minds about moving. They changed their minds about everything, which means I'm stuck in this house, in this fucking house, until I can get a university on a white horse to rescue me.

My mouth is doing the thing where it doesn't wait for my brain's input. It says, "You lied to me."

Mom says, "Honey—"

And that, like, why is that the thing that makes me absolutely snap? It wasn't them arguing at the dinner table and during every car ride, or Mom's passive aggressive reminders when Dad forgot things, or them going to an adults-only Halloween party when I was still young enough to want to trick or treat. It wasn't the constant and utter disregard for anything school-related. It wasn't asking me to help them repair their marriage—or them finally admitting it's beyond repair, or them putting the house on the market without even bothering to give me a heads-up.

It's them *getting back together.* It's them deciding they're going to fight for love or whatever the shit.

And I just—I've just had *enough of their bullshit.*

"Do you have any idea how unhappy I am?"

Silence.

"Of course you don't." I drop my bag on the floor right where I'm standing and throw my arms wide. "Of course you don't, because all you see is each other and your fucked up marriage. You don't see me, and you never have, and— Jesus Christ."

My dad tries first. "Abbie—"

"Did you know I have a girlfriend? Did you know I got accepted to Florida International University, and then I got my acceptance rescinded because I was bombing my AP US History class? Did you know I was taking an AP class? Do you remember what grade I'm in?"

Mom's turn. "Now, Abigail—"

"Did you even want to have me?"

"Abbie!" My dad is shouting. My dad has never shouted at me. And I don't know if he's shouting at me, or if he's shouting to me, because I'm obviously—even to them—really god-damn upset, and he's just trying to get a word in.

So I shut up, I guess. Because what can I change about any of this?

"We love you," he says, more gently. "We—we haven't always been the best parents, probably, and that's not your fault. That's our fault. That's something—" he glances at Mom "—we want to try to fix."

You don't have to take that shit from your oppressors, Mendel said. It's maybe a little dramatic, but like...maybe it's not.

"No," I say. "No. It's too late. I'm graduating from high school in three months and I'm not spending those three months here."

Well. There it is, then.

"No," Mom says. "We're your parents, and you're living with us."

"I am eighteen, and no I am not," I snap. "Margo Zimmerman's parents said I could stay in their house because you said you were divorcing and moving and I had nowhere to go, so they offered me somewhere to live until I graduate so I don't have to re-enroll three months before graduation in some new high school in god knows where. I am staying with them, and that's final."

"You don't get to decide what's final," Mom yells.

"Barbara." Dad puts a hand on her arm and looks at me. Really looks at me.

He says, "You've been unhappy for a long time."

It's not a question.

I whisper, "Yeah," because that's the best I can squeeze out through the tight spot in my throat. And then I'm crying, I guess. I'm crying because my parents will never be Margo's parents, but also because Margo's parents will never be my parents, and because I've never really felt like I've had parents, and that somehow this leggy redhead on my swim team became the gravity in my universe, the only thing that keeps me from spinning out. The only thing that keeps me from throwing my hands up in the air and saying fuck it, nothing matters, because she knows things matter and that I matter.

I matter, and my happiness matters.

Dad says, "Can I hug you?"

I nod, and he comes over and wraps his big dad-arms around me and my nose presses to his chest too hard, but it doesn't matter, because god, I would have given anything just to have one of my parents hold me while I cried. Either of them. I would have given everything.

He says, "Stay with your friend Margo's family."

I didn't need permission, but I did. In my heart.

I would have given anything for it. I would have given everything.

Thank god I didn't have to.

Track meets at S.W. Moody are kind of a big deal, which is why Margo and I decide to make an appearance. We sit with Margo's *Gossip Girl* friends a couple rows down from the Queer Girl Crowd. Nobody says anything when we show up together, but why would they? We've been hanging out a lot. People are used to it, I guess.

What they're not used to is me sliding my arm around Margo's waist and tugging her against me and pressing a kiss against the hinge of her jaw. She's so much taller than me, even sitting down, that it's all I can reach, but I don't care because I get to do it and no one else does.

We don't spend the whole time attached at the face. I've got friends in the stands and on the field, and I'm not one of those people who disappears just because she lands a significant other, because she thinks romance is more important than friendship. Plus, like, don't stare into my eyes that much. It's uncomfortable. Also holding hands is probably one of the least comfortable intimacies anyone can engage in? Sweaty palms and weirdly spread fingers. Hard pass.

Until I hear from two rows behind me, I hear, "I didn't think Margo Zimmerman was the type to go through a *phase*." I think it's Adriana's ex-girlfriend Brooke, which works out great because honestly, Brooke's always been kind of shitty.

My jaw clenches but I don't say anything because I don't think Margo heard it. She's turned kind of away from me, talking to Robbie and Manny, but her hand is resting on my leg.

Jordan says to Brooke, all slow, "That's just like, your opinion, man," and kind of laughs to themself.

Brooke doesn't seem to get the reference, because she says, "Look. Chad's right there, and she's talking to those two idiots. Look at how she's dressed. She's not here for—"

I turn around and say, loud enough for them to hear down on the field, "SHE'S GAYER THAN YOU ARE, JAN."

Silence falls over our little crowd, and Jordan bursts out laughing.

I turn back around to face the field and feel Margo's eyes on me. Well, I feel *everyone's* eyes on me but Margo's are the only ones I care about. I look at her and say, in a much more measured tone, "What's up?"

She says, "Uh…" and kind of holds her hands out in an almost comical shrug. And that's it.

Robbie stage whispers, "Holy shit, buddy."

Manny glances back at Brooke and starts laughing, too. She's texting, or pretending to.

Robbie says to Margo, "We know it's not a phase, dude."

"Yeah," Manny says. "People change and shit."

Margo says, "Thanks," and it's quiet, a little emotional for an affirmation that ended in the word *shit*. But like, I get it.

"Or they stay the same," Robbie says. "Chad's been a phase for everyone."

Margo chokes out a surprised laugh.

Manny says, "*Everyone.*"

Robbie's brow briefly furrows. "What, bro?"

"All we're saying," Manny says, "is that love is love."

"Yeah, man. Love *is* love."

"Plus, like, your girlfriend is really hot."

I can't. I'm laughing too hard, because I see why Margo is friends with these two wholesome jock boys.

"Totally," Robbie says, "but not like, in a weird way."

Manny's face is very serious. "Not like we want to watch or something. That's not cool, buddy."

"No," Robbie agrees. "We respect you."

"But she *is* hot."

"And you're hot."

"You're a fucking power couple," Manny says. "You're both hot."

"But not because you're girlfriends."

"No, we're feminists."

Robbie nods emphatically. "Yeah, we're feminists, bro."

"We love that there's a woman vice president."

"I mean, we don't love that she's a cop."

"No, buddy, we do not."

"But we love that she's a woman."

"A woman's place is in the House," Manny says, and Robbie jumps in to help him finish: "And the Senate!"

He high fives Margo, then high fives me, then Manny grabs his arm and shouts, "Dude! Trevor just nailed his vault!"

"Fuck yeah, Trev!" Robbie whips his shirt off, and I see a number painted on his chest, which, I don't know? Is Trevor's? Are there numbers in track and field?

Manny pulls an air horn out of his pocket and blasts it. His shirt is off, too, with the same number painted on it, and then he and Robbie bump chests and it's all just pretty surreal, I guess.

I lean over to Margo and say, "They're pretty sincere, huh?"

She laughs. "Too good for this world."

"Brooke's an asshole," I tell her. "Free bonus gay lesson— some gays are assholes. Don't listen to them." It's something I have to keep telling myself, too. Charlie's like, two bleacher rows behind us and she hasn't even tried to talk to me. And that's fine. I mean, we haven't really talked much since that night she called Margo a nutjob.

I regret nothing.

"I mean, in fairness," she says, her eyes on the field, "it's not exactly like this sundress and these strappy sandals scream *gay*."

I roll my eyes. "Who cares? They're you, and you're gay, so they're gay, and Brooke's an asshole."

She raises an eyebrow and half smiles. "This from the girl who told me I needed to start wearing plaid?"

"Don't tell anyone, but sometimes I'm an asshole, too."

She bumps my shoulder but doesn't back off after. Just leans there and says, "You're just saying that because you're into all the leg these sundresses show."

"Sundresses are proof that G-d loves us and wants us to be happy."

She kisses me, kind of laughing into it. It's probably the best way to be kissed.

CHAPTER 33

Margo

Three months later

I haven't seen Abbie this dressed up since she showed up in room A24 with a syllabus—she's in slacks and a button-down with the sleeves rolled up because her mission in this life is to take me out of it. But honestly, Abbie in rolled-up sleeves. What a way to go.

I lean back in the passenger's seat and squint into the setting sun. Flowers everywhere because it's spring and spring is graduation, and oh my god. Oh my god, we're graduating. Like, imminently.

I've waxed poetic about it enough times that Abbie actually threatened to slap me if I went there again, so I don't say, *Wow, it's over, how crazy is that?* for the millionth time in the last month. I just kind of smile and think it to myself because, it *is* crazy, *Abbie*, that it's all over.

As it turns out, Abbie's parents decided to *not* get divorced. For now. Despite the Sokoloffs still having a house in the school district, Abbie still moved into the FROG. I couldn't blame her. But that is probably why she's hit her limit on my "graduation shit." I am in the FROG with her. A lot.

Talking about graduation. And also not.

I say over the music in the background, "Hey, any word on Florida International?"

Her hands tighten on the wheel, and I hold my breath. "Well," she says, "I wasn't going to mention it until this weekend, but it seems like between the freshly diagnosed ADHD and Mr. Cameron's impassioned speech to the admissions board, I've been accepted as an incoming freshman for the spring semester." She can't control her face anymore, and the smile that cracks it is wide and bright.

"Oh my god, yes!" I say.

Abbie says, "Oh my godddddduuuhhhh."

I backhand her shoulder.

"Okay but really," she says, "I just want you to know how grateful I am for all your help in that class. I don't even care that I didn't pass the stupid AP test. I really appreciate all of it."

My cheeks get a little warm and I just shrug it off. "Well, the favor was mutual. Without your instruction, how would I have known to sit like this?" I throw my feet up on the dash and she slaps them off.

"That's dangerous in *those*."

My feet hit the floor, and I'm laughing.

"I can't believe you wore heels to this thing," she says. "Do you understand how long graduation ceremonies are?"

"What was I supposed to wear with this dress? House shoes? Come on."

"You know the answer to that," she says. "It's Converse. It's always Converse."

I snort. The song coming from Abbie's phone ends, and when the new one starts, I clasp my hands to my chest and say something I've never said before, which is: "Aw, babe!"

Abbie makes a face like she just smelled a ruptured skunk. "Uh, what is it? *Babe*."

She's only got one hand on the wheel, the other on top of the gear shift, and I just let this slow cheesy smile spread over my face, and slip my fingers over her hand, curling them together. Interlacing them. One. By. One. Softly, desperately, sappily romantically. A real John Mayer move, if there ever was one.

I swear, she's actually panicking.

Her eyes are a little wide and she's facing forward as though there is absolutely no such thing as peripheral vision.

"It's our song!" I say and turn up the volume.

"Oh my god," she says, and the release of tension is almost *audible*.

As Andy Samberg tenderly raps about *The Chronicles of Narnia*, we drive down the interstate into the sunset—*into our future*—hand in fucking romantic hand.

★ ★ ★ ★ ★

ACKNOWLEDGMENTS

Writing a book is never a solo endeavor—which might seem obvious when, well, you cowrote one. But it took so many more people than the two of us (and the tireless baristas at both the stunningly, beautifully gay coffee shop and bookshop in town) to make *Margo* happen.

First, we want to thank our inimitable agent, Becca Podos, whose guidance, whip-smart commentary, and constant willingness to engage in (or instigate) gonzo meme exchanges and not instruct either of us to walk the plank really made this wild, gay little book possible. Thanks for letting us slide into your DMs.

Claire Stetzer, thank you so much for taking a chance on us, for falling in love with Margo and Abbie the same way we did, for adding so much depth and heart to the story of two girls we knew beyond a shadow of a doubt we could trust you with. We are so glad that we did. Vegas odds say there's probably some pic of Rhys and Taika landing in your inbox right now about it.

To our film agents, Madeline Tavis and Holly Frederick—we are so lucky to have you in our corner. There is no one in the business who works harder than you do, or who makes their clients feel more truly championed and taken care of.

To Sara's husband, for all the kids-wrangling shifts so we could get in the quality hyperfocus time needed to turn this book into what you see here.

And last, but the very opposite of least, thank you to Ross Birdsall and Tim Ephraim Stone for giving us a secret key to Gay Dude World so that we could use it to really beautifully ruin Margo's life. Though your advice extended to more than the following, Ross, we particularly want to acknowledge your contributions in leather jewelry and short shorts. Tim, for teaching us about Sean Cody, and subsequently sending our agent's day spiraling into chaos when they Googled it and screamed, learning that Sean Cody was not "a gay singer you use as code, you know, how like we mention Girl In Red to each other." Thank you to Sarah Abu-Ali for teaching us to swear in Arabic. And to Ash Roseman for adding a dose of gay Zoomer culture to our tragically millennial understanding of the world.

To our friends, our readers (our readers!!!), and everyone else who has helped along the way with a text, a Twitter thread, a cup of coffee, or a dinner while we stayed up too late to create a world, thanks so much for helping us get here.

—Sara and Bri